THE VIADUCT KILLINGS

WES MARKIN

First published in Great Britain in 2022 by Boldwood Books Ltd. This paperback edition first published in 2023.

1

Cover Design by Head Design

Cover Photography: Shutterstock

A CIP catalogue record for this book is available from the British Library.

Paperback ISBN: 978-1-83533-939-8

Hardback ISBN 978-1-80483-749-8

Ebook ISBN 978-1-80483-747-4

Kindle ISBN 978-1-80483-748-1

Audio CD ISBN 978-1-80483-755-9

MP3 CD ISBN 978-1-80483-752-8

Digital audio download ISBN 978-1-80483-746-7

Large Print ISBN: 978-1-80483-750-4

Boldwood Books Ltd.

23 Bowerdean Street, London, SW6 3TN

www.boldwoodbooks.com

To Jo

PROLOGUE

THEN

Malcolm's Maze of Mirrors.

A sign hanging on the kiosk at the maze's entrance said:

Welcome to the unknown.

Emma Gardner, ten years old and full of curiosity, was not one to turn her back on the 'unknown', even if it was almost six o'clock, and nearly everybody else had vacated the theme park.

'Please, Daddy.'

Her father looked down at her. 'The eyes?'

She fluttered her eye lashes.

He pinched one of her pigtails and then slid his fingers down it. 'Are you sure, honey? Are you ready for the "unknown"?' He made quotation marks with his fingers over the word. 'And you'll be going it alone...'

'I love the *unknown*,' Emma said, still working her eyelashes. 'And I work best alone.'

Her father pressed two pound coins into her hand.

'Sucker,' her mother said and laughed.

'The *best* sucker in the world,' Emma said, turning around to look up at her mother.

Her mother had her hands on her younger brother's shoulders.

Speaking of unknown, she thought, looking down at Jack's gaunt, pale face.

The eight-year-old boy didn't meet her eyes. He stared off into space, completely lost to his own thoughts.

'You want to take Jack with you?' her mother asked.

Not really. 'Of course, Mum.' She smiled. She was a good, compliant girl. Always had been. It gets you what you want. *Generally*. She wasn't about to mess that up by refusing to do her bit with the weirdo brother who always ignored her.

Her mother leaned down, so her lips were level with her son's left ear. 'You want to go in with your sister?'

Jack sucked noisily at his bottom lip for a moment to suggest he was thinking about it. It was a con. He looked up at Emma. 'No, thank you.'

When she was certain that her mother's eyes were on her father, rather than her, she mouthed 'weirdo' at Jack. He must have missed her criticism because he made no response.

She headed to the kiosk and stared up at the elderly woman with purple hair and large glasses. Emma thought she looked remarkably like that presenter her parents liked to watch on television. *Dame Edna Everage. Or was it actually a man dressed as a woman?* She seemed to recall her father telling her something like that a year or so back.

'Now, babber, you do realise we're closing in five minutes?' Edna said.

'It'll only take me five minutes,' Emma replied, standing up straight and opening her hand to reveal the two pounds.

'Confident, aren't you?' Edna smiled and took the money. Her teeth were the whitest Emma had ever seen. She wondered if they were real. 'You'll be all alone in there, you know? Not the hardest maze in the world, but lots of funny mirrors, and strange lights. You sure you wouldn't like to take that little man over there with you?' She nodded back over at Jack and her parents.

I'll be more worried with him in there with me, she thought, shaking her head.

'Through the curtain then, babber... Don't linger... If we get to five past six, then my manager will have my guts for garters!'

Emma threw a wave at her small family and then lined herself up with a large, grinning clown's face painted on the side of the structure. She suspected the clown was supposed to be Malcolm. The entrance was through Malcolm's mouth, and the curtain that admitted you looked rather like a long black tongue hanging over his bottom lip. It trembled in the light breeze.

Well, you wanted the unknown, Emma, she thought, *and the unknown is certainly what you're getting.*

She lifted the curtain and entered.

She expected it to be dark; however, the tunnel of mirrors stretched before her, bathed in a green glow.

Apart from the faint humming sound of the lighting equipment, and the occasional whistle of the breeze through the old slats that formed the frail structure, she could hear little.

Edna had been right. She was completely alone. Not that she was nervous about it. If anything, she was overjoyed, and chuckled loudly to herself as she walked the corridor, knowing that nobody could hear her foolish sounds.

In the mirrors, she observed herself in many shapes and sizes.

Emma the turnip. Emma the pencil. Emma with a head like an aubergine.

She reached the end of the tunnel and opted to turn right over left. Several steps later, she opted for left over right.

A strobe light kicked in.

She paused at a mirror that made her look like Tweedledum and did some dance moves in front of it.

She did The Brooklyn Shuffle from *Staying Alive*. It was her mother's favourite film and, by default, one of Emma's.

Tweedledum doing The Brooklyn Shuffle in slow motion. This one brought out the loudest chuckle yet. When her amusement passed, she weaved further into the maze, but the flickering lights were making her feel nauseated.

She sighed in relief when the strobe light stopped—

Quick footsteps. *Somewhere further in front... No... perhaps, further behind?*

With the realisation that she didn't know where they were coming from, her breath caught in her throat.

Disorientated, she turned in a full circle. *Which way had she been walking again?*

The footsteps stopped. She paused and listened...

Humming lights... whistling breeze...

She looked at her reflection. A balloon head and a stick-thin body. She wanted to cry.

'Hello?' she called. This felt sensible. She did it again. 'Hello? Is anyone there?'

No response.

Had it been sensible?

She felt her stomach turn over, and put a hand to it, as if that could stop the discomfort.

Get a grip, Emma. She darted forward in the blue glow. She took a right turn, then another right. There was a chance one direction could lead her to the exit, wasn't there?

When she reached a dead end, she stopped and pressed her palms to the mirror, and looked at her reflection – she was one eyed and her face was squashed beyond all recognition.

Her heart pounded in her chest. She opted for a word her dad was notorious for saying but would cost her a week's pocket money. 'Shit!'

The strobe lights kicked in again.

She turned from her monstrous reflection and ran. 'Help me!'

She weaved left and then right this time. 'Help me—'

She slammed into a mirror, and then backed away, clutching her nose. As she turned from the dead end, she checked her palm. No blood.

The strobe lights stopped.

Jack was standing in front of her with his hands behind his back.

'Jack!' she cried. 'Thank God, Jack!'

Yes, he looked peculiar standing there, staring at her with his empty eyes, but he *always* looked peculiar and, besides, his presence here meant that she wasn't being stalked through a maze of mirrors by Malcolm the clown or any other psychopath.

'You changed your mind then?'

He didn't respond, but this was typical.

'It's quite a laugh.' She took a step forward, so she was standing directly in front of him. 'Hard to find your way out. Maybe we can do it together?'

He didn't change the position of his head, or eyes, but he did let his hands – which were behind his back – fall to his side.

There was a large stone in his left hand.

'Jack, what have—'

Her brother swung the stone upwards and everything turned white. She staggered backwards, the pain pulsing in her forehead. The mirror stopped her, and she slipped down it until she was sitting on the floor.

Her vision was blurred, so she rubbed at her eyes with her

sleeve. When she pulled her arm down, she saw blood soaked into her cardigan.

She looked up at him. He was holding the stone by his side, and still wore that empty expression.

He let the stone fall to the floor with a thud.

'Weirdo,' he said, before turning and walking away.

From that day forth, Emma Gardner no longer craved the unknown.

Trouble is, it always had a knack of finding her.

* * *

Now

Detective Chief Inspector Emma Gardner locked the car with her fob and then looked up at the twelve-storey high-rise estate.

'It's seen better days,' Detective Sergeant Collette Willows said, shielding her eyes from the glare of the sun.

'Every high-rise from the sixties has seen better days,' Gardner said, starting towards the brick carcass.

'Wiltshire is beautiful, boss, and yet for the last ten years, I've only ever seemed to end up in the gloomiest of places.'

'Well, try twenty, Collette!' Gardner said. 'And I've yet to land anywhere exotic, myself.'

'You really know how to make a girl feel happy with her choices in life.'

Gardner laughed and pointed down at the smudged stamp of a ladybird on the back of Willows' hand. 'You've nothing to complain about. Clubbing on a school night. Life of bloody Riley.'

'Ladybirds is an LGBT club you know?'

'Yes, I know. What's your point?'

'The point is that clubbing is a necessary evil. I'm looking for a partner. I'd rather be tucked up at home all cosy-like, blissfully watching Netflix like you and Mr Gardner.'

'Well "blissfully" is an overstatement. Have you met Barry? Anyway, let's not go there. Besides, isn't the internet a safer bet for finding Ms Right these days?'

'Nah. The ones I meet on those sites are only ever after one thing.'

Gardner raised an eyebrow. 'And what are they after at the clubs? It's certainly not the conversation. I mean, can you actually hear anything in there? I've driven past Ladybirds and my windows nearly shattered on my car.'

They walked past several youths circling one another on BMXs and pulling wheelies.

'They should be in school,' Willows said, sizing them up.

'That's not why we're here,' Gardner said, 'Eyes on the prize.'

'What's the prize?'

'I don't know yet.'

And she didn't. This was hunch work. Pure and simple.

Two days back, local deadbeat, Nirpal Sharma, had been murdered behind a pub. A sawn-off shotgun had been the weapon of choice. Always a good choice for a murderer, but never the best choice for the relatives who would have to identify the poor sod.

The case, as it so often did when it involved reprobates operating outside the law, had quickly careered to a dead end. However, before the head-on collision, Gardner had a hunch.

Nigel Harnett.

Nigel used to run drugs for Nirpal. Only a few years back. So, who knew? Maybe he'd have an inkling as to what had gone down that night behind the Old Nag's Leg in Tidworth?

Gardner sighted the entrance, and they crossed a small garden which was scattered with rubbish.

'Jesus – this is practically fly tipping. On your own back yard of all places,' Willows said, kicking an abandoned bike wheel out of her path.

'After we speak to Nigel, we can stop by the two hundred or so residents and update them on your thoughts if you want?' Gardner said, cocking an eyelid.

'How have I coped with your sarcasm this long, boss?' Willows asked, rolling her eyes.

'Are you keeping to the recommended units of alcohol a week?'

'Of course not!'

'Precisely.'

When they reached the entrance, Gardner saw that the metal door was ajar, eradicating the need to buzz. She pushed the door open and winced at the sour smell. To say this was the smell of piss would be over-simplifying it. There were a great many other odours at play here too.

'Maybe I should have worn a stab vest,' Willows said.

'Maybe.'

'Are you being sarcastic or serious?'

Gardner shrugged. 'I don't know.'

'This is like a scene from *The Wire*,' Willows said.

'Is this *Wire* a crime series?'

'Yes.'

'Why would I watch crime? I live it every bloody day. I opt for period dramas.'

'*The Crown*?' Willows asked, a smile tugging at the corner of her mouth.

'Yes. And *Bridgerton.*' Gardner said with a raised eyebrow. 'You like what you like.'

'*The Wire* is about some high-rise estates called "the projects" in Baltimore. Lots of drug-dealing, guns and murder.'

'You're always so dramatic! This isn't America, Collette! And certainly not Baltimore. Mainly just petty thieves and small-time dealers here. All of the aforementioned still claiming benefits to get by. Anyway, stop, we have a decision to make.'

The squat, dark haired DS stopped and raised an eyebrow at Gardner.

'Stairs or lift?' Gardner asked.

'He lives on the eighth floor, boss, so that'll be the lift.'

Gardner looked at the yellowing steps littered with crisp packets and empty beer cans. She looked at the lift, which was covered in graffiti tags. One of the doors looked crooked, and the button was also missing, meaning you had to reach inside the hole to click the sensor to summon the lift. 'Risk your life with that then.' Gardner mounted the first step and kicked an empty tin of Skol out the way. 'I'll see you on the eighth.'

Gardner heard Willows mounting the steps behind her and smiled. On the second floor, she turned back to her. 'You didn't fancy the lift then?'

'And risking my life? Not really.'

Gardner laughed. 'It's only a lift! You've taken a bullet before now. You're made of Teflon.'

Willows laughed. 'You're intolerable, boss. No wonder you've lost weight – that sarcastic brain of yours is working flat out to wind people up!'

Gardner patted her six pack as they reached the next floor. 'If this is the result of my sarcastic brain – thank God I developed a sense of humour when I did.'

They relaxed the conversation until they reached the eighth

floor, or rather, Willows did. She was concentrating on her breathing.

They went through the door, and Willows leaned on the waist-high balcony to catch her breath. Gardner came up alongside her and stared down at the debris-strewn garden. It was a long way down.

Gardner waited for Willows to get it together. 'This is why you need to opt for the stairs more often.'

'Give me strength! You're just like Jenny was! Harping on about my health.'

'Jenny. I liked that girl. She had character.'

'As you regularly remind me.'

'Just saying.'

'With all due respect, boss—'

'Ah, here it comes. That means the comment will come with no respect whatsoever.'

Willows smirked. 'With all *due respect*, boss, it doesn't matter how many times you tell me how much you like my ex, the flames can never be rekindled.'

Gardner nodded and sighed.

'Those flames,' continued Willows, 'are well and truly out.'

Gardner continued to nod. 'I see.'

'So, can we have an embargo on the word *Jenny?*'

'It was you who brought her up!' Gardner turned and started to walk. 'Anyway, what if a suspect with that name turns up? We can't possibly have an embargo on it then!'

'Intolerable,' Willows muttered.

Gardner worked her way to the sixth door along and knocked. She almost didn't recognise the man who opened the door. Apart from his lank, thinning hair which begged for a trim, and the pallid worn skin, a hangover from a youth full of drug abuse, Nigel Harnett was a man transformed.

His eyes seemed sharper. He'd put on a healthy amount of weight, and he stood with an air of confidence that didn't come to someone who was under the colossal weight of substance abuse.

But what was most staggering was his Royal Mail uniform. The hunched-up drug addict she'd arrested in Tidworth many years back appeared to be gainfully employed!

'Nigel Harnett?'

'Who wants to know?'

She showed her badge. 'DCI Emma Gardner.'

'I remember you.'

'You have a good memory, Mr Harnett.' She gestured to Willows. 'This is DS Collette Willows.'

'I hope she's nicer to me than you were,' Nigel said, sneering, and showing his yellowing, broken teeth.

'You were under arrest for assault, Mr Harnett. A man was on life support,' Gardner said. 'How nice could I really be? I brought you coffee if I remember?'

'Coffee!' Nigel grunted. 'You kept me in that room nearly all night!'

'And you needed a fix... but as I just said, not really my fault. You were a drug addict, and a man was on life support.'

'I didn't do it.'

'And you were released as soon as we knew that.'

'Anyway, what do you want? Life's different now. I'm different now.'

'I can see that. I'd like to say how glad that makes me.'

'Don't be polite to me now that I fit into your definition of society. You treated me like rubbish when I needed help. Get to the point... What do you think I've done this time?'

'Nothing, Mr Harnett. We're here to ask for your help actually.'

Nigel laughed. 'Unbelievable. Is this what getting clean and a job gets you? More attention off you lot rather than less?'

Gardner shrugged off his aggressive tone. These days, it was commonplace out on the street, and wasn't a precursor to failure. 'I believe you can help us. Of course, you're under no obligation, but if you think about how far you've come? Your help today could also help stop others making the same mistakes.'

'Spare me the bleeding heart! Come in if you must.' He turned and walked into his flat. 'But if you're here to turn me into some sort of grass, you might as well leave now mind!'

Gardner and Willows exchanged a glance as they followed him in. Willows closed the door. 'Shoes on or off?' Gardner called after Nigel, who was taking a door on the left of the corridor.

'Would you take them off at your door?'

Gardner slipped her shoes off.

'Hospitable,' Willows whispered as they followed him into his lounge.

The lounge was sparse, but very tidy. His walls were freshly painted, and he had some potted plants around the room.

Good on him, Gardner thought.

'It looks nice.'

'Well, you offered me a coffee all those years back, DCI, so I guess I'll return the favour.'

'Tea please,' Gardner said.

'I'm fine, thank you,' Willows said.

Five minutes later, Gardner and Willows were sitting on a sofa which sagged in the middle and made them slide towards one another. Gardner looked down at the teabag swimming in her oily tea, and then put it on the floor beside her feet, hiding her disgust.

Nigel sat down in a rocking chair, sipping his own tea.

Gardner wondered if he had left his teabag in to stew as well, or whether that was just the way he treated unwelcome guests.

'Mr Harnett, we'd like to ask you about Nirpal Sharma,' Gardner said.

Nigel rolled his eyes. 'I bloody well knew it.'

'Believe me when I say that we have exhausted other lines of inquiry—'

'The man is a monster. I want nothing to do with him or whatever he's done.'

Gardner exchanged a glance with Willows, then looked back at Nigel with a raised eyebrow. 'You don't know?'

'Know what?'

'It's been all over the news. He's dead. Murdered.'

Nigel shrugged.

'You don't look surprised,' Gardner said.

'Why on earth would I be surprised? I just told you the man was a monster, didn't I? How does it usually end up for people like that?'

Gardner sighed inwardly. Her hunch was starting to look like a dud. 'I wondered if you'd heard anything?'

'Are you not getting the message here? I walked away from that life a long time ago.'

'While you were still mixed up with Nirpal, all those years back, can you remember anyone bearing a grudge against him?'

Nigel laughed. 'Try a million people. Including myself!'

Gardner sighed outwardly this time. She'd had an inkling that her hunch was going to hit a brick wall. Nigel wasn't about to drag himself back into a world he'd fought to escape.

Willows touched Gardner's leg. 'May I, boss?'

May as well. Gardner nodded.

'Mr Harnett, we suspect someone has murdered Nirpal Sharma to move in on his business. If you can tell us something now to help us identify this murderer, we may be able to get them off the street. Just think of the young people who would benefit from that... One less person forcing children to deal drugs.'

'No one was there to help me!' Nigel shook his head. 'Anyway, you take one out, another steps up. It won't make any difference. Surely, you know that better than anyone?'

Very much so. But that doesn't give us the right to stop trying. 'You have to start somewhere though. You *always* have to start somewhere.'

Nigel slammed his cup down on a small table beside him. Tea splashed out onto the black wood. 'Do you even know what you've done by coming here today?'

Gardner felt a sudden chill in her spine. 'I don't follow—'

'The danger you've put me in?'

'We've come in plain clothes, Mr Harnett.'

'How bloody naïve are you? Do you think that will fool anyone around here? Plus, you were waving your badges around on the doorstep like my maneki-neko!'

'Sorry. Your what?' Gardner asked.

He pointed at a white figurine of a cat on the mantlepiece that was waving its hand. 'A Japanese good luck cat.'

'Ah, I see,' Gardner said, nodding. 'I—'

'Get the hell off me, man!' Someone was shouting just outside Nigel's flat.

Gardner stood and moved towards the lounge window.

'Don't bother. Kids,' Nigel said. 'Always at it. Even worse at night when I'm trying to bloody sleep.'

The shouting continued and Gardner pulled aside the net curtain and looked out the window. Sure enough, two lads were fighting outside. Neither of them could be older than fifteen.

Seeing how close they were to the balcony made Gardner's stomach turn.

She marched past Willows. 'Stay here please, DS. Continue the interview. I'll break this up.'

'Waste of bloody time,' Nigel called after her.

Gardner slipped on her shoes, opened the door and stepped out. She surveyed the danger and was seized by adrenaline. A Southeast Asian lad was waving a knife at a black lad, who had his hands in the air. 'I'm sorry... I'm sorry...'

The plea was ignored. The aggressor thrust the knife towards the scared lad. Fortunately, the youth was nimble enough to evade the blade.

Gardner was rooted to the spot as a cold burn spread over her chest. She put her hand to the precise spot where, years ago, she had been left in a critical condition from a knife wound. She took a deep breath. 'Oi! Police! Put the knife down!'

It worked. The boy with the knife looked at Gardner, widened his eyes and started to back away.

Revealing her identity at full volume on this estate felt reckless, and she suspected paranoid Nigel would be emitting an anguished groan. However, needs must. And her decision had yielded results. The terrified boy was out of danger.

'I said, put the knife down!'

The boy complied. The knife bounced off the floor.

She sighed. Her decision was vindicated.

With her palms out, showing she was unarmed, she moved forward. She placed a hand on the terrified lad's shoulder and steered him around the back of her. Then, she continued forward. The other boy appeared unarmed, but appearances, as she well knew, could be deceptive.

'Listen,' Gardner said. 'I stopped this before it got out of hand. We can put this right—'

The Asian boy turned and ran.

'Wait!' She looked at the knife on the floor, and back up at the fleeing lad. She needed him in custody. Next time, if he tried again, she wouldn't be around to ensure the right outcome.

She gave chase. *Maybe you were right about the stab vest, after all, Collette.* She yanked her radio from her belt and radioed in for assistance.

Control told her there would be a five-minute wait, but she planned to have it in order before then.

She skidded around the corner in time to see the lift doors closing. *'Wait!'* She looked above the lift door at the glowing down arrow; there were no lights for floor numbers. She flung herself at the stairwell.

The stairs were another sixties throwback. Steep and narrow. Going down at some speed, she kept her fingers trailing the bar for security. She kicked aside empty beer cans and swerved discarded mushed food.

At the bottom of the steps, she used her momentum and the end of the stairwell bar, to spin ninety degrees right to where the lift doors were.

Closed.

She looked up. No arrow indicating up or down. She slipped her finger through the hole where the button used to be and pressed the sensor with a click. The doors didn't open. The down arrow above the doors glowed again.

Shit... He'd got out on another floor.

She slammed the wall beside the lift door with the side of her fist. She waited for the door to open, confirmed the Asian lad wasn't in there, and entered. It surprisingly smelled better than the stairwell, considering it was a very enclosed space. Gardner hit the button for the eighth floor.

Catching her breath, she watched the floor numbers glow one by one.

One – two...

There were six floors in between one and eight. Fifteen or so flats on each.

Three – four...

She'd summoned assistance. So, as soon as they arrived, she'd get them to work, searching door to door...

Five – six...

Even if it took Gardner all day, she'd find him. She knew what he looked like, and he was in this high-rise somewhere.

Seven...

She wasn't having a stabbing on her watch.

Eight.

The door opened and the sound of screaming pierced her.

Shit... shit... Collette?

There was more screaming, and some shouting now. She broke into a sprint, spinning around the corner.

The noise seemed to be coming from down below, outside. She felt some relief. Collette was up here. In flat 111. With Nigel.

She chanced a look over the balcony. Nothing in the debris-strewn garden down there. But the noise of people was coming from down there somewhere – she was sure of it. Maybe the other side of the high-rise?

As she sprinted past flat 110, a thought occurred to her, and she tasted bile. After she'd taken the lift, had the lad completed his journey down the stairs, and then finished what he'd started with the other kid?

She reached Nigel Harnett's flat out of breath, but with no time to catch it. The door was wide open. Had she left it that way? Even if she had, wouldn't Nigel have felt the draught and come to close it?

'Mr Harnett?'

No answer.

She felt her old knife wound sting again.

'DS Willows?'

Still no answer.

Had they heard the noise from below and gone to see what was happening?

She looked down at Willows' shoes by the door.

She recalled Nigel's words. 'Do you even know what you've done coming here today?'

Have I brought danger to his doorstep? Surely not; I've only been gone a minute or two.

She looked left, where she'd interrupted the fighting lads.

A distraction.

God, no...

'Collette?'

She bounded down the corridor. The lounge door was open. She looked inside.

Nigel was face up on the floor in a pool of blood. His eyes unblinking. His face ghost-like. His throat cut.

Gardner could hear her heart pounding against her ribs. The burning in her scar was merciless.

'Collette! Please, where are you?'

She looked right towards a closed door.

The screaming and shouting seemed to be quietening down outside now.

'Collette?'

She opened the door. The noise outside was louder again. It was coming from the other side of the high-rise. Gardner looked around the immaculate kitchen, and then let her eyes settle on the open patio door. A curtain whipped about in the breeze.

She clutched the scar on her chest and willed herself not to stop. She approached the curtain and drew it aside.

A small balcony. A few potted plants. A wicker chair.

A waist-high balcony.

'Collette?'

Tears starting up in her eyes, she looked over the balcony.

Directly below, a crowd of anxious people had gathered on the estate's children's playground.

At the centre of the crowd, lying on the roundabout, was the body of her Detective Sergeant.

Emma Gardner slipped to the floor, stared up at the sky, and cried.

* * *

Three months later...

'It's been over three months, Emma,' Superintendent Joan Madden said, reaching into her drawer and pulling out some yellow bicycle clips. She put them on the table beside her pen holder.

'Yes, ma'am,' Gardner said, looking her boss up and down, admiring how slim and toned she was in her lycra cycling gear, despite her fifty plus years.

Am I envious?

Yes. Probably.

But at least the envy might get her arse into gear again. She could barely remember what it felt like to work up a sweat. In fact, the last time she had done so was on that high-rise...

She rubbed her forehead as she thought about Willows'

broken body, far below. She didn't fight the memories. Her counsellor had warned her not to. It just made them worse. Better to let them do what they must. Even though they felt like a ravenous cancer.

'Three months,' Madden said again. '*Over* three months.'

'Yes, ma'am,' Gardner said, realising she was repeating herself.

'So, you won't mind if I call time on it?'

'Time on what?'

'Time on blaming yourself.'

Blunt.

But that was Superintendent Joan Madden to a tee. She was certainly no counsellor, offering you a tissue while advising you to embrace those feelings!

Gardner sighed. 'I shouldn't have left her.'

'You had a reason.'

'I left her and she's dead.'

'She's dead because of Lewis Petrich. And he's in custody.'

'I put her in harm's way.'

'Emma! How many times? You witnessed a knife crime. You pursued the perpetrator to stop them hurting anyone. Besides, if you were to blame, you'd already be out of a job. And you're not.'

Gardner rubbed her forehead again. 'If I could go back in time, I would do it differently.'

'Well, I'm glad you can't, or you'd be dead too!'

Jesus! Blunt was an understatement!

'It's over now,' Madden continued. 'Mike and his team found Petrich. Petrich gave up his boss, Rob Mitchell. Mitchell admitted to killing Nirpal Sharma. There's no revenge mission for you to have. I'm not saying you must forget. Nobody here will ever forget Collette – she was one of our own. But you have to call time on the moping. You're a DCI.'

'Thanks, ma'am. I'm almost there. I promise. My work isn't suffering.'

'Nor is it being conducted with any enthusiasm.'

'I'm going to get my act together, ma'am. Have you seen how much weight I've put on?'

'I hadn't noticed.'

Was that a hint of subtlety? No. The tone of voice was completely insincere.

'Two stone! Point is, I'm determined to take control back.'

'Good. Which takes me to the solution then.' She looked at her watch. 'Although, I'll have to be quick; don't want to be cycling in rush hour.'

'Solution?'

'Secondment.'

Gardner gripped the edge of the table. 'Sorry?'

'Secondment. You. A fresh start. Some experience. Eventually, when you get back here, I will have my DCI back.'

'I'm kind of rooted here. Anabelle's settled at school. My husband—'

'Works from home and can move.'

'Yes, but back to Anabelle...'

'Don't take them then. Seen many a family man happy for the break from his wife.'

'Thanks for thinking of me, ma'am, but really—'

'You don't even want to know where it is then?' Madden asked as she started to fit her bicycle clips.

Emma shook her head.

'Probably best you know as you're going.'

Blunt bitch. Gardner bit her lip and looked down.

'Lovely neck of the woods,' Madden said. 'North Yorkshire.'

'North Yorkshire!'

'Beautiful. Look at these.'

Madden opened a brown folder and dropped some photographs in front of Gardner who picked one up. It was an aerial photograph of a sprawling river dotted with cafés, with a railway bridge over it. The second photo was a picture of a castle. The third showed an assortment of large rocks, all piled on top of each other, forming awe-inspiring shapes – a geologist's wet dream. 'Knaresborough; Ripley Castle; Brimham Rocks. I've done a lot of cycling around the Yorkshire Dales.'

'It looks lovely, but—'

'Near Harrogate too. Bettys café. You won't find better afternoon tea.'

Gardner nodded. She recalled Willows' admiration for Harrogate. She used to go once a year to the Theakston Old Peculier Crime Writing Festival to see all her favourite crime writers speak. Emma felt a cold ache in her stomach.

'I don't suppose you will let me decline.'

'I've stuck my neck out here for you, Emma.'

Here we go. The emotional blackmail.

'I didn't ask—'

'Told them up at Harrogate that I had the perfect person for the vacant DCI job.'

Emma sighed and looked down.

'Things are in motion. You're from Wiltshire, Emma. Where rural, wealthy and *poor* lives, all meet in one heady collision! They were salivating over the prospect of receiving you.'

Now the flattery.

'They have a similar world. Similar imbalances. Similar beauty. They need someone like you to keep it all together.'

I'm not applying to be the prime minister!

'Make me happy, Emma. Twelve months tops. If you make this work, good things will be coming your way.'

Finally, the manipulation...

Gardner inwardly sighed. The thought of leaving her family filled her with despair. 'I really—'

'Okay. I'll let you think about it. But know that it's all on track. We have a place ready for you in Knaresborough. Wait till you see it!'

My world is about to be turned upside down, isn't it? Gardner nodded.

'Brilliant, Emma,' Madden said, starting to fix her helmet to her head. 'Now, unless there's anything else?'

Gardner nodded again. 'Ma'am.' She stood and turned to leave.

'You're going to love it. The position starts on Monday. Celebrate this weekend, then pack, and your accommodation details will be over by email.'

Gardener left and went to sit in a cubicle in the toilets.

Madden had given her approximately thirty seconds thinking time.

Emma Gardner was going to North Yorkshire whether she liked it or not.

There it was again. The unknown. Always pouncing on her when she least expected it.

1

Doug Brace's golden retriever, Lancelot, gave the lead one hell of a yank and managed to bury his nose in a bag of half-eaten chips.

Doug tugged Lancelot back gently so as not to hurt him, but the dog whined regardless. 'Stop faffing, you mardy boy!'

Ahead of the two companions, illuminated by the moon behind it, was Knaresborough Castle. First built by a Norman baron c. 1100 on a cliff edge, it now stood ruined, following its taking by Parliamentarian troops in 1644 during the civil war. It wasn't destroyed because of the warfare, but rather from a brutal insidious order from Parliament to dismantle Royalist castles. Some of the castle stone had made it into the town centre's buildings, keeping the soul of the castle burning strong in Knaresborough's heart.

Doug didn't believe there was a better place in the world for a midnight stroll than Knaresborough Castle. However, he was born and bred here, and so was most certainly biased!

Doug led Lancelot through the central two imposing solid towers in the enclosure wall, and down the path framed by the Castle Yard, which was two large patches of grass, one of which had been set up as a minigolf course – an irritant to the hundreds of picnickers that flocked here on a summer's day.

They walked past the bowling green, which he personally found far more enjoyable than the minigolf, to the five-sided keep. Like the rest of the castle, the keep was largely ruined. Doug had visited the interior on several occasions and admired the vaulted basement and the upper storeys which were roofless, so you could climb up and catch some rays.

Lancelot cocked his leg and let fly on the doorway to the keep.

'Give me strength, boy! This was where the lord of the castle used to reside.'

Lancelot regarded him.

'You don't have a bloody clue what I'm on about, do you?'

Lancelot approached him, placed his paws on his owner's stomach, and received a loving pat for his lack of manners.

Despite it being in the latter half of spring, the weather wasn't giving up any summer warmth just yet, so Doug fastened the top button of his parka when the keep no longer provided him a wind block, and came upon the cliff edge.

There, he paused, as he *always* paused, to admire the view of the Knaresborough viaduct, striking over the river Nidd.

At night-time, the view was even more special due to the moonlight dancing on the Nidd; and, of course, the absence of snap-happy tourists who came in their droves.

The many cafés and houses alongside the Nidd were dormant at this time, and the swollen trees and blooming flowers swayed joyfully in the peace and quiet.

Lancelot whined and pulled at his lead.

'What 'ave you seen now, boy?'

Lancelot whined louder and pulled harder. Something had his attention on the patch of grass ahead.

'You'll be the death of me, Lancelot,' Doug said, negotiating the steep gradient of the grassy patch. They drew closer to the cliff edge, but it wasn't dangerous. There were barriers up, protecting them from a tumble into shrubbery and onto the steps that led down to the river Nidd. However, Doug still didn't fancy taking a tumble on this slope. His bones were old and his specialist was forever crooning about a hip replacement. 'While I can walk, I can walk,' was his mantra.

His specialist's mantra was different. 'If you don't have to walk in pain, why walk in pain?'

Doug would always agree to think on it. A process that would last until he'd driven out of the hospital car park, before promptly forgetting all about it. It was bad enough spending an hour at hospital; why would he want to spend a few days there under a bloody knife?

Doug stopped and squinted. His eyesight wasn't all that sharp, but he was sure he could see a pair of trainers poking out from behind the back of the keep.

Lancelot's whining and tugging continued.

'Lancelot, be quiet, and be still for pity's sake.'

Doug inched nearer and, when he was near enough to conclude that they were trainers, and that they were *still* on someone's feet, he took a sharp deep breath.

Exhaling, he looked up at the view, which over the years had left millions spellbound, before looking down again at the feet. 'Dear God,' he said.

Together, the two companions drew level with the back of the keep and saw a young man, wearing a jogging suit, lying on his back. Doug took a step towards him. 'Son, are you okay?'

There was no reply, so he chanced a few more steps, shortening the lead and keeping Lancelot close to his side.

Eventually, Doug was close enough to see the boy was too

pale to be alive. His open, lifeless eyes were further confirmation of his passing. Then, came the recognition. 'Bradley Taylor. Dear God.'

Only seventeen years old.

Lancelot stopped tugging, sat down, and whined.

2

Detective Inspector Paul Riddick struggled to get the key in the lock.

It wasn't because he was drunk, but rather because his date, Cynthia, was clamped to his face, and her hands were under his leather jacket, working at his shirt buttons.

Riddick broke away, gasping for air. 'Slow down.'

Her drunken eyes were half-closed; lipstick was smeared over her face.

'Give me a chance to get the door—'

Cynthia went for the buckle on his belt.

He put his hands on hers and forced them away from his trousers. He'd drunk far more than his date; however, lately, his tolerance exceeded that of most people, and so he was able to exercise much better self-control. 'I've neighbours.'

He turned his attention back to the door. The key slid home. The door opened and he sighed with relief. But before Riddick had even cleared the threshold, Cynthia was forcing her mouth onto his again. *What the hell; when in Rome*, he thought, allowing her to pin him against the hallway wall and kicking the front door closed with his foot.

They slid across the wall in a passionate embrace.

However, when Cynthia made another attempt to undo his belt, he again stopped her.

'Why?' Her frustration was clear.

'I...'

'Shall I go?' How quickly frustration could turn to anger!

'No. I want you to stay. Go upstairs, first door on right. Let me get some drinks.'

'Drinks *after*,' she said, leaning in and nuzzling his neck.

He worked himself away from her. 'Please. I just need a moment...'

She pulled her head back and looked him in the eyes. 'Ah... I see.' She smiled and winked. 'You don't carry one in your wallet, do you?'

That's not what he'd meant. But it would do. He shook his head. 'No, I'm a fool.'

'No worries.' Cynthia kissed him slowly.

He heard her take a deep breath through her nose.

As she backed away from him, she chewed her lip for a moment and then said, 'Don't keep me waiting.'

'I won't.'

Riddick watched Cynthia ascend the stairs, noticing that her tights had laddered during their clinch.

He headed into his kitchen, quickly checking that his trousers were still fastened. He made straight for the island where an opened bottle of Merlot awaited him. He reached for the glass, stained red from use earlier this evening, and filled it. He drank greedily, sighing when the glass was empty, and the alcohol was topped up in his bloodstream.

'Was everything all right tonight?' Riddick asked, pouring himself another glass.

'The usual argument,' Rachel answered. 'Molly wanted Julia Donaldson. Lucy wanted Dr Seuss. A bit of both, and they settled.'

Riddick turned to look at his wife. She was sitting at the table in her nightie, crocheting.

'Making anything nice?' he asked.

'A bunny rabbit for Louise.'

'That'll be one happy niece.'

Riddick took a step towards Rachel, taking another mouthful of Merlot. His wife didn't look at him. She was too engrossed in constructing a carrot for the bunny.

'I brought someone back with me,' Riddick said.

Rachel nodded. 'Who?'

'Cynthia. She works at Earl's Estate Agents in town.'

'Do you like her?'

'She's nice, I guess, but I don't know her all that well.'

'Where is she now?'

'Upstairs in the spare room.'

'You should go to her.'

'I wanted to see you first.'

'Go, Paul.'

'Are you sure? I mean, I could open another bottle of wine?'

Rachel shook her head. 'Paul, we've talked about this. Go upstairs.'

'I'm sorry.'

Rachel stopped crocheting and turned to look at him. 'You've nothing to be sorry for. Now go, please. I want to get this done for the morning. And take her a glass of wine, too. She's a guest!'

* * *

Later, after Riddick had made love to Cynthia, he headed into the twins' room in his dressing gown. He approached Molly first. He smiled at her Disney Princess bedsheets. They were faded through over washing, but she was determined not to give them up, despite incessant offers from Riddick and Rachel to buy her any cover she wanted.

He turned and looked at Lucy. She was just as attached to her Marvel bedsheets. He smiled at the *Oh, the Places You'll Go!* by Dr Seuss open on her bed.

Chalk and cheese these two.

Lucy opened her eyes. 'Daddy?'

'Sorry honey, you go back to sleep.'

She smiled. 'Are you okay?'

Riddick paused.

'Daddy?'

He nodded. 'Yes, honey, I'm fine.'

He turned for the door before she could see his tears.

3

The phone call from Chief Constable Rebecca Marsh had been a bolt from the blue, and not only because it came in the middle of the night.

Suspected murder!

It'd been a long time since that'd happened around these parts.

Riddick opted to walk. It was only a fifteen-minute stroll to Knaresbough Castle, and he dreaded to think how over the limit he was. The breeze had picked up pace since his date with Cynthia earlier, and he wished he'd slipped a jumper on between his shirt and leather jacket.

Throwing some extra-strong mints into his mouth, he entered via the car park that attached itself to the side of the castle grounds. He saw the black incident van, several patrol cars, and a couple of sporty Audis owned by some of the bigwigs who would now be in attendance. He also saw a couple of vans he recognised. *Shit. The press.*

The castle grounds were well lit by the full moon. Due to recent spring showers, the soil was soft under foot but not muddy. Not far ahead, he could see the crumbling façade of the keep, and a blue-and-white police cordon tape strung between a rusty gate beside the keep and a bench beside the bowling green.

There was good news and bad news regarding a small group of people in front of the rusty gate. The good news was that they were on the right side of the cordon. The bad news was that they were reporters, and if there was one person reporters didn't like, it was him.

He avoided eye contact as he passed.

'DI Riddick?'

Eyes forward, he chewed on another mouthful of mints.

'DI Riddick, do you know who the body belongs to?'

He growled.

'Is this your first crime scene since the Winters case?'

Riddick stopped and turned his narrowed eyes on the female reporter who'd asked that question. Marianne Perse. Freelance journalist. Always selling to the highest bidder and bids were obviously high – she drove a Bentley.

He fixed her in his stare.

She smirked. 'Well, DI Riddick, *is* this your first crime scene since?'

Riddick took a deep breath through his nose and exhaled slowly.

Muttering 'piss off' under his breath, he turned to the cordon and surveyed the scene. Among the scouring white-suited Scenes of Crime Officers, he spotted Ray Barnett, who was in his white paper suit. The tall, black DS was holding a logbook in his large hand. Riddick gestured him over. 'Evening Ray.'

'Sir.' He nodded and scribbled Riddick's name into the logbook.

Behind him, Riddick could hear his name being called by the newshounds.

'They're relentless,' Barnett said.

'Rabid is the word you're looking for,' Riddick said with a smile. 'Don't suppose you fancy putting the diseased animals down for me?'

Barnett smiled back. 'Alas, I'm unarmed, sir.'

'That's a big bloody logbook, Ray, and I've seen you arm wrestle. I'm sure we could come up with a solution—'

'As I live and breathe,' Chief Constable Rebecca Marsh said, 'it's my most prized detective, doing what he does best, rebelling against the convention of punctuality. Ray, leave us a moment please.'

'Yes, ma'am.' The large man walked away, weaving over the plates laid by forensics to protect the scene.

Chief Constable Rebecca Marsh was nicknamed 'Harsh Marsh' by some due to her short temper, and 'Dr Frank-N-Furter' by others due to her short black hair, masculine appearance and leanings towards dark make-up. She was unaware of either nickname, but many felt she would appreciate the first. Not so much the second.

'Was better to walk, ma'am,' Riddick said, throwing another mint into his mouth. 'I had a few sundowners earlier.'

'Doesn't matter how many mints you chew, Paul, I can tell from your eyes, your hair, and the colour of your skin that you've been painting the town red again.'

'Hard to paint Knaresborough red—'

'Are there bars?'

'Yes, but—'

'When there're bars, there's capacity to paint. And you've been painting all night. *Again.*'

Riddick nodded.

'Notice how I keep using the word *again*?'

'Ma'am, I'm fine to do my job.'

'Good. Because we've a bad one here. MCU has not seen one like it in its five years of existence.'

The Major Crime Unit in Harrogate mainly dealt with kidnap, rape and cold cases. Murders were rare in this neck of the woods.

'DI Riddick? Chief Constable Marsh?' The press continued unabated.

'They were bad before you got here,' Marsh said. 'But not like this. You really know how to rile them.'

Riddick rolled his eyes. *I didn't bloody say anything!*

'Fortunately,' Marsh said, 'Joe is on his way.'

Joe Bridge was the Press Relations Officer, and he was like the Pied Piper when it came to rat infestations like this one.

Barnett came back over with a wrapped bundle and handed it to Riddick who tore it open and slipped on his white paper suit and his overshoes. Then, he stepped under the cordon. 'What do we have, ma'am?'

'IC1 male, black hair. He's tall, skinny, young.'

Riddick took a deep breath. 'How young?'

'It's Bradley Taylor.'

Riddick breathed out. 'Good God. Are we sure?'

'Yes. There're enough officers here that recognise him.'

'Not surprised. He's one of our local louts. He's also a kid.' Riddick glanced at the press and sighed. 'Which means they'll be very hungry.'

'Ravenous, no doubt,' Marsh said. 'However, Bradley recently turned eighteen – Doug Brace had it wrong. At least, he's no longer considered a child.'

'Cause of death?'

'Don't know. The pathologist has yet to arrive.'

They started to walk along the path of plates. Riddick nodded a greeting at the Chief Forensic Officer, Fiona Lane, who was currently overseeing the pouring of resin into something on the grassy area. Other officers, including Roy Reid, the Exhibits Officer, were helping steady the tent they were erecting over the grass and the side of the keep in case a spring shower should suddenly ensue.

'You must have an inkling?' Riddick said.

'No,' Marsh said. 'No marks on the body.'

'Natural causes?'

'Maybe... except, why was he around the back of the keep?'

'Bradley Taylor? I can give you any number of reasons. The clear favourite being that he was smoking something he shouldn't have been smoking,' Riddick said.

'He's never shied away from doing that out in the open! Besides, there's no one around here at this time; why hide away?'

'Drag marks on the ground?'

'The grass did look flattened nearby, but I've let forensics crack on with that.'

As they approached the back of the keep, Riddick cast his eye over the striking viaduct and the moonlight dancing on the Nidd. He wondered, briefly, if Knaresborough's most famous view had been ruined forever.

'By the way, you're not the Senior Investigating Officer,' Marsh said.

At that point, a woman wearing a yellow raincoat underneath her paper suit stepped out from behind the keep. She was looking down at something. Riddick traced her eyes and saw she was looking at the white trainers poking out from behind the keep.

'DCI Emma Gardner,' Marsh said. 'She arrived yesterday.'

'Nice raincoat. No rain, like.'

'She's from the south. Wiltshire. Not used to the drizzle.'

'West Country? Wow. Not a fan of the accent.' *I'm also not a fan of someone new. Especially considering the chaos that is about to descend on Knaresborough.*

'And what do you think she'll make of your accent?' Marsh asked.

'That it's full of northern soul?'

'Northern, yes, Paul. The soul, questionable.'

'You know, ma'am, I did think you'd be tapping me up for that DCI job.'

'Did you want it?'

'Of course not.'

'Didn't think so.'

However, neither do I want to be working for someone new. Especially a southerner wearing a silly raincoat. 'It still would have been nice to be asked though.'

'I'll introduce you to—'

'No thanks, ma'am. I got this.'

4

Gardner knelt down to look at the trainers. One foot was tilted inwards, and she could see that it was muddy and grass stained.

'What've you found, ma'am?'

Gardner looked up at a tall man with a medium build, black hair, and a five o'clock shadow.

'And you are?'

'DI Paul Riddick.'

Gardner nodded. 'DCI Emma Gardner.'

'I know… the chief constable filled me in.'

'Good stuff… Just call me boss, please – I can't handle the ma'am.'

'Okay, boss. I'll be the assistant SIO.'

'I was told.'

Riddick smiled. 'Told or warned?'

Gardner felt the two stone she'd recently put on as she rose from her haunches. 'Irrelevant. With me, everyone starts with a clean slate. Hope I get the same courtesy.'

'Of course.' Riddick took a step forward and looked at the pale, wide-eyed corpse. Doug Brace hadn't been wrong – it was

Bradley Taylor. 'You were looking at something when I came over?'

'The victim was dragged. Mud and grass stains on the back of the trainer. Of course, I'm not forensics, but I've seen it before. I'm not arguing natural causes anyhow.'

'Depends how you look at it,' Riddick said.

'Pardon?'

'Well, it's perfectly *natural* that someone would want to kill him.'

Gardner raised an eyebrow.

'This is Bradley Taylor, boss. Known to many as a *right little shit*.'

Gardner took a deep breath. *Should I hold back, or let fire? This is a child lying dead.* She let fire. 'I don't appreciate the tone, DI; he's only seventeen!'

'Actually, that's wrong. Bradley turned eighteen recently. However, eighteen, seventeen or even fifteen; it makes no odds, boss. I'm telling you; Bradley Taylor was a little shit of the highest order.'

It had taken Gardner less than two minutes to realise that her new assistant had a questionable attitude.

Behind them, forensic halogen arc lamps burst into life. Everything glowed, including the whites of the dead boy's eyes.

'Okay, as you seem to know so much about Bradley Taylor, Detective Inspector, tell me more?'

'Please, *boss*, call me Paul.'

He'd emphasised the word *boss*. Was he mocking her?

'Possession of marijuana,' Riddick said. 'Underage drinking – until he turned eighteen, of course. A couple of assaults. Suspected dealing.'

'Suspected?'

'Yes, as in, we *suspected*, but no evidence was found.'

'Let's deal in facts then please Paul.'

'Facts? Here's one. Neil Taylor, Bradley's father, is a *convicted* drug dealer. No suspicions there! He's also a local bully. All round bad man. As a youngster, he was also a *right little shit* too.'

'Why's he not in jail?'

'He was. Until two months ago. We're just waiting for his first slip-up, so we can send him back.'

'Unless he goes on the straight and narrow?'

Riddick shook his head. 'Neil lives and breathes crime. If not for the budget cuts, and a reduction in the number of eyes we can have on him, he'd be back inside already.'

Gardner looked down at the body. 'Do you think he has it in him to kill his own boy?'

Riddick looked down too. 'The thought had crossed my mind.'

'And Doug Brace, the man who found him?' Gardner asked. 'Do you know much about him?'

'Yes. Polar opposite to Neil Taylor! Doug is everyone's hero. Especially to the kids round here. He has run an ice cream shop since before I was born. He also manages the local children's football team – Knaresborough Celtic.'

Gardner nodded. She was pleasantly surprised. He knew his community. Not only did that make him an asset, but it also showed that he cared about the people he was paid to protect.

'Can you think of any reason local good guy Doug and local bad boy Bradley may have come to blows?'

Riddick shrugged. 'I think that may be a non-starter, boss... Also, has anyone told you what time Doug found Bradley?'

'The emergency call was logged at 12.03 a.m.'

'A midnight stroll for Doug, then.'

Gardner turned and looked out over the view. 'Why not, with such incredible scenery?'

'Yes,' Riddick said. 'But the scenery does cause most of our problems.'

'Sorry?' Gardner said, looking back. 'Problems?'

'*Tourists.* Droves of them.' He pointed in the distance at a rocky formation. 'That's Mother Shipton's Cave. People go there to see things magically turned to stone.'

'I don't understand.'

'Over time, the high mineral content that runs down the cave walls calcifies objects. Queen Mary did her shoe there in 1923. If that doesn't float your boat, the magician Paul Daniels calcified his wife's toy rabbit there wearing his bow tie.'

'Sounds fascinating.'

'It really isn't, but my point is, we're bursting with tourists, but we aren't bursting with murder. There'll be a simple explanation for all of this.'

Several SOCOs were calling over to one another. Gardner looked over. One of them was holding a condom up in the glow from the halogen bulb, before dropping it into an evidence bag.

'A sex game gone wrong, perhaps? Simple enough,' Riddick said.

Gardner turned back to Riddick and shook her head. 'I come from a very similar place to you, Paul. And in my experience, murder is anything but simple.'

* * *

After talking with Chief Forensic Officer Fiona Lane, Emma hopped over the protective plates to the cordon. At one point, she almost lost her footing, but she didn't feel irritated. Protecting the crime scene to within an inch of its life always paid off. Fiona's cast of a clear footprint was testament to this.

Up ahead, the press was issuing questions, rapid-fire, at a

young, suited man with a large quiff. He repeatedly brushed them off with ease. Mainly with comments such as, 'We will let you know as soon as we can'; 'We have no conclusions regarding that yet'; 'As always, we will provide a full and frank briefing once the crime scene has been processed.'

After every brush off, the officer adjusted his quiff, before turning his attention to the next fevered hound.

Gardner felt someone stepping up alongside her.

'Joe Bridge,' Marsh said. 'No one can pacify the press like that boy.'

'He certainly looks like he's got it under control.'

'He has. But sooner or later, Emma, you'll have to step into the limelight. However, if what Superintendent Madden told me over the phone is anything to go by, I've got nothing to worry about.'

Gardner gulped. 'I hope so.'

'Of course, I've been lied to more times than I can remember. You know how many secondments I've had pushed on me with glowing references? Too many. It seems we're a dumping ground.'

It didn't take a genius to realise that these words were laced with hostility. What could she have possibly done to wind up her new boss already? Unless this was just her way of laying out her expectations?

'However, I'm confident that's not the case here,' Marsh concluded.

'It won't be, ma'am,' Gardner said, feeling relief.

The chief constable smiled at her. Her dark make-up made her look ghoulish in the glare of the halogen lamps. 'I hope you and DI Riddick hit it off?'

Like a house on fire.

'We've had initial discussions regarding the victim. His knowledge of the area will be valuable.'

'Yes, in some ways. In other ways, it'll be a hindrance.'

'Sorry, ma'am?'

Marsh turned her attention from Gardner. 'I'll let him fill you in. He's good at what he does. Just comes with baggage. Keep the baggage out of the equation, and you have the best assistant SIO in the business.'

'How do I keep this baggage out of the equation then?'

'Well, for a start, you keep him away from *them*.' She pointed at the press. 'Or, more likely I guess, you keep *them* away from *him*.'

'Ma'am, that may be diff—'

'DCI Smith!' A female reporter shouted.

'DCI Smith, a moment please?' another reporter called.

This mysterious DCI Smith had upstaged crowd-pleaser Joe Bridge. The circle of reporters lost their shape and started to swarm behind a man moving slowly towards the cordon.

'What the hell is he doing here?' the chief constable muttered.

'Who's that?' Gardner said. 'I didn't realise there was another DCI?'

'There isn't. He's your predecessor. Anders Smith.'

'Retired?' Gardner said. 'I don't understand... What's he doing here then?'

'Good question,' Marsh said, starting forward.

Gardner moved alongside her. This was her crime scene. No one would be touching it without her say-so. And certainly not a retired detective!

Ex-DCI Anders Smith was a tall, strong-looking man, but he was beholden to a wooden cane, making his approach slow. He was wearing a buttoned shirt, a denim jacket, and some ripped jeans. Gardner and Marsh met him at the cordon.

'Anders,' Marsh said. 'It's almost two in the morning. Can I ask why you aren't enjoying your well-earned retirement? Unless traipsing around in the middle of the night is your idea of fun.'

'Night was when I always came alive, ma'am. I always did my best work then if you remember.'

'Did someone call you here, Anders?'

Anders must have been mid-sixties, but his hair was a striking blond. More than likely it was dyed, but Gardner had heard of some people who kept that shade deep into later life. He shook his head. 'No one called me.' He pointed off in the direction of the viaduct. 'I live on the river remember. When you fired up the halogen bulbs, I was halfway through some Horlicks in my kitchen. I drove up. Taking on those steps up the cliff is not something I'm attempting with this back these days.' He smiled. His face creased all over.

'Sorry, sir, can I ask why you came up?' Gardner asked.

His smile fell away and he turned a stunned expression towards her. She could also feel Marsh's eyes burning into the side of her head. It'd probably not been her finest hour in endearing herself to hardened locals such as this one. However, needs must. Anders Smith was now retired, and so was a civilian, and had no place here.

'To see if I could offer a hand, love,' Anders said.

Gardner had never been a fan of being called *love* anyway but being called *love* in a senior position by someone who should know better considering his background, was just downright demeaning. And deliberate. 'I'm not—'

'Anders,' Marsh interrupted. 'We appreciate your concern, and your offer to help, but you know that wouldn't be appropriate. We've enough staff to cover it.'

Anders laughed. 'We've never had enough staff to cover anything!'

'Thanks for stopping by, Anders,' Marsh said, 'but we really must press on.'

'Who is it?' Anders asked.

'Sorry—'

'Who's dead? I'm assuming someone's dead – I doubt you'd be making this song and dance over an accident.'

Gardner had heard enough. 'You know we can't tell you that. Now, please sir, I'm the SIO on this case, and you must move on. You're currently a civilian. We have a hard enough time keeping the press at bay as you probably know—'

'Wait!' Anders snapped. '*SIO*?' He looked at Marsh. 'Is this really my replacement?'

'Yes, I am. *Love*,' Gardner said and forced back a smirk. She glanced at her chief constable and thought she detected a ghost of a smile on her face too.

Anders scowled. 'I see my recommendation regarding Paul went unheard then?'

'He wasn't ready, Anders... *Besides*, this really isn't the time for this discussion.'

Have I stepped on Paul Riddick's toes then? Gardner wondered. *Have I upset the natural order by swanning in here and claiming the DCI role?*

Judging by her initial impressions of Riddick, it may just be a good thing.

Marsh continued to wave off Anders. 'Now, I'm going to have to insist—'

Anders lifted the hand that wasn't on his walking stick. 'No need, ma'am. I understand. Once a cop, always a cop and all that. Couldn't just sit there and watch trouble on my doorstep without so much as offering a friendly hand.'

Marsh nodded. 'I understand.'

'And the offer is still there if you want to give me a bell—'

Gardner heard footsteps behind her. 'Ey up, sir.' It was Riddick.

'Now then, me old cocker,' Anders said, and gave a deep-throated chuckle.

Riddick drew up alongside Gardner and Marsh. 'Thought it might be you when I heard the fiery conversation!'

'Well, you know me, son. Always like to tackle the fire head on.'

Clearly, Gardner thought, *despite it being wholly inappropriate... Now piss off!*

'And enough of the sir, Paul. I'm a civilian now. As my *replacement* saw fit to remind me.'

Gardner narrowed her eyes.

The press drew closer behind Anders. Joe Bridge, despite the accolades shovelled on him by Marsh, was now failing miserably to contain them. His quiff was out of sorts, and he looked flustered.

'Anyway, nice to see you all,' Anders said. 'Paul, I'll be in touch about that pint.'

Riddick gave him a mock salute.

Anders waved farewell, turned and slowly moved away. The wooden stick looked as though it had seen better days, and Emma wondered how long it would hold the weight of such a big man.

As he neared the press, they parted like the Red Sea to allow him through.

Gardner expected them to close in on him when he reached the centre of the path they'd formed, but the ambush never came. Gardner had never seen journalists so respectful with a target.

Before he'd reached the end of the pathway, one of the journalists chanced it. A smartly dressed woman with a glamorous haircut and eyes shining with youth and energy darted out in front of him. 'DCI Smith? Do you have anything you can share with us?'

'Sorry, love, your name?'

Gardner rolled her eyes – the man was from the dark ages.

'Marianne Perse.'

'Well, Ms Perse, I'm afraid I cannot help you. I'm retired. Did you not get the memo?'

'The memo?' Marianne said.

Anders chuckled. 'Must have got lost. No, I'm all done. On account of this back. However, if you need someone to talk to' – he turned and pointed at Gardner – 'she's yer lass.'

Gardner reddened from a combination of embarrassment and fury.

Prick.

She spun and disappeared back onto the crime scene before the hounds descended on her.

* * *

Gardner was introduced to the forensic pathologist, Hugo Sands, who was in his mid-thirties, and didn't respond to questions immediately. Instead, he had a disconcerting way of staring at you for a few moments before answering.

It soon became clear though that he wasn't doing this because your questions were stupid. He was doing this because his response, when it finally came, had been given serious consideration.

'Was there a struggle?' Gardner asked.

There was a long pause. 'Too early to say, but if there was, it wasn't a great one. This was over quickly.'

'Does this suggest the victim knew the killer?'

There was an even longer pause, which was ridiculous considering the monosyllabic response. 'Maybe.'

Gardner tried to keep the frustration out of her voice. 'How do you think he died?' Gardner resisted the urge to break eye contact with him as his brain ticked over.

Eventually: 'I need him on my table. You don't want guesswork.'

'I would take a guess at this stage... *anything*.'

Hugo shook his head. 'It really would be finger-in-the-air stuff.'

Gardner resisted the urge to tap her feet. 'Please.'

'Asphyxiation?'

'There are no marks on his neck though?'

'I've seen something similar before. A headlock doesn't always leave marks. Not initially anyway...' He then paused for a while as if he'd asked himself a question. 'If he was *dragged* in a headlock as the ground and trainers suggest – this could have killed him...'

'Making the killing unintentional?'

Hugo raised an eyebrow. She waited, but he clearly wasn't going to answer this.

'Okay,' Gardner said.

'If you'll excuse me, ma'am, I'd like to go back and examine the body some more.'

'Of course.'

She turned to Riddick, who'd remained quiet throughout that strained conversation. 'Manslaughter would certainly be more realistic in an area not renowned for its murder rates.'

Riddick nodded. 'However, Bradley kept bad company. *Very*

bad company. And such company is notorious for taking people from A to B.' He drew a line across his throat to indicate what he meant by B.

Gardner nodded and then looked out over the view again. 'I can see why your place brings the tourists, Paul; it's beautiful.' She thought for a moment before turning back to Riddick. 'The condom,' she said. 'Was Bradley up here with someone he shouldn't have been up here with?'

'If it even belongs to him... The DNA test needs to be fast-tracked,' Riddick said. 'I imagine quite a few couples head up this way to romance in the moonlight – we don't want this to be a red herring.'

'However, if it is his, we could have a good old-fashioned cuckold here?'

Riddick smiled. 'If he was interrupted mid-flow by a headlock would his pants not have been around his ankles? Although, I guess our perp could have waited until he was dressed to pounce?'

'Or dressed him after?' Gardner said.

Riddick nodded.

'Either way, it would be a quick case to close,' Gardner said. 'We'd just have to find the witness who had sex with him.'

'I hope so, because you do know that the list of people with motive will be a long one. Bradley was—'

'A right little shit, Paul. I heard you the first time.'

'And when there's one little shit, there're a million other little shits.'

'Very philosophical.'

'Realistic, boss. And you only have a team of twelve or so. The little shits vastly outweigh the team.'

Gardner sighed.

This is my first day, I have a murder – which is completely unheard of in these parts – the press is now gunning for me thanks to the pompous prick with the cane, and it is almost three in the morning! Please, Paul, could you just allow me to retain a small modicum of confidence?

She was glad she hadn't said this out loud, but she still felt irritated enough to press him on Marsh's warning. 'The chief constable said you had some baggage.'

'She said that?'

Gardner nodded.

'Ignore her. She's got it in for me. They don't call her Harsh Marsh for no reason.'

'Actually, she spoke very highly of you.'

He sneered. 'She's lying. She'd cheer if she saw the back of me!'

'Why do you think that, Paul? What's this baggage?'

Riddick turned to face her and raised an eyebrow. He then turned from her and started to walk away. 'We all have baggage, boss. If I show you mine, you can show me yours.'

She rolled her eyes and caught up with him. 'At least tell me something about this Anders Smith?'

'What do you want to know? That his mother was Scandinavian, hence the rare first name? Or that his dad was local builder, Trevor Smith, hence the common surname?'

'That wasn't the first thing on my mind… How about what he's doing at our crime scene?'

Riddick shrugged. 'How would I know?'

'Well, you seemed very friendly with him.'

'Everyone is friendly with the Lionman.'

'Lionman!'

'The translation of Anders – his nickname.'

'I've heard of ironmen, but never lionmen. The man can barely walk!'

'Toughest cop you ever met, Lionman,' Riddick said. 'Back in the day, of course.'

'Tough cops don't impress me much.'

'Well, he certainly impressed many around here.' He stopped and faced Gardner. 'He pulled a couple of kids from a burning house once.'

Gardner was speechless. And rather worried. She'd just come to blows with the local hero.

'Why the surprise, boss?' Riddick said with a ghost of a smile on his face. 'Just because everyone loves him, doesn't mean they'll dislike you. Anyway, relax; you struck gold. You're with me now, which will take all the attention off you, believe me.'

'How so?'

'Follow me and I'll show you.'

* * *

They left the crime scene and pulled off their paper suits.

Gardner surveyed the press, relieved to see that Joe Bridge had enlisted the help of a few plain-clothed officers to get them under control again.

'What're you planning to show me?' Gardner asked as they headed in the direction of the car park.

'It's coming... wait for it...'

'DI Riddick!' someone called.

'As promised,' Riddick said. 'The SIO on the bloody case is officially immune! You now have your very own human shield, boss.'

Gardner said, 'I don't understand. Why're they so interested in—'

'A few questions, DI Riddick?' It was the female journalist

that had stopped retired DCI Anders Smith in his tracks. *Marianne Perse.*

'No, Ms Perse, you may not,' Riddick called back.

Gardner looked at Riddick. She could see the fury in his eyes. She put a hand on his arm. 'Best to be polite, Paul. We don't want to create a scene.'

'Polite?' Paul raised an eyebrow. 'They don't even have that word in their chuffin' vocabulary!'

'DI Riddick!' shouted a male journalist.

Riddick strolled straight ahead. Gardner followed closely.

'Two minutes of your time!' another called.

'Piss off,' Riddick muttered.

'If this is a murder, DI Riddick,' Marianne called, 'will you be moved off the case?'

Riddick stopped. Gardner looked at him. Those furious eyes had narrowed. She didn't know what the hell was going on, but she didn't want him biting. She touched his arm again. He shrugged it off and kept walking. Gardner inwardly sighed with relief.

Once Gardner and Riddick had drawn level with the back of Bridge and his assistants, Marianne Perse called out again. 'The Winters case is still fresh in everyone's minds, DI.'

Riddick stopped and pointed. 'Fresh in *your* minds. The world has moved on.'

'Easy to move on for you, Detective Inspector. Not so for others,' Marianne said. 'Lives were turned upside down. Can we have a comment?'

'This is the only comment I have, Ms Perse,' Riddick said, still thrusting his finger in her direction. 'You don't care about anyone's life being turned upside down! You're chasing money; move on to something else.'

'Fine!' a male journalist said. 'Could we have a comment on *this* case, then?'

'We'll have a press conference in due course,' Gardner replied. 'Until then, could you keep your questions for Officer Bridge.'

That wasn't enough for the press – obviously – who continued to bark questions, and rile Riddick, but Gardner carried on walking with her hand on the small of her partner's back.

At the car park, she stopped and waited for him to turn and face her. 'So, human shield, do you want to fill me in on what's going on?'

Riddick shrugged. 'Not really.'

'Don't you think it's important for me to understand—'

'It's nothing to do with Bradley Taylor. This case is completely unrelated.'

'It'll be easy enough for me to look up. The Winters case? Fractured community relations often have a bearing on any investigation.'

He sighed.

'Do you have your car?' Gardner asked.

'I walked.'

She pressed her key fob, and the lights on her BMW glowed. 'Hop in then, and you can fill me in on this Winters case on the drive to Harrogate.'

'You're okay, boss,' he said, turning. 'I'll grab a taxi. Don't want to put you in the way of fractured community relations.' He strolled off with his hands in his pockets.

Shit.

Relations were certainly fractured all right!

5

Kelsey reached up and touched the certificate her mother had pinned to her bedroom wall: English Literature. Most committed student. Congratulations! Mrs Bradford.

She stared at it for almost ten minutes.

It was an accolade earned through countless hours of dedicated hard work, a token of admiration and respect from Mrs Higgins, her English teacher, and the head teacher, Mrs Bradford, and a symbol of her parents' immense pride.

Kelsey resisted the urge to tear it from the wall.

This award had been more ammunition for those evil bastards.

She went up to her bedroom and perched on the end of her bed. She rolled back her sleeve and stroked the old scars on her upper arm, avoiding the fresh ones that still stung. She looked up at her bookshelf, where the knife was hidden inside an old maths book that no one would ever think to check. She gritted her teeth, fighting back the call for distraction – those sharp stabbing pains that made her forget her woes, if only momentarily. She rolled down her sleeve, closed her eyes, lay back on her bed, and sought out another distraction instead.

Richard Hill.

Someone else who liked English Literature!

Someone who always had a kind word for her when very few people did...

Someone who was popular but didn't allow it to twist his kind nature.

Richard Hill.

She recalled the moment, several weeks ago, when they'd partnered for a science experiment, and he'd said, 'Call me Rich.' He'd smiled. His teeth were perfect and glowing.

She smiled now. Richard 'Call me Rich' Hill. The most perfect of distractions!

Another distraction was her phone. She read the news on the BBC app first, before checking her Gmail. Afterwards, she headed over to Facebook, and...

She felt the world around her suddenly jolt.

She saw a picture of herself receiving her English certificate in assembly. The headteacher was shaking her hand. Over the bottom of the image, someone had drawn an image using a computerised red marker.

It was clear what that image was. A tongue licking an arse.

The world felt as if it was turning the wrong way.

The image had attracted 107 laughing emojis already, and many comments.

She looked through the names. A fair amount of Year 11 students, and some from Year 10 had dropped likes or emojis. The same names. Those who had been torturing her for years.

The comments were nasty, but most were posted from the usual people.

However, someone had posted:

What yer reckon, Rich, still fancy her?

Richard 'Call me Rich' Hill's response:

As if 😂

It was at that point that Kelsey's world stopped jolting and turning, and simply collapsed around her.

6

Moments before the briefing was due to start, Gardner looked at her reflection in the bathroom mirror. *You've got this. When it comes to incident rooms, you've learned from the best.*

Her heart racing in her chest, she marched from the bathroom and into IR1.

In her mind, she'd imagined that everyone in the incident room would fall silent when she entered – just like they always did for her friend, and mentor, DCI Michael Yorke down in Wiltshire. However, they didn't. The eleven officers in the room continued to chat incessantly. From the front of the room, she surveyed them. Many officers, as was often the case, were male. They looked excited. Murder was hardly ever on the agenda, so she forgave them this discretion. However, enough was enough, so she coughed. *Loud.*

The majority looked in her direction. Some of the older men continued talking though.

The detective she respected above all others, Yorke, could organise and control a team without breaking a sweat. For a moment, she felt the anxiety of imposter syndrome, but then she recalled the pep talk she'd given herself in the bathroom mirror. *Snap out of it, Emma!*

She held her hand up. 'Sorry… your boss, a female, is at the front of the room.' This stopped the arrogant display, and the responsible officers looked on with red faces. Their colleagues chuckled though, and so she chalked her introduction off as a success.

'Good morning, everyone. I've not had a chance to meet most of you yet. I only arrived yesterday. And, no, before any of you ask, I didn't bring this victim with me. I'm as surprised as any of you - I was hoping for a quiet start!'

Some murmurs and laughter.

'My name is Detective Chief Inspector Emma Gardner and I will be the SIO on the case.' She looked through the crowd for Riddick. He was sitting at the back on his own. The lone wolf or the outcast? Judging by the press earlier, she assumed it to be the latter. She nodded in his direction. 'Detective Inspector Riddick will be my deputy.'

Murmurs and laughter were replaced by hushed whispers and sneers.

It appeared that Riddick's unpopularity wasn't confined to the media hounds; those closest to him also seemed to have an axe to grind.

Riddick slumped back in his chair, and put his hands behind his head, trying to look as nonchalant as he could.

'You'll be able to tell from my West Country accent that I'm a rural girl, or a *lass*, as you may prefer to call me here.'

She noticed some laughter from the red-faced older officers. Was she winning over her more hardened section of her audience? She felt a sudden surge of confidence.

'Now, as I told DI Riddick earlier, I'm not a ma'am. Never got on with it. Boss, please. I'd also like to introduce Matthew Blanks, our HOLMES 2 operative. This is his first day in the job. And what a day to start.'

Matthew Blanks, hunched over his laptop, raised a hand but said nothing. He had more facial hair than a yeti, and Gardner briefly wondered if it was weighing him down and preventing him from looking up to greet his colleagues.

She walked over to the large investigation scene board. At the top was written *Operation Eden*, the operation name randomly spat out by the computer. She pointed to the picture in the centre of it. 'Bradley Taylor. Our victim.'

They'd used Bradley's Facebook profile picture. He stared into the camera aggressively with half an eyebrow shaved off. It was clear what persona Bradley was trying to convey, but Gardner didn't want to dwell on it – she already had a sense for current opinions of the victim. She'd need to get some sympathy for him to instil some drive in the team. Beside his image were his name, address and date of birth written in marker pen.

Beneath those details: *Body discovered at Knaresborough Castle Keep. Reported 12.03 a.m.*

Alongside those details was a photograph of Doug Brace standing proudly outside his ice cream shop, posing for a press release. His details were also carefully written beside him.

'The family have yet to identify him, but he was recognised by both Doug,' – she pointed to the picture of Doug – 'DI Riddick, and several other officers. I think we can now move forward certain that the victim is indeed Bradley.'

She was looking at the board when she thought she caught someone murmur, 'Good riddance.' She turned to survey her audience, unable to determine if she'd imagined it, but doubting very much that she had.

'Listen. I'm going to be blunt now, but I do think some of us in this room may need to hear this. I've already heard Bradley

Taylor referred to as a "right little shit" this evening' – she didn't look over at Riddick as she said this so as not to undermine his already fragile authority – 'and we're going to have to knock these views on the head. He was young, only just eighteen.'

A hand shot in the air. It was a small male officer without a hair on his head.

'Sorry, could I get your name?' Gardner asked.

'DS Phil Rice, boss.'

'Thanks DS Rice. Fire away.'

'Bradley ran our people ragged these past years. Him and his friends.'

'I understand that, but he was not that long ago a child. He'd a future ahead of him. A chance to change—'

Someone grunted. She looked among the many faces looking up at her but couldn't identify who it was.

'This was someone's child…' Her eyes darted back and forth, ready for the next grunt. It didn't come.

'It is our job to provide justice to him, and justice to his family.'

Rice's hand shot up again.

'DS Rice?'

'Speaking of his family, boss, his father is right piece of work. Neil Taylor.'

'Thanks DS. DI Riddick has already made me aware. Neil recently got out of jail and has also been a drain on our budget… However, this still changes nothing. Look, if it makes you feel better, let's get justice for his mother. And if that still doesn't help with it, let's fall back on the old classic.'

'The old classic?' Rice said with a raised eyebrow.

'Doing your job, DS.' She'd toyed with the idea of adding goddamned before *job*, but figured that might make her sound too aggressive, and rather American to boot. 'Now, DI Riddick, shall we go through what we have so far?'

'Yes, boss,' Riddick said, rising to his feet. 'Bradley Taylor, aged eighteen. Left school at sixteen with no GCSEs. Was supposed to stay on and retake his English and maths in sixth form. He never bothered. I don't think the school were that concerned about pushing the issue and forcing him in.'

There was a chuckle, but Gardner let that one slide.

Riddick continued. 'So, in that time, he's been picked up for underage drinking, vandalism and shoplifting. Nothing serious enough to land him in a detention centre. He was suspected of dealing drugs, but there was never evidence to make this stick, but I'd say it was highly likely, especially considering his family history.'

Matthew Blanks, the HOLMES 2 operative, tapped away incessantly on his laptop, recording details. His long hair swinging back and forth as he did so made him look like a head-banger at a heavy metal gig.

'Bradley lived with his mother, Honey Taylor,' Riddick said. 'She's divorced from Neil. Consequently, she's all alone. We have the family liaison officer with her.'

'Sorry, DI Riddick, can I just interrupt. I'd like to extend my gratitude to DS Ross and DC O'Brien for delivering her the awful news. A task none of us envy.'

Ross and O'Brien were given pats on the back.

'And of course,' Riddick continued. 'The news was also delivered to Neil Taylor.' He looked over at DS Ross. 'How did he take it?'

'As expected, there weren't any tears,' Ross said. 'Just a few angry growls, and a flat-out refusal to have a family liaison officer.'

'I wonder why!' Rice quipped.

Family liaison officers were often the eyes and ears of the team. Neil Taylor would be well aware of this, and if he was, as many believed, still dealing drugs, he wouldn't be welcoming anyone into his house.

'Cause of death is suspicious,' Riddick continued. 'There is evidence of the body being dragged to its resting place behind the keep, so initial thoughts are that the death wasn't natural; unless, I guess, whoever was with him was spooked by a sudden death and hid the corpse anyway. Although, that'd be the last thing I'd do if someone dropped dead of a heart attack in front of me. The pathologist has him on the table now, and he will touch base with us as soon as he knows any more.'

'Thank you, DI Riddick. Doug Brace,' Gardner said, pointing at his picture, 'phoned the discovery of Bradley in at 12.03 a.m. Forensics are still working the scene as we speak. On the grass beside the keep, where many stop to admire the view of the Nidd and the viaduct, they've uncovered a used condom. DNA testing will ascertain whether it was used by Bradley and, if so, we can start to work out who he had intercourse with. They've also recovered a size-nine boot print from a patch of mud on this grassy area. Again, it is too early to tell if it has any relevance – but it's something, nonetheless. We need to gauge Bradley's movements before he met his fate in the castle. And, of course, anyone else that entered the grounds around the same time.'

She moved along the board to a large, aerial image of the castle grounds.

'There are a number of different routes into the castle grounds.' She traced the route that Doug had taken between the large solid towers on the enclosure wall – the main entrance. She then traced the route in via the car park that she and the other investigators had taken. 'Finally, from Waterside here by the viaduct, and up these steps to the castle grounds. The steps end right by the keep. Three ways in for Bradley, and his killer. We need to gather as much CCTV footage from these areas as we can. There is a public house here on the corner of the car park – so there will be some there. There will also be some along Waterside as there are a lot of homes. Speaking of homes, we need to go door to door. Did anyone see the victim? If so, when?'

She looked around at the eager faces. She no longer felt nervous, and they were no longer looking at her as though she was an alien. She must have succeeded in presenting herself as someone who knew what she was doing. She forced back a desire to shout hallelujah!

She decided to bring this briefing to a close while the going was good and let her people loose on this mystery.

'Until we know otherwise, we work on the assumption that this was a killing, and it wasn't random. You all know as well as I do that motive is the best place to start. So, if Bradley was targeted, we need to find out why. And this is where I appreciate it will get messy. Because, as many of you have been at pains to point out, he has caused a lot of problems in the past. This means we need to build up a picture of his life. Who did he knock around with? Was he involved with gangs? County lines? Conflicts? Did he have a girlfriend? Girlfriends? Who? He was unemployed, so he must have been accessing money somewhere. His mother's benefits, or illegal activity? Unfortunately, his mobile phone is missing, but we can access records. Social media is always a treasure trove. Medical problems? Unlikely at his age, but let's look. And the school? Let's find out what he was like, and what he was up to while he was in attendance.' She paused for breath. 'I could go on, but according to the chief constable, I've inherited a fantastic team, so I'm confident you'll just get to it.'

A few eyebrows were raised. They were either surprised that

Marsh had passed on compliments regarding them, or they simply thought she was fibbing.

Of course, it was a fib. Marsh had never made any compliments, but Gardner knew the value of motivation and positivity.

'DI Riddick and I will speak to the parents. Suspicions are high regarding Neil Taylor's place in all of this, so it seems an important and logical starting point. I have assigned tasks and pinned them to the wall. We will reconvene at 6 p.m. I appreciate that you've lost sleep tonight, so subject to what we learn, I will try to claw back some time for you. Thank you.'

She was first out the door. Marsh was standing there, smiling. 'Didn't want to cramp your style, so I listened out here, Detective Chief Inspector.'

'Ma'am... How did I do?'

Marsh clutched her upper arm, smiled and winked. 'Not bad for a woman, Emma. Not bad at all.'

7

Family Liaison Officer Sandra Fletcher opened the door of Honey Taylor's house for Gardner and Riddick.

Sandra had a young, warm face, still unweighted by the trials and tribulations of great loss. It would be in stark contrast to the woman awaiting them in the lounge.

Honey Taylor vaped with a trembling hand, while perched on the edge of the sofa, tapping one foot anxiously.

The room was a mess. There were a couple of open pizza boxes on the table and a couple of empty cans of beer. There was also an odour of rotten food in the air. An odour that many stable people would struggle to live with. Gardner suspected that Honey wasn't a well woman at the best of times, and that Bradley's death would be the straw that broke the camel's back.

Bradley's mother hadn't even noticed the detectives walk in.

'Honey?' Sandra said.

After lowering her red vape pen, Honey turned to look at her visitors. Her eyes looked glassy and unfocused. 'Yes?'

'This is Detective Chief Inspector Gardner, and Detective Inspector Riddick.'

She pointed the vape pen at Riddick and shook it. She also narrowed her eyes. 'I know who you are.' She looked at Gardner. 'Never seen you before, mind.'

'I'm so sorry for your loss, Mrs Taylor,' Gardner said.

'Are you absolutely sure it's him?' Honey asked.

'Yes, ma'am. He's been identified by a number of people now. I'm sorry.'

She turned away and continued to stare off into space. 'Well, everyone knew who he was. You don't need me to identify him, then?'

'A formal identification would be welcome, but, of course, we could ask someone else if you'd prefer?'

'Don't be asking his father.' She turned back and waved her vape pen at Gardner this time. 'I mean it. Don't be asking his father.'

Gardner nodded, but this wasn't an agreement. It was just an acknowledgement that she'd heard the request.

'Can we take a seat, Mrs Taylor?' Gardner asked.

Honey nodded at the sofa opposite hers. 'But call me Honey. Mrs Taylor makes it sound so... I don't know... so...'

Dramatic and real? Gardner thought, taking a seat with Riddick beside her.

'I'll get us all a cup of tea,' Sandra said.

Everyone explained how they took their tea, which turned out to be the same, and then Sandra vacated the room.

Gardner readied her notebook. From the corner of her eye, she noticed that Riddick hadn't readied his. This irritated her. 'Here.' She handed him her notebook and pen.

He took them without looking at her, no doubt trying to hide his own irritation with her.

'He was a little shit, you know,' Honey said.

Gardner resisted rolling her eyes, and instead nodded sympathetically. 'Children can be troublesome sometimes, Honey—'

'No. He was a *little shit*. I'm not surprised this happened.'

Gardener and Riddick exchanged a look. Honey was staring in the direction of Riddick and Gardner's feet rather than their faces, so she wouldn't have noticed.

'Could you elaborate on that, Honey? Why did you think that?' Gardner asked.

She vaped and continued tapping her foot for a moment before replying, 'He pissed people off all the time.'

'Anyone in particular?' Riddick asked.

'Everyone,' Honey said.

Gardner nodded. 'How would you describe your relationship with your son?'

Honey lifted her free hand in the air and gave a so-so gesture.

'Up and down?' Gardner said.

'Yeah,' she said. 'We'd have blow-ups, but it always settled afterwards. We were close, I reckon. But he was too much like his bloody father.'

'How so?' Gardner asked.

'Attracted to trouble.'

'What kind of trouble?'

She shrugged. 'He liked to steal. Stole from my purse... Never much in there, mind.'

She then looked as if she was welling up, so Gardner said, 'Take your time, Honey.'

The moment passed, and Honey sighed. 'He'd no need to steal from me. I'd have given him anything he asked for.'

Gardner offered her a sympathetic look despite the fact that she wouldn't notice it – she was still gazing downwards.

'I knew he was struggling, but he'd never mention it. I think he thought he could get away with lifting a few quid from me and

I wouldn't notice. I did, of course. You always notice when you don't have much, do you know what I mean? Anyway, he had pride, I'll give him that.' She looked up for the first time in a while. 'He got that from me. Not that arsehole of a father!'

Gardner continued to probe Honey over her relationship with Bradley, casting regular glances sideways at Riddick, relieved each time to see him taking notes. When it became clear that Honey either knew little about what her son was up to outside her house, or was just unwilling to share anything, Gardner changed focus. 'When was the last time you saw your son, Honey?'

At that point, Sandra came into the room, holding a tray with three cups of tea. She placed the tray on the small table between the sofas. 'Three teas with milk, no sugar.' She smiled and took a seat next to Honey.

Honey breathed out a lungful of vapour and said, 'Yesterday. He came in and raided the fridge, as he does most days, and then disappeared through the door. He asked me for a lift, but I was already over the limit by then. Never like to break the law. I always left that for the bastards I fell for.'

'Where did he want a lift to?' Gardner asked.

'Crown Inn.'

Riddick said, 'That's a Wetherspoons.'

Gardner nodded. 'What time did he make this request?'

'Around half eight, I think. Roughly. I was just about to start the second episode of *Corrie*. Another reason I didn't want to give him a lift... the main reason to be fair. He ended up walking.'

'How long is the walk into town from here?' she asked Riddick.

'Twenty-five minutes, give or take.'

Which gave them a window of between five to nine, and three minutes past midnight – the time Doug phoned the murder in.

Gardner allowed a moment for Riddick to take some notes, while she indulged in a mouthful of tea. The tea tasted different. Gentler and smoother than she was used to. She looked down. It was also lighter in colour. 'Nice tea. Thank you.'

'Yorkshire Tea,' Sandra said. 'Only the best, of course.'

'Nothing to do with that,' Riddick said. 'Water is just softer up here than down south. Yorkshire Tea still comes from Asian plantations. It's not cultivated on the dales!'

Sandra looked embarrassed.

'Just saying.' Riddick shrugged.

Gardner inwardly sighed over the irreverent interaction. 'Thank you. So, Honey—'

'Where were you between nine and midnight yesterday?' Riddick asked.

Gardner had to stop her mouth from falling open. *Woah man!*

'Where do you think I was?' Honey said, glaring at Riddick. She reached over to pick up her tea and, for one horrible moment, Gardner worried that she might just launch it over Riddick. 'I was here.'

'Can anyone verify that for us?' Riddick asked.

Sandra was looking down at the floor now. Gardner felt compelled to interject. 'These are standard questions, Honey. You are in no way under investigation. We rule everyone out before proceeding.'

Much to Gardner's relief, Honey took her hand from the hot tea. Again, she waved her vape pen at Riddick. 'This one's a bad 'un.' She looked at Gardner. 'Do you know that?'

Gardner shook her head. 'DI Riddick is just doing his job, Honey. The question is a necessary one—'

'I'm not talking about the question. I'm talking about him in general. A bad 'un. He shouldn't be working after what he did.'

Bloody hell, Gardner thought. *Here we go again! What have you done, Paul?* She felt annoyed with Marsh for not telling her more about the man she was working with. Later, she'd have to start digging.

'Honey,' Riddick continued. 'Could you please answer the question?'

She narrowed her eyes. 'Try the pizza delivery guy. I got a pizza around ten.'

'That doesn't account for the entire time,' Riddick said.

'Then, you'll have to arrest me... bad 'un.'

This was getting out of hand. Gardner leaned over and whispered in his ear. 'Outside, Paul.'

Riddick stood up. He handed the notebook to Gardner and turned to leave.

'Out on your ear,' Honey snapped. 'That's what should have happened to you.'

'Nice,' Riddick said, opening the door. 'Some of us have mortgages to pay, Honey.'

'You saying I don't!' she called after the departing DI. 'You think I enjoy being on benefits?'

Once Riddick had left, Gardner turned back to Honey. 'I'm sorry that got out of hand. DI Riddick was acting with the best intentions.'

Honey laughed.

'You aren't under suspicion, Honey. And we're going to do everything in our power to find out who did this.'

Honey now looked angry and frustrated, rather than distressed.

Gardner tried to revive the interview, but due to the sharp altercation, it now felt as if it was winding to a close. She still managed to press Honey further on Neil.

'The man's a rat. He's only just got out the nick, and he's hooked up with someone. Living in their house and everything.

On Hay-A-Park estate.'

'What kind of relationship did he have with his son, Honey?'

'You'll have to ask Neil that. Not great. However, none of his relationships ever are.'

Gardner continued to ask questions as she finished her tea, but when it became clear that there was little else to discuss – at least for now – she gave her farewell.

Outside, Riddick was sitting on the bonnet of the car.

'Enough's enough, Paul. You need to fill me in,' Gardner said.

'It's personal,' Riddick said. He raised an eyebrow. 'Although everything is online.' With that, he hopped down from the bonnet and climbed into the passenger side.

8

The journey to Hay-A-Park was short despite feeling incredibly long. Such was the impact of the stony silence in Gardner's car.

As she rounded a corner into the estate, past an empty children's playground, Gardner couldn't hold back any more. 'We're not going to get far if you wind up the witnesses!'

Riddick's expression darkened. 'I'm pretty sure I didn't start it.'

'She could have been throwing stones at you for all I care. You never rise to it.'

Riddick looked out of the passenger window, clearly hiding his fury from his superior.

Gardner took a left turn. Riddick wasn't offering any directions, but it didn't matter too much because Gardner was using her Sat Nav. She counted off the numbers on the houses she passed, before stopping beside the driveway to Number 26.

She killed the engine and reached for the handle.

'I asked for her alibi,' Riddick said. 'I was reasonable.'

'No, you interrupted me. You knew I was working it gently. You took it upon yourself to go for the jugular.'

Riddick shook his head.

Gardner sighed. 'Listen, if you want to fill me in on what this is all about, I'm all ears. Otherwise, let's press on for now. I'd prefer to hear your version of events before I finally get five minutes to google this infamous Winters case, but I've got very little patience in breaking down your stubborn veneer. Talk to me or just help me! That before, in Honey's house, doesn't help anyone. The chief constable speaks highly of you, Paul, so I'm keen to keep you by my side, but' – she looked at the house where Neil Taylor was currently residing – 'mess this up, and I'm talking to the boss back at HQ.'

Riddick looked at Gardner. 'Something you should know.'

'Go on?'

'I went to school with Neil Taylor.'

'Great.' Gardner raised an eyebrow. 'Do you have history with this man?'

'Not as such, no. I'm just acutely aware of what a shit stain he is. It's hard for me to guarantee I'll tiptoe around him.'

'Paul, for pity's sake, he's just lost a son—'

'The man is a drug dealer! The number of lives he's destroyed is unfathomable. If you want to sympathise with him, be my guest, boss. But I won't be finding it in my heart.'

'Am I best going in alone?' Gardner asked and sighed.

'I'm not letting you go in there alone.'

Gardner guffawed. 'My hero!'

'I don't mean it like that. Don't worry! No one has ever made me so acutely aware of how well they can handle themselves as much as you have! It's just that I know this dickhead. I can see through the lies he's about to tell you. And I promise you, they'll be nothing but.'

'Okay,' Gardner said. 'Just don't swing for him. Please. Do I have to beg?'

Riddick smiled and made the Scout salute. 'Scout's honour. But I still can't promise I'll be polite. However, after five seconds in this man's presence, you'll struggle too.'

Riddick opened the door and stepped out.

Gardner shook her head and smiled. She genuinely couldn't decide if she liked him or not. One minute she wanted to brain him, the next minute she admired his fire.

When they reached the front door, they heard shouting from a man and a woman inside. The actual reason for the quarrel was unclear as the only discernible words were profanities, driven forcibly through the wooden door due to the emphasis being placed on them.

'It's only bloody gone breakfast,' Riddick said. 'Wonder what it's like by teatime!'

'Between this and his neurotic mother, Bradley had a crap life.' Gardner sighed. 'People should bear that in mind.' She didn't look at Riddick as she knocked on the door, making it clear that he was one of the people she was taking aim at.

'Met plenty of wealthy kids who were right little shits too,' Riddick said. 'I don't discriminate based on background.'

An answer for everything!

The door opened. A man stood there in a pink, frilly dressing gown. He had chiselled features, but they were far too sharp and angular to be considered handsome. The chest hair exposed due to the loosely tied dressing gown was repulsive.

Gardner held up her ID.

'For pity's sake.'

Gardner looked left at Riddick who was forcing back a smile. She acted like she hadn't heard the inappropriate welcome and continued. 'Neil Taylor?'

'Uh-huh.'

'I'm Detective Chief Inspector Emma Gardner and this is—'

'Can I stop you right there? I told you people earlier – did you not listen? Do you know what we've been through today? What *I'm* going through? And don't give me that supportive bullshit.' He pointed at himself and then at Riddick. 'We've never been friends. So, just because my kid has died, doesn't give us a reason to form any bonds now. I said no, and I meant no.'

Gardner took a deep breath. 'Mr Taylor. This is not about the family liaison officer.'

Although it would be a major coup to get one in here.

'So, what you want?'

'To ask a few questions.'

'Why?'

'We question everyone who's close to the victim. I'm assuming you'd want us to help find whoever is responsible?'

'What time did my boy die?'

'We suspect it was between nine and twelve.'

He clapped his hands together. 'I was in bed with Mandy the entire time. You can ask her if you want.'

'We'd like to,' Gardner continued.

'Can you do it over the phone?'

'Not really. Listen, Mr Taylor, we understand what you're going through, but we're not here suspecting you, we are here to build a picture of who your son was, and try and identify who would want to—'

'Neil, do you have something to hide?' Riddick asked.

Shit, Gardner thought. *Here he goes again!*

'And why would you ask that, Paul?' Neil asked.

'Because in my experience, witnesses who are abusive and dismissive, usually have something to hide.'

A smirk spread across Neil's face and he took two steps backwards. 'Best come in and sit for a while then if that's what it's going to take. You did a great job of stitching me up last time.

Ended up inside for the best part of four years. Probably best I don't let you do it again, eh?'

'Thank you, Mr Taylor,' Gardner said, following Neil into the house.

'Whatever.'

Gardner looked back at Riddick and fought back the urge to tell him to wipe the bloody 'I told you so' expression off his face.

* * *

Mandy Spencer might have owned the bricks and mortar, but Neil Taylor had made this home his. He had his feet on the coffee table and Gardner thanked her lucky stars that the dressing gown went all the way down to the top of his calves. It wouldn't be the first time a witness had accidentally exposed themselves during an interview, but Neil's modesty was a particularly nauseating prospect.

What was even more nauseating was watching Mandy wait hand and foot on Neil's every need. In less than ten minutes, he ordered her to open the window because he was warm, demanded a cup of coffee, and even had the gall to send her to their bedroom for his cigarettes.

Gardner watched Mandy's movements, trying to determine whether this was due to adoration or fear. Gardner's eventual conclusions terrified her more. It was gratitude. She'd seen this before in people who bounced between abusive relationships. They were so desperate not to return to their old life, they swerved the warning signs that a repeat of what had gone on before was just around the corner. Gardner had read the background on Neil. There was no doubt Mandy was caught up in a very toxic relationship with a very toxic man.

When Mandy handed the cigarettes to Neil, Riddick said, 'I'd prefer it if you didn't smoke.'

'Whose house is this anyway?' Neil threw them on the table beside his feet and the ashtray. Mandy sat down alongside Neil and fidgeted.

'What was your relationship like with Bradley?' Gardner asked.

Neil looked at Mandy, smiled and then looked back at Gardner. 'Shite?'

Gardner put her pencil to her notepad but thought better of writing this down. 'How so?'

'Well, he couldn't be bothered to visit me inside – so that's four years you can chalk off right there. Even before I went down, I barely saw him. Used to wander the streets, getting himself into all sorts of bother. I lost count of the times your lot brought him back to the house.'

If you'd been any kind of father to him, he may have had a reason to stay in.

'Yes, he did get into a lot of trouble,' Riddick said, reading from his notes. 'Social workers were involved. He was almost taken into care on one occasion.'

Neil nodded. 'At the time, I suggested that might be a good thing to Honey.'

'Why?' Gardner asked, feeling the nib of her pencil snap as she pushed too hard into the pad.

'That'd show him actions have consequences. Teach him a lesson. He'd have been back, one day. Disciplined, you'd hope.'

'Going into care is not the same as going into the army, Mr Taylor,' Gardner said.

'Speaking of actions having consequences, Neil,' Riddick said. 'How did Bradley feel about you going to jail?'

Gardner looked at Riddick. *Easy does it; not too much now...*

'Well, like I said, he didn't visit me, so put two and two together. Besides, I was stitched up, as you well—'

'No. You were found guilty,' Riddick said.

'Doesn't mean I am.'

'Would you consider yourself rehabilitated, Neil?' Riddick said.

'Rehabilitated from what? I was innocent!'

Riddick snorted.

Okay, that's enough. You're winding up the witness again, Paul. 'This is all on record, Mr Taylor. We just want to ascertain if it is relevant to what happened to Bradley.'

'It's not. Do your lot even know how he died yet?'

'No, I'm afraid not,' Gardner said.

'So, you don't even know if he was murdered?'

'The circumstances around his death are suspicious,' Riddick said. 'That's as much as we're permitted to say right now.'

'Drugs?' Neil asked.

'Did Bradley take drugs?' Gardner asked.

Neil shrugged. 'How do I know? Hardly saw him. He was a skinny streak of piss, but aren't most teenagers?' He put his hand on Mandy's thigh.

'When was the last time you saw Bradley?' Riddick asked.

'Couple of days ago. He stopped by the house. Afternoon.'

'Why?'

'To cause problems!' Mandy said. It was the first time she'd spoken.

Gardner noticed Neil's knuckles whiten as the bastard tightened his grip on Mandy's leg.

'He wanted a loan,' Neil said. 'Was sick of living at his mum's. He wanted a handout so he could put down a deposit and pay a month's rent somewhere.'

'And did you help him?' Gardner asked.

'Help him!' Neil said. 'How would giving him almost two grand have helped him? He'd have blown it before he'd even got to the estate agent.' He looked between the two officers. 'I know what you're thinking, chip off the ol' block! But I'm telling you, I worked for everything I ever made; no one ever gave me a handout!'

'So, you refused to help him then?' Riddick said.

'I *advised* him to get a job.'

Riddick made a note, purposefully murmuring, 'Declined support.'

You can't help yourself, can you? She shook her head in his direction.

Concerned about the way Neil had gripped Mandy's leg, Gardner addressed her next. 'Was that all he wanted?'

Mandy nodded. Neil relaxed his grip and then withdrew his hand.

'Do you know if Bradley had a girlfriend?' Gardner asked.

Neil shook his head. 'I keep telling you, I hardly knew him! He wasn't about to confide his intimate affairs to me, was he?'

'How about friends? Enemies, perhaps?'

Neil shrugged.

'This is your son, Neil,' Riddick said. 'You're connected. Let's not beat around this. You must know some of what your son may have been up to!'

Neil glared at Riddick. 'Read my lips, Paul. I. Genuinely. Do. Not. I've been squeaky clean since I was paroled ten months back. Been breaking cars down the garage. Fetch quite a few quid old parts on eBay!'

Gardner heard the squeaking of floorboards. It sounded as if someone was coming down the stairs beyond the lounge door.

'Is anyone else in the house?' Gardner asked.

'Just my daughter, Cherish,' Mandy said, standing. 'I'll go and see if she's okay.'

'How old is Cherish, Mrs Spencer?' Riddick asked.

Mandy suddenly paled and looked at Neil as if to seek permission for answering the question.

Neil rolled his eyes and looked down; he would know how suspicious her response looked.

'Eighteen,' Mandy said.

'Eighteen.' Gardner made a note. 'Similar age to Bradley, then?'

'What's that got to do with anything?' Neil said.

'They might have some similarities in social groupings, perhaps? At the very least, she may have known some of his friends.'

'Chalk and cheese them two,' Neil said. 'You won't find anything there. Mand, love, go and see if Cherish is all right... She's been feeling under the weather a bit these last—'

The door opened and a heavily pregnant young woman came into the room.

Gardner stood. 'Cherish?'

'Yes... Who're you?' the woman said, stroking her rounded stomach, exposed due to an ill-fitting T-shirt.

'DCI Gardner, and this is DI Riddick.'

She nodded down at Riddick, influencing him to stand too.

The only person now not standing was Neil, but he was staring ahead, looking thoroughly pissed off.

Gardner approached Cherish, noticing immediately that her face was red and blotchy. She nodded down at the bump. 'How long to go?'

'Six weeks,' Cherish said, and rubbed at her tears.

'You must be excited?'

Cherish started to well up. Mandy came up alongside her and

put an arm around her shoulder. 'She's not been feeling the best. Have you dear?'

Cherish shook her head. Tears were running down her red face.

'Would it be okay to ask you a few questions, Cherish?' Riddick asked.

Neil finally stood. 'No, it would not! Have you seen the state of the lass?'

Gardner turned and looked at the angry father of the victim, and then looked at Riddick. She gave him a swift nod. She hoped he interpreted it for what it was. *Leave it for now. We can pick this one up later.*

Gardner looked back at Neil. 'I totally understand, Mr Taylor. We can see what a day it must have been for you all.' She looked back at Mandy. 'We'll do everything we can.' She glanced at Cherish. 'Bradley's death is a tragedy—'

Cherish gave an anguished cry, turned and buried her face in her mother's chest.

Bingo.

* * *

Outside Mandy Spencer's house, Gardner climbed into her BMW.

Riddick opened the passenger door to climb in beside her, then hesitated.

'What're you waiting for?' she asked.

He didn't reply.

Nor did he get into the vehicle.

For pity's sake...

She climbed back out of the car and looked at him over the roof. He was glaring at Mandy's house.

'Marching back in there isn't the best—'

'She's pregnant with our victim's baby.' He looked pumped. She could see the desperation on his face for the truth.

'Get in the car before you reveal all of our cards in the centre of this bloody housing estate!'

He grumbled but complied.

Only upon exiting Hay-A-Park estate did Gardner see fit to raise the subject again. 'Did you see her? Poor girl was a mess. Putting pressure on her while Neil is watching over is not the best move.'

'Someone has been murdered!'

'Take a couple of deep breaths and think.' She drove under the railway bridge and onto Chain Lane. 'Better? Do you see where I'm coming from now?'

'Not sure. I'm still thinking the same thing – someone has been murdered, and that girl, Cherish, is the best lead we have.'

'And Neil knows that too. Which is why he is being as secretive as they come, while Mandy is choosing her words very carefully so as not to piss him off.'

'Did you see his hand on Mandy's leg! Jesus Christ!'

Gardner nodded, feeling the anger well up inside her again. 'What is that bastard hiding?'

'Well, he's not protecting Cherish. Did you see that poor girl struggle into the room? She's almost eight months pregnant. She certainly wasn't lurking up by the castle keep, overpowering Bradley, and then skipping away before Doug's dog pissed on the crime scene. That man has only ever cared about himself.' Riddick clenched his fist.

'I looked at a pair of his boots on the way out.'

'Let me guess, size 9?'

'Yes, but let's not get too excited – it's a common size. Anyway... which way to the hospital?' Gardner asked.

'Take a left at these lights,' Riddick said.

'Let's not jump to any conclusions on Neil's involvement in the murder. The man has a past, and after assessing his character in there, I strongly suspect he is up to no good in the *present* too. I also suspect that he just doesn't want us sniffing around his business. He'll think that as soon as we know that his current partner's daughter is pregnant with Bradley's child, we'll be all over him like a rash.'

'Yes – when are we planning on that rash-like approach?'

'Well, the post-mortem is due to finish any time now. Let's confirm it was a murder first. Then, we can have our briefing, and set the dogs on Neil and Mandy – find out why they want to keep the truth from us.'

'Dogs?' Riddick said, and snorted. 'Hamsters have more bite than them lot.'

'Well, I don't need any more rottweilers,' Gardner said, and fixed Riddick in a stare.

9

Caught up in a traffic jam on the way to the hospital, Gardner received a call asking her to hold off on the post-mortem for another thirty minutes.

'Just as well,' Gardner said, tapping her hand on the steering wheel. 'How long does this bloody train take?'

Gardner and Riddick, among many others, were stuck behind a barricade that had come down with very little warning. Despite being at a standstill for almost five minutes, there was still no sign of the train that had put the brakes on their journey.

Gardner gestured at The Prince of Wales public house, which was doing a thriving trade in its concrete, roadside beer garden, despite it only being early afternoon on a weekday. 'I can see why they built this pub. Having a train cut through my town would drive me to drink too.'

Riddick smiled.

'What?'

'Who's the grumpy one around here after all?'

'Last time I checked, grumpiness and impatience were two

very different things.' The barricade rose. She looked up at the roof of her car. 'Thank you, lord.'

'Well, as there's no longer a rush, there's a Costa on the left…'

'Most sensible thing I've heard from you all day.'

After parking, Riddick treated her to an extra-large Americano. She opted out of milk. He, himself, opted for a medium cappuccino. He plonked the tray down on the table in front of her.

'Coffee in a soup bowl,' Riddick said. 'Counts as a gym session carrying that over! We only have ten minutes, you know?'

'Won't take me ten minutes.'

'You drink that in under ten minutes, your bladder will burst.'

Gardner noticed his open wallet on the tray. There was a picture of Riddick with a woman, presumably his wife, and two young girls. She pointed at it. 'Cute family.'

Riddick looked down at the picture and scooped it up. He closed it, lifted himself from the chair, and slipped it into his back pocket.

'A wallet in your back pocket? Sense, man! You're a copper!'

'Precisely. And everyone knows that around here – so who'll try?' Riddick said. 'Plus, haven't you seen the way everyone steers clear of me like I'm the local leper?'

'Yes.' *And it's actually odd for someone who is quite likeable.* 'Maybe you can now enlighten me as to why that is?' She picked up her bladder-bursting soup bowl with both hands and took a large, red-hot mouthful.

Riddick raised an eyebrow. 'Good job we're heading to the hospital, I hear they're good with third-degree burns.'

'Told you, no patience. My husband calls me *asbestos mouth*.'

'He sounds romantic.'

Gardner snorted. 'I wish! So, tell me about your family. Like I said, they look cute.'

Riddick looked away. 'Yes.'

'The girls a similar age?'

'Twins. Lucy and Molly.'

'Lovely. What they like?'

'Total opposites.' Riddick smiled, staring off into space. 'One goes potty over princesses, the other loves to wreak havoc with a Nerf gun.'

Gardner laughed. 'And your wife?'

Riddick looked at Gardner. 'Is this our "getting to know each other" meeting, boss?'

'Well, I suppose we best have a go at some point.'

'Don't be offended; never been one for talking about myself.' He took a mouthful of cappuccino.

'At least tell me her name?'

'Rachel.'

'What does Rachel do?'

He looked away. This was clearly something he didn't want to engage with. Not wanting to give him the opportunity to wriggle out of another conversation, she said, 'Her job?'

'Her job is to looks after us... Me in particular!' Riddick said, looking back.

'Behind every great man is a great woman and all that?'

'She's the only great one. You have me pegged all wrong.'

Maybe, Gardner thought. *One thing that I am picking up on though is that you're incredibly down on yourself.* 'Why is there so much self-pity?'

'I hadn't noticed.'

Yeah, right! 'You know Chief Constable Marsh speaks very highly of you.'

'Just like she spoke highly of your team?'

'Yes, that was bullshit, but I'm not fibbing about this.'

Riddick laughed. 'Believe me, Marsh would sooner I were

gone.'

'Why would she put you on the case then? Not like murders are ten-a-penny around here. Pretty sure she wants it solved. Pronto.'

'You like to talk, boss. Maybe you should cut back on the caffeine?'

'Talking is good for you. Caffeine not so much.'

He took a large mouthful of his lukewarm cappuccino. 'Never found talking much use.'

'Jesus – you really are a barrel of laughs! You've a beautiful family. Thank your lucky stars. How many people can say that? Fewer than you think.' She took another sip of her Americano. 'I'll tell you about mine. I have a husband, Barry, who unlike your better half, does very little for the family. However, in fairness, he does bring in a decent income... Anabelle, my daughter, is six, going on thirteen.' She rolled her eyes.

'Girls are like that,' Riddick said with a smile.

'Seems so. I've lost control of her wardrobe.'

'Independence and young people. It's the promised land.'

'Yes. But wearing multicoloured tights to school is a land I'd prefer to avoid.'

Riddick laughed. 'Are they coming to join you soon then?'

'Barry is just tying up loose ends down in Salisbury, and then they'll be up here.'

'You must hate being without them?' Riddick said, looking down at his cappuccino, and swilling it around his cup.

'Yes, I hate peace and quiet.'

'You're investigating a murder – hardly peace and quiet.'

Gardner nodded.

Riddick looked at his watch. 'Speaking of murder, boss, you need to speed up. Our victim will have been opened and closed by now.'

Gardner drank the rest of her bucket of coffee.

10

While waiting in the scrubs area, Riddick paced. 'They could do with some bloody windows.'

'In my experience, mortuaries are always in the arse-end of hospitals,' Gardner said, tipping some tic tacs into her hand.

'No sunlight. It'd be like *seasonal affective disorder* in this dungeon all year round!'

'I've met plenty of pathologists who prefer it this way.' She crunched the tic tacs.

'Hugo has always been an odd ball.'

'Let me guess, you went to school with him too?' Gardner asked.

Riddick nodded. 'Although, unlike Neil, he isn't a dickhead, just odd.'

'You're very good at putting people into labelled boxes. What's the label on mine?'

'At the moment you defy classification, boss.'

She smiled and nodded. 'I like that.'

Riddick continued pacing. 'Forget the dark, how could anyone work with this smell of detergent—'

The door opened, and Hugo walked in, wearing his scrubs.

He had his blood-stained gloved hands up in the air. Was this a clear warning to all concerned not to offer him a handshake? 'Afternoon.' He pulled off his plastic gloves with a snap, pinned his foot to a lever on his bin, and threw the offending items away. He then went to the sink and scrubbed his hands.

Gardner launched her notepad over to Riddick who caught it in both hands. 'Notes.'

He saluted her. 'Actually, I take back what I just said… I do actually have a clearly labelled box for you.'

Gardner spoke to Hugo's back. 'So, what have we got?'

Hugo reached for a towel, and turned to look at her, drying his hands as he did so.

Here we go again, Gardner thought. *It's like having a conversation with a bloody sloth!*

She felt like saying, 'I thought it was going to get easier when you had him on your table,' but forced her words back.

Eventually, he spoke. 'I can tell you, without a shadow of a doubt, that the cause of death is asphyxiation.'

Hallelujah, a conclusion! 'I see.'

'Marks on his neck have actually started to show. This usually happens when the skin begins to dry. It becomes more transparent and marks to the tissue become more evident. There are also contusions on his windpipe. I've taken swabs, but I don't think you'll find any DNA. We have some fibres, though. You see, he was strangled in a choke hold. The police, yes, *that would be you*, used choke holds to subdue suspects once upon a time. It was stopped after a spate of accidental deaths.'

Gardner exchanged a glance with Riddick. Hugo's accusatory tone could suggest that he believed the current crop of police officers had the same capacity for police brutality as the old – total nonsense of course.

'What other conclusions have you reached?' Gardner asked.

She waited for his measured response. 'The pattern of the emerging bruising and contusions does suggest dragging. I'd say your assailant was taller than the victim, and strong. I'm not ruling out a woman, but a man is more likely. Bradley would have lost consciousness before he died. So, the assailant could have stopped when he went limp. In wrestling, they used to call it a sleeper hold for that reason.'

'We know the time of death was between nine and twelve,' Gardner said. 'Are you able to narrow it down more for us?'

'I'd say closer to twelve than nine,' Hugo said. 'If it'd been nine, the bruising would more likely have shown up at the crime scene.'

'Okay, thanks, that's useful.'

'Oh, there's also some evidence of a struggle. The victim reached behind himself to grab at the arms cutting off his oxygen. We have recovered some more fibres from the fingernails, but no skin or blood I'm afraid.'

This was disappointing. She usually gathered more from the post-mortem than this. The fact that the murder weapon was someone's covered arm didn't help matters. Face-to-face strangulation using hands often brought DNA.

'Had he had sex recently?' Riddick asked.

'Yes,' Hugo said. 'Very recently – within the time frame we've already mentioned. There was also evidence of spermicide. I suspect he used a condom.'

Gardner and Riddick exchanged another look.

The used condom at the scene. Who had Bradley been having sex with by the castle keep, overlooking the viaduct?

'There's something else,' Hugo said. 'The crème de la crème, actually.'

Gardner was taken aback by his use of figurative language. He actually smiled too, which came across as somewhat creepy.

'Our clearest indication that this was deliberate and pre-meditated. You see, the assailant left a mark on the victim's lower back, underneath where his belt sits. The mark is only about two inches long and one inch wide and was done post-mortem. They used a sharp knife and then taped a gauze pad over it. That's why it went unnoticed at the crime scene, and there was no blood on the shirt. The mark looks like the letter *E* to me.'

Gardner exchanged another look with Riddick. His look said it all: in *Knaresborough?*

She felt a cold sensation in the bottom of her back, in the same spot that Bradley had been scarred. 'We need to see it.'

'I know,' Hugo said, nodding at some scrubs hanging on a rail at the back of the room. 'That's why I got these ready for you.'

11

Paranoid after the events of the day, Neil rose from the sofa, went into the kitchen, and reached into the dishwasher for the kitchen knife he'd used last night.

He turned it over beneath the light bulb.

See... sparkling... not a trace of blood... now stop being ridiculous!

His mind turned to the jumper outside in the dustbin.

Should I burn it rather than leave it for the binmen?

He dismissed the idea. He'd probably attract more attention with the fire!

No, the best thing you can do right now, Neil, is have a beer. The police have a knack for getting you rattled.

He heard a loud knocking sound and looked up at the ceiling where Cherish's room was.

Haven't you learned your lesson yet?

There was another loud knock.

Unbelievable.

He shouted, 'Don't I have enough to worry about?'

He paused, waiting to see the impact of his words. Nothing. Blissful silence. Good. They were really winding him up—

Another knock.

What the hell do I have to do to get some peace around here?

He bounded up the stairs, reached into his pocket for a key, thrust it into the lock on Cherish's bedroom door and opened it.

Cherish, clutching her exposed, pregnant belly, stood there, staring at him. Her face was blotchy from incessantly crying all day, but there was now fire in her expression. Her lip was pulled back in a snarl, and her teeth were exposed.

'*Now* you show some balls, lass!'

'I *hate* you.'

Neil laughed. 'It's a shame you couldn't show them when Bradley was walking all over you. We might have had one less problem to deal with.' He nodded down at her bump.

She stroked her stomach. 'You can't treat us like this.'

'I can't?'

'Doesn't matter who you are,' Cherish said.

'Doesn't it?' Neil stepped to one side and looked over at Mandy, who was sitting on the end of their bed. She was holding a bag of frozen peas to one eye.

Neil gestured to the open door. 'Okay, Cherish. I'll leave this door open on one condition.'

'Anything,' Mandy said and then winced.

Cherish shook her head in disgust.

'The police will be back. They *always* come back. And when they do, just keep your bloody mouths shut, okay?'

'Yes,' Mandy said.

Cherish narrowed her eyes.

'Cherish?' Neil said.

'Whatever.' Cherish stormed past him.

'Good girl.' Neil smiled.

12

It'd been an eventful day, but such events could easily continue unabated throughout the night, and Gardner knew the importance of keeping her team fresh. If something pressing did come up for the MCU, then she and Riddick would take up that mantle; she didn't want to get the backs up of her new team.

She looked up at *Operation Eden* on the large whiteboard. It had undergone developments.

To the right of the board was a large aerial image of the castle grounds, and close-up photographs of the three entrances: between the large solid towers of the enclosure wall; the car park at the side entrance which provided the shortest route to the crime scene at the keep; and the steps that led down to Waterside beneath the imposing viaduct. Additionally, there were further aerial shots of the winding Waterside which led from Bond End on one side, all the way to Bland's Hill on the other.

Bradley remained at the centre of the board, frozen in that aggressive pose with a shaved eyebrow.

Frozen forever.

Red lines sprang from the victim, linking to Neil Taylor, the drug dealing father; Cherish Spencer, potential mother of his unborn child; Honey Taylor, beleaguered mother. There were other characters in this developing story that had earned a blood-coloured route to the victim. Bradley's best friend, Dan Lotus, was a new addition. They would be hearing more about that troublemaker later in this briefing.

Additionally, on the board were images of areas that Bradley had been known to hang out with friends: the park near the Knaresborough community centre and the field near the rugby pitch, to name a few. One of her officers had also pinned a map of Knaresborough to the bottom corner of the board, and meticulously, with a green pen, drawn out the most common 'routes' that Bradley's gang would walk on a day-to-day basis.

Gardner turned away from the board back to her team of eleven, who looked, on the whole, surprisingly perky despite a day of pounding the pavement. She'd never be grateful for a murder, but she was happy to see many of her colleagues fired up with purpose. Too often, their jobs could be slow and ponderous and not full of the excitement and glamour promised on the average crime TV show.

Riddick was currently working his way through the forensics so far. He'd handed every officer a photograph of the two-inch E carved into Bradley's lower back. 'The lack of clotting suggests it was done post-mortem. It wasn't to torture the victim. We suspect it could be a message of some kind.'

Up in the air went the hand of DS Phil Rice. The officer who, earlier, had been intent on justifying that Bradley's demise was a blessing to the local community.

Riddick nodded at him. 'Phil?'

'His signature?' Rice said, rubbing his bald head as if he were coaxing these ideas out.

'Nothing's off the table at the moment,' Riddick said. 'We do believe the "E" to be part of a message.'

'Ecstasy?' Rice said. 'Bradley and some of the others were involved with drugs.'

'As DI Riddick said, nothing is off the table, but let's keep it very factual for the moment.' Gardner nodded over at DC O'Brien and DS Ross who were sitting together. 'Lucy and John are investigating the Knaresborough gang culture, and they can debrief us in a moment.'

Matt Blanks looked up from the computer. Gardner was sure she caught the HOLMES 2 operative's eyes roll beneath his mane of shaggy hair. The case had a lot of angles and inputting the data would be wearing on him. She was pleased to see him quickly get over it though and return to banging away on the keyboard.

'Forensics on the fibre under Bradley's nails, and the DNA samples from the condom aren't ready yet, but they are being fast-tracked. Tomorrow is unlikely, but we can live in hope.'

'Thank you, DI Riddick,' Gardner said. Despite his unpopularity, he was handling the room well. People here probably thought the same of him that the chief constable had. Capable, but unhinged. Gardner had seen nothing to contradict this in his behaviour today.

'Ray next.' Gardner nodded at the tall, black officer. 'His team have been very effective in putting a timeline together.'

'Thanks, boss,' Barnett said, rising to his feet. Gardner was glad that in this day and age, incident rooms opted for spotlights rather than hanging bulbs. Barnett must have been six foot seven.

He went over to the pictures of Knaresborough on the right side of the board. He tapped the map of the town centre. 'According to Honey, Bradley's mother, he left home at 8.30 p.m.

We have CCTV footage of him arriving at The Crown Inn at eight fifty. He meets with best friend, Dan Lotus.' Barnett moved across the board and tapped the picture of another angry looking youth with his finger. 'Together, they enter. We have photographs of all other known associates of Bradley that entered the public house after that time. Including Bradley, there were five in total.'

Gardner nodded. She turned to face the officers and singled out one of the few females in attendance with her eyes. 'Louisa. Have all four friends been interviewed?'

DC Louisa Marks flipped open her notebook. 'Yes. All of them provided information that supports the timeline established by DS Barnett so far. They all left together at twenty-five past ten.'

Gardner looked back at Barnett, who was nodding. 'Staggered out more like. But that was the time we have on CCTV. They then headed over the road to Rizza Pizza. They went into the takeaway and placed their orders.'

'Yes, they confirmed that,' Marks said.

'The pack then rolled out of the takeaway,' Barnett continued, 'headed into the ginnel at the side of the store and rolled three spliffs.'

'None of the four witnesses mentioned this,' Marks said.

'Wonder why?' Rice said.

'They obviously had no idea about the CCTV camera in the ginnel,' Barnett said, pointing to an image of the five youths smoking together.

'That, or they didn't *care*,' Rice said.

Gardner nodded.

Rice, who'd been working with Barnett today, said, 'And this is when it gets spicier – and I'm not talking about the pepperoni pizza.'

Did you really just make that joke? She regarded Rice with a raised eyebrow.

Unbelievably, several of his colleagues chuckled.

Maybe the bar for a cheap laugh is lower up north?

'The proprietor Marco Russo,' Barnett said, tapping a picture of a large man in a suit, 'came out to challenge the young men about smoking drugs outside his shop. CCTV footage shows an argument between Marco and Dan Lotus. It never gets violent. And, if anything, footage shows that Marco was the most likely to swing as it rumbles on. Eventually, Bradley steps in and actually calms it down. He throws his spliff down, stands on it, and instructs two of the others, who are holding the spliffs, to do the same.'

'Bradley the leader?' Gardner said. 'And, seemingly, someone who has respect for others?' She regarded her audience, hoping that this would help endear the victim to the more grizzled officers.

'Or maybe he just wanted his pizza?' Rice said.

Gardner inwardly sighed. 'Continue please Ray.'

'Yes, boss. After they've eaten the pizza, Bradley breaks away from the group.' Barnett traced the high street with his finger. 'His friends head this way towards Bond End. And Bradley' – he poked the town centre proper – 'heads into the centre via a side street.' We have CCTV footage of him on the bench by Blind Jack using his mobile.

'Blind Jack?' Gardner asked.

'A bronze statue of John Metcalf on one of the benches. He has a surveyor's wheel beside him,' Barnett said.

'Local legend, boss,' Marks said. 'Blinded at six by smallpox, he still became one of the fathers of the modern road. Responsible for 180 miles of turnpike road.'

'Thanks,' Gardner said. 'What was Bradley doing on his mobile?'

'Can't tell,' Barnett said. 'My guess: he was texting, because when he gets a response, he's quick to his feet.'

'That'll be sex, then,' Gardner said.

'Sorry?' Barnett said.

'Sex. He just arranged his booty call. I expect we will find his DNA in the used condom. I also doubt he texted Cherish Spencer, as she is far too pregnant to be wandering around at this time for a secret rendezvous in a fourteenth-century ruin. Have we located Bradley's mobile yet?'

'Sorry, boss,' Barnett said. 'Still no sign.'

Gardner sighed out loud on this occasion. 'What time are we on in this timeline, Ray?'

Barnett consulted his notes. 'Five to eleven. So, Bradley heads down Market Place' – he continued to trace the route with his finger – 'onto Castlegate, right onto Castle Yard, and he approaches the castle entrance. So our last sighting on CCTV is at one minute past eleven.'

'A one-hour window for him to be murdered in,' Gardner said. 'Potentially, by the person he has sex with?'

Rice thrust his hand in the air. He didn't bother waiting to be asked. 'Didn't the pathologist say he suspected a male as the killer?'

Gardner shrugged. 'Why couldn't Bradley have been having sex with a male?'

Rice looked confused. 'Not really in character, boss?'

'Your view of his character is fairly two-dimensional, Phil. Already, we have a boy who has shown leadership abilities, de-escalated an argument with an angry shop owner, and could be gay? Isn't it in our job description to build up profiles rather than make assumptions?'

Rice looked down; so did several of his colleagues. She wondered if that would stop them hanging off his arrogant coat-tails too much.

Barnett continued. 'No one came into the castle via the same route over the next hour. No one. Eleven fifty-six p.m. is our next sighting. Doug Brace walking his dog.'

'Okay, so how about Castle Yard car park, where we came in?' Gardner asked.

'Again, no one,' Barnett replied.

'Really?'

'Yes. A weeknight in Knaresborough is fairly quiet around the town centre.'

'So this leaves Waterside?' Gardner asked.

'Yes.' Barnett nodded. 'But this part is a work in progress. People do like to take late strolls on Waterside. From Bond End all the way to Bland's Hill is about two miles. There're a lot of homes and cafés on this stretch, which is positive for CCTV footage, at least on the side nearest Bond End. However, there is a lot of activity. Including cars going down here.'

'Can't you just narrow it down to those taking these steps up to the castle?' Gardner asked, pointing them out on the aerial image.

'Unfortunately, there is no CCTV on the steps, or on Waterside *after* the steps before Bland's Hill. So, we cannot work out if anybody opted to climb them.'

'Anybody opted?' Gardner said. 'Ray, we know someone opted to climb them – this isn't in doubt.'

'Yes, boss.'

'We have a small window, Ray. If Bradley did text the person he was meeting at five past eleven, then we start the clock then. Our killer approached the steps from one of these two sides.' She pointed at Bland's Hill first. 'If they approached from Bland's Hill, we have no footage, so you need to go further back, onto Bland's Hill itself.' She then pointed at Bond End. 'If it was Bond End, then we have a lot of footage prior to the steps, and we'll nail them eventually.'

Barnett nodded. 'Lists are being prepared. Those who live there, and so drive, park and walk on the Waterside regularly, and those passing through, either by vehicle or on foot.'

'Good work. How's door-to-door?'

'In hand,' an older officer called from the back of the room.

'I'm sorry,' Gardner said. 'I haven't got everyone's name down yet.'

'DC Will Holbeck, boss.'

'Okay, Will. What have you found?'

'It's been frustrating, I'm afraid, boss. Much like Ray. People don't pay much attention from the windows of their houses on Waterside. It's a busy old place. They're used to it... There was one thing though...'

'Go on.'

'Mrs Seren Hamilton heard a man arguing on his mobile. Lots of effing and jeffing. It was eleven-thirty. Nothing much draws this lady to the window, but she said he was shouting that loud, she was worried someone was getting mugged. When she got to the window, he was wrapping it up.'

'Can she give a description?'

'Dark clothing, tall with a hoodie drawn up. Nothing much else, I'm afraid.'

Gardner looked back at Barnett. 'Have you correlated this with CCTV?'

'Yes,' Barnett said, reaching into his notes. He pulled out a photograph of a hooded figure. 'He walks the entire stretch from Bond End to our last CCTV point prior to the steps.'

'Can you get the image to the forensic video team?' Gardner said. 'Enhance it.'

'Already in hand, boss,' Barnett said. 'But I don't think it will do much good. The quality of this footage is crap, and it is dark down there.'

'It's something,' Gardner said. 'Okay, I am going to spend the evening scouring the detailed statements we have from Doug Brace, and the four friends that spent the evening with Bradley before he was murdered. Myself and DI Riddick will be looking more closely at Neil Taylor and Cherish Spencer tomorrow. And Ray and his team will be tearing up trees on Waterside. I suspect tomorrow will be even busier than today, so I want you to all go home and rest. Back here, first thing. Six a.m. Hopefully, I'll be sharing the final findings from SOCO, who have just completed a search of Bradley's home. Preliminary reports suggest little, but I haven't spoken to them in a couple of hours. Well done, team. Get some rest.'

13

Gardner had been set up with some accommodation in a newbuild property on the edge of Knaresborough.

She wandered around the three-floor property, marvelling at the space and the modern furnishing before settling into her new kitchen. It was still light, so she gazed out over a trim garden.

I could get used to this. She poured herself a large glass of red wine, thinking about their poky little affair down south with its garden full of muddy patches.

She looked down at her mobile phone. There was little reception, and no sign of either 3G or 4G. The price of being so far out of town. Worse still, the internet in the house was not yet connected. *Bloody admin department!* Lovely house, yes. Great décor, indeed! But the logistics! How does an SIO run a case without the internet?

She phoned her husband Barry, who sounded his usual bored self, but she didn't pass comment. Even before this move up north, she felt as if the marriage was heading past the point of no return. Usually, a reminder of her struggling marriage would send her spiralling into anxiety; however, right now, she was halfway through a bottle of Merlot, and everything had started to glow a little. Eventually, the bore fed back on Anabelle's success: a certificate from her class teacher for her remarkable progress with phonics. This added to Gardner's warm feeling.

Throughout most of the call, her mind was elsewhere, and at the end she hit him up with a favour. It was the least he could do for his persistent lack of interest in her. 'I want you to google the Winters case in North Yorkshire. I also want you to google Detective Inspector Paul Riddick.'

'Why?'

Because I asked you to. 'He's my deputy SIO. There's some history. Big history, I expect. He hasn't been forthcoming, and as I told you before, I have no internet.'

'Couldn't you just have found out from someone at work, or better still used the internet when you were out and about?'

Marsh wasn't exactly forthcoming! Add to that I've had barely five seconds since I arrived. However, strike any excuses, you're my husband so... 'Could you just do it please?'

He reluctantly agreed.

'And phone me back as soon as, please.'

'Okay, love you,' he said and hung up.

Do you? she thought. *In fact, do I love you?*

In the fading light, she watched a magpie dig for worms in her new garden and worked her way through the remainder of the bottle. She'd picked up a microwave meal on the way home, but after arriving home, she'd not fancied a red-hot Madras any longer and had chucked it into the fridge, along with a bottle of Chardonnay she was saving for tomorrow...

Her phone rang. She looked down and saw with a small burst of excitement that it was the man responsible for nurturing her career, DCI Michael Yorke. If anyone knew the perfect things to say to her right now, it was this man!

'Mike!'

'Emma, how're you?'

'Okay. Two days and you're missing me already?'

'Exactly right.' He paused. 'Have you got a minute?'

Something was wrong. 'You sound even more serious than usual and that takes some doing.'

'Thanks.' He sighed. 'It's about Jack...'

Her mind went blank. 'Jack who?' It was a defence mechanism. She knew well enough who Jack was.

'Your brother.'

Her chest froze. She closed her eyes. She was in Malcolm's Maze of Mirrors again. Jack was in front of her, holding his stone. She clutched her bleeding head and stared into his cold, dead eyes.

She opened her eyes. 'Are you sure? Jack *Moss*?'

'I'm sure, Emma. I'm looking at the report on screen now. *Jack Nathan Moss.* He's out. Good behaviour.'

'Shit. Where's he now?'

'A halfway house in Tidworth... Listen, Emma, this doesn't have to be your problem. You don't owe him anything.'

'You're damn right!'

'I just thought you should know.'

'Thanks.'

'I understand that this may be a bit of a shock to you, so shall we schedule a catch up tomorrow night instead? Give you time to get all those new colleagues of yours eating out of the palm of your hand? Then you can dish the dirt on life up north?'

She laughed. 'That would be great, Mike.'

After the phone call, she emptied the remainder of the bottle into her wine glass. A bit splashed over the rim and onto the wooden tabletop.

Jack Nathan Moss.

Her younger brother.

Again, she recalled those cold, dead eyes regarding her in Malcolm's Maze of Mirrors.

As a child, the doctors had diagnosed him with a multitude of learning difficulties. Her parents had fawned over him. But Gardner had seen the truth that day. He lacked emotion.

Actually... *he lacked soul.*

A teenager with no qualifications, no hope, and a significant lack of empathy was always going to fall in with the wrong crowd. By the time he was in his twenties, that crowd became just plain bad. Gardner had learned enough about Jack's past to know that her cold, empty brother became a go-to for jobs that were often dirty, and violent.

Unbelievably, he was only tried for one killing, and this was downgraded to manslaughter.

Because he 'accidentally' drove a car over someone from a rival gang. As you do.

Of course, Gardner knew the truth. Not only because she'd seen it in his eyes that day in the maze while he was holding that bloody stone, but she'd seen it countless times since.

On the day of their mother's funeral when he didn't shed a tear, for example.

And the day of their father's funeral when he didn't even bother attending.

She thought of the bottle of Chardonnay cooling in the fridge and looked at the bottle on the table she'd demolished in less than an hour.

Be sensible, Emma. Briefing at six.

She went into her new lounge and threw herself onto the sofa. It was too soft and certainly wasn't the highlight of the luxurious home she'd received gratis. She'd already tested the television earlier, so knew it would work when she hit the remote.

She was just in time for the regional news on ITV.

There was a photograph of Bradley Taylor on the screen. Shaved eyebrow. Aggressive expression. The same one that was on the *Operation Eden* whiteboard.

Well, that will endear him to the public I'm sure...

She sat up and cranked up the volume. She was at the end of the broadcast, but she caught this: 'Emotional locals paid their respects.' A camera panned over flowers that had been laid at the entrance to the castle. There was a soundbite from an elderly man. 'We've never seen the like... not here... not in Knaresborough.' He pulled off his glasses and wiped an eye. Then, Marianne Perse, the irritating journalist who'd confronted Paul Riddick at the crime scene, offered her thoughts on the matter. 'The police are referring to him as the Viaduct Killer.'

'No, we're not,' Gardner said to the screen. 'Why in God's name would we do that?'

Sure enough, the presenter interviewing the freelance journalist asked a similar question. 'But Bradley Taylor was found behind the castle keep wasn't he?'

Marianne shrugged. 'The Viaduct Killer. That's what my source tells me. Maybe it's to do with the view of the viaduct from the crime scene?'

'You don't have a bloody source,' Gardner said.

'My source also informed me that the victim was strangled.'

'You do have a source you bloody bitch!' Gardner stood.

She watched the end of the broadcast with her mouth hanging partially open. It concluded with a telephone number for the public to contact with any information.

Gardner killed the television.

Again, she thought of the Chardonnay. 'You have a briefing, Emma!'

Her phone rang from the kitchen table. She sighed as she headed back for it.

Barry.

Ah shit, she thought. *The Winters case and Paul.* It'd completely slipped her mind following the revelation regarding Jack.

'Barry?'

'Bloody hell, Em, I didn't expect that.'

At least he sounded more enthused than usual. 'Go on.'

'Where do I start?'

'Right now, I feel nowhere, so start *anywhere.*'

'Most of it's tragic... In fact, it's all tragic.'

'Do I need to sit down?'

'Do you have wine?'

'No,' she lied. 'Just get to it, please.'

So Barry told Gardner all about the Winters case. As promised, it was a tragic tale.

'Awful,' Gardner said. 'Just bloody awful. And it makes a lot of sense. No wonder he's public enemy number one.'

'I wish that were it,' Barry said.

'Really, there's more? You must be over the worst by now.'

'I wish...'

Gardner felt a cold chill work its way up her spine.

'What is this Paul Riddick actually like?' Barry asked.

'Well, that's a question and a half. He's kind of a mixed bag. Standoffish. Angry and aggressive a lot of the time. Erratic, but passionate.'

'Sounds like most detectives.'

Gardner rolled her eyes. 'There are moments when he seems more tender, gentle even. It's hard to explain. There's definitely something gnawing at him.'

'You can say that again.'

'Just get to the point, Barry.'

'That man will be seriously damaged, Em. In fact, if that were me, I wouldn't even be working. Hats off that he is *actually* working.'

'Barry, for pity's sake.'

So, Barry told her, and when he'd finished, she was forced to end the conversation because the tears were coming, and she was struggling to find the words to speak.

She did, however, manage to go to the kitchen and retrieve the Chardonnay from the fridge.

And while she drank the white wine, she thought about, in no particular order: her brother's cold eyes, Riddick's tragic history, Bradley Taylor's lifeless body, and Collette Willows lying dead on the roundabout far below her.

14

Over the kitchen table, Anders Smith fixed Riddick with a stare.

'I know that look, boss.' Riddick licked salt from the back of his hand.

'Good,' his former DCI replied, running a hand through a mop of blond hair. 'Pay close attention to it. And stop calling me boss.'

Riddick drank another shot of tequila. There was no lemon to dive for. Bitter fruits repulsed him. 'Well, if you're not my boss any more, why do you keep telling me what to do?'

'Well, I may not be your boss in the police, mucker, but you are crying out for some guidance on life.'

'You remember the Game of Life?' Riddick snorted.

'I do. I played it a few times, until the shit plastic spinner broke. Why?'

'I was good at it,' Riddick said, refilling his shot glass.

'Is anything serious with you?' Anders played with the top of his walking stick which was leaning against the table.

'New stick?' Riddick said.

'Yep. The last one was falling to bits.'

'Looks expensive. *Shiny.*'

'Well, I'm beholden to it so thought it was worth the investment... Anyway, stop changing the subject... I'm being serious here, pal... You're drinking too much.'

'I've had a tough day! A murder in Knaresborough! How can that not put you on edge?'

'You drink every day, Paul.'

Riddick sighed.

'And not just a little bit, mate.' He nodded at the bottle of tequila.

'It's getting me through the day,' Riddick said.

'That's my point. When you start getting through the day after drinking what *you're* drinking, then you know there's a problem.'

'If I didn't drink, my problems would be worse, believe me—'

'You sound just like me,' Anders said. 'Or at least, the me from five years back.'

'You spent most of your career pissed, boss. And you didn't do such a bad job of it!'

'Ha!' Anders said, sitting up straight in his chair, groaning over the discomfort in his ruined back. 'Just because I saved two children from a burning house doesn't make it a good career.'

'It's a pretty good place to start!' Riddick said, pouring more salt onto the back of his hand.

'Right place, right time, son. Has nothing to do with the way I treated people at work, the way I treated my family.'

'You were direct, so what? You got things done.' Riddick licked the salt from his hand.

'I was a grumpy bastard, and no one liked me.'

'They loved you.'

'*No*. They pretended to love me, Paul. Really, they *hated* me.'

'Well, I liked you.'

'Yeah, but that's very different.'

'How so?'

'You're like me, as I keep saying.'

'An alcoholic?' Riddick drank the shot.

'Damaged.'

Riddick smiled. 'You say you were hard work when you were pissed all the time. You're not exactly uplifting now, are you?'

Anders smiled. 'You want to know the two reasons I finally stopped drinking?'

Riddick shrugged, pouring himself another shot.

'Firstly, rosacea.' He pointed at his bulbous red nose. 'Have to take antibiotics every day, and it still looks like this. You think everyone respects me, Paul? They call me Rudolph at the chuffin' golf club!'

Riddick laughed. 'Second?'

'Family.'

Riddick reached for the salt.

'They left me. I lost everything.'

Riddick shook salt onto his hand.

'I destroyed my family, mate.' He lifted his new cane and pointed it at Riddick. 'So, I quit.'

Riddick drank his third shot in ten minutes, and then pushed the bottle away. That would do for now. He looked up at Anders and sighed. 'I can live with a red nose.'

* * *

After seeing his old boss out, Riddick staggered into his lounge.

He steadied himself against the windowsill and watched Anders, who hadn't touched a drop, drive away in his diesel-gulping Land Rover.

'Recovering alcoholics are bad for the environment,' he slurred.

He turned around and stumbled into the wall. Again, he had to steady himself. Consciousness was on its last legs.

He looked at a picture of Lucy and Molly standing under an overhanging rock with their arms raised to give the illusion that they were lifting it.

'Brimham Rocks,' Rachel said, coming up behind Riddick.

He felt his wife's arms slip around his waist.

'The only place in modern Britain where health and safety has been chucked out the window,' Riddick said and snorted.

'Was fun to watch them climb all over them, though,' Rachel said.

'Watching my children running around on a ten-metre-high rock with sheer drops on either side wasn't my idea of fun.'

Rachel kissed his neck. 'You had their backs.'

That time, Riddick thought. *I had their backs that time.*

He reached out and touched Molly's face, and then Lucy's.

'Brimham Rocks, eh?' Riddick said as a tear ran down his cheek. 'I bet the Air Ambulance curses its existence.'

'Go to bed, honey,' Rachel said. 'You're drunk again, and you have work in the morning.'

'Okay.'

'Oh, and did you call Cynthia? To arrange another date?'

'No,' Riddick said. 'I wasn't feeling it.'

'Well, sleep on it. I think it'll be good for you.'

'Whatever you say, Rachel. I love you.'

'I love you too.'

15

Kelsey looked down at the scars criss-crossing her upper arm, and then up at the bookshelf where she once hid her knife in a maths book, until her mother and father had managed to find it.

She missed the cutting. Badly. The distraction had been ever so welcome. But Dr Evans and her parents had been right. It'd needed to stop. And now, for seven days at least, it had.

Her phone beeped. She read Andy's message:

Chin up. Don't let them get the better of you. These pricks will all come to nothing.

She threw her mobile aside and sighed. Easy for him to say. He hadn't heard the chanting in the corridors today en route to the library – the only safe space in the entire school. Arse-licker... arse-licker... arse-licker...

Not exactly original, but it did the trick of sucking the air from her body. Especially when one of those chanters was now Richard 'Call me Rich' Hill.

The boy she'd loved before discovering that he was just another mean bastard.

Downstairs, she could hear her parents arguing again. She couldn't make out exactly what they were saying, but she knew it was about her.

It was always about her.

In fact, her mother had said as much earlier when Kelsey had been unable to eat her dinner. 'It's always about you, Kelsey. Always.'

She wouldn't be surprised if this was the reason for the argument raging downstairs. Her father always had Kelsey's back. Apart from Andy, there wasn't really anyone else...

And then Kelsey had an idea.

At first, it seemed a rather black and horrible idea, but as more and more shoots sprang from the darkest hollows of her mind, it lightened, and seemed to make a lot of sense.

And, just like that, all of a sudden, it was a good idea. The best.

She went through into her parents' bedroom. They wouldn't hear her over their raised voices. In her mother's bedside drawer, Kelsey found the bottle of pills. Her mother had, on occasion, given her one of these tablets to help her sleep. She was under strict instructions to never tell her father about this. He certainly wouldn't approve. The doctor didn't want Kelsey to have sleeping pills, fearing that she would become psychologically addicted.

She emptied about half the bottle into her hand and counted.

Fifteen pills.

Simply holding those pills offered her something that was like staring up at that bookshelf when the knife had still been in that book.

There was no small measure of relief in knowing she had an option.

Back in her room, she laid the pills beside her laptop. She toyed with the idea of leaving a message on social media, but why? They would probably ridicule her decision.

'It's always about you, Kelsey. Always.'

She did, however, text Andy a farewell message.

A couple at a time, she swallowed the pills with water, and then reached for her favourite book.

Alice in Wonderland.

Her father used to read it to her when she was small. Once, they'd even seen it at the theatre as a family.

She didn't get far.

The White Rabbit appeared wearing a waistcoat.

'Oh dear! Oh dear! I shall be too late!'

And Kelsey followed him down the rabbit hole.

16

Rather unsurprisingly, Gardner didn't sleep well.

She gave up completely at 4 a.m., and then opted for a run along Waterside at 5 a.m. while the sun was rising.

A sleepless night and too much wine weren't conducive to an athlete's lifestyle, but she wasn't trying to clock up serious miles, or ridiculous speeds. She had two aims. To shift some of the weight she'd put on since Collette's passing, and to de-stress following the revelations about Riddick, and the news of her sociopathic brother's release.

There was a car park opposite the entrance to Waterside. She didn't bother with music, but had her phone pinned to her arm just in case someone tried to call her. She was also tracking the route.

There was no coincidence in her choice of run; Bradley's killer had been here somewhere on the night of his murder.

She started at the Ugly Duckling Tearoom, grateful it wasn't yet open; a hot coffee and a warm Danish would probably have been one temptation too many. She then crossed over Bond End, which was effectively a large hill that led up into the town, eyed up the Worlds End pub, which was also, fortunately, closed, and broke into a sprint.

If you could call an eleven-minute mile a sprint.

She gazed over the Nidd as the sun continued to break the darkness overhead. The river, adored by the locals, meandered along, peacefully, glittering under the first of the day's rays. The fauna and broad-leafed trees that lined the banks were enjoying the spring weather, both swelling and blossoming. Rowing boats, from five-seaters to ten-seaters, lined the bank, ready for the punters to descend.

She passed rows of thatched housing on the right side, perched on the riverbank. On her left, were larger, impressive houses pushed further back at the end of long driveways. Some were raised high, allowing them staggering views of the Nidd. There were also large craggy cliff faces imposing themselves on the beautiful gorge.

Did the killer walk this way? If so, someone saw him. There were houses, CCTV cameras outside the numerous quaint cafés. It was only a matter of time before Barnett and his team identified him.

She thought of the hooded figure arguing on the phone.

Was that you?

She paused, gasping for air, beneath the eighty-foot viaduct. She looked up at the stone structure that took away the breath of many an observer. She didn't quite get it. A glorified railway bridge in her opinion. The area around it was awe-inspiring, and she certainly 'got' the staggering view from the castle grounds, but she couldn't help but feel that this element was overrated.

Mind you, she felt like this about all man-made structures. Being from Wiltshire, she lived for the greenery. And this place did have it in abundance.

She continued along the killer's potential route until she

reached the foot of the steps that wound up to the castle. She recalled Barnett's explanation. From this point, there was no more CCTV, at least no more working CCTV, until Bland's Hill. So that hooded figure could very well have continued alongside the river at this point into irrelevance.

Alternatively, he could have turned off and walked up these steps to commit murder.

She started to run up the steps, but when it became very clear that they were far too steep for such a gung-ho approach, she slowed. When she reached the top of the steps, she was out of breath despite moving at a snail's pace for most of it.

Okay, Emma. You are cutting down on the booze, and you are getting fit!

Still gasping for air, she looked at the fourteenth-century crumbling keep. She touched the blue-and-white police cordon which led right around the viewpoint beside the keep. It should keep people off the scene until SOCO were happy that they had harvested all they could.

She looked at the yellow markers. Number one for the used condom. Number two for the footprint on the patch of mud.

She threw a glance over at the shade behind the keep where Bradley Taylor had ended his days. Then, she turned to face the staggering view again.

The clouds had cleared now, and the sun burned heavily in the sky.

She watched a train soar over the viaduct and made a promise to herself to do that train journey when this was all put to bed.

She reached for the phone in her pocket and contacted Barnett first.

'Ray, briefing is cancelled. I want you and your team down on Waterside first thing. Our killer walked that route. I can feel it.

Do what you have to. Pound on the doors until they're hanging off. Scrutinise every person picked up on CCTV. Find out who the hooded chap is. Widen CCTV as far as you can. We will reconvene at six tonight in Harrogate.'

'Yes, boss.'

'Also, the press. The Viaduct Killer? Who did that? Any ideas?'

'No, boss. It didn't come from me or anyone in my team, I assure you.'

'Are these leaks common?'

'Not really. Chief Constable Marsh runs a tight ship.'

'Any idea who could have spoken to Marianne Perse?'

A pause. 'No, boss, sorry.'

Being careful, eh? Fair enough, no one likes a snitch.

During her sleepless, drunken night, she'd taken the liberty of inputting the numbers of important members of her team into her phone. She phoned them to inform them that the briefing would only be once today, and to also set them relevant tasks. This included: visiting the local school and fleshing out Bradley's background; preparing detailed statements from all of his close friends; interviewing the bar staff working at The Crown Inn; interviewing, again, the aggrieved pizza takeaway owner, Marco Russo. She also let the antagonistic DS Phil Rice loose on Bradley Taylor's criminal history. He was grateful for the responsibility. She wondered if he was usually overlooked. Wouldn't surprise her.

Then, she phoned Riddick, her heart slumping in her chest as she did so. Today was the day she'd be having a conversation with him about what she'd found out from Barry, and it filled her with dread.

'Boss.'

'Morning Paul. Briefing is cancelled. I want to meet for coffee. When's the earliest we can do that?'

'You've finally been online then?'

Well, my husband did. And it cost me a decent night's sleep. 'What's the earliest, Paul?'

'Seven a.m. Town square. Caffè Nero. It's opposite Blind Jack's statue.'

From beside which, Bradley potentially contacted someone for a late-night rendezvous, she recalled.

'Okay,' Gardner said, trying not to sigh as the anticipation of their conversation weighed heavily on her.

'But I warn you, boss. They don't do soup bowls of coffee in there.'

'I'm aware of what Nero sells, Paul. I'm from Wiltshire, not the Outer Hebrides.'

17

'So, here we are for the second time in two days, blowing our income on overpriced coffee,' Riddick said.

Gardner drank from her grande Americano as she looked at her deputy SIO. The café was almost dead at this time, and they'd dived for the leather couches in the corner.

Riddick looked more unkempt than he had done yesterday. He no longer had an enigmatic five o'clock shadow. Today, he just needed a shave. Normally, she'd accuse him of boozing the night away. However, right now, that would just be hypocritical.

She took a deep breath. 'Okay, Paul, I—'

'Know all about the Winters case?' Riddick said with a raised eyebrow.

'Yes.'

Riddick sneered and took a mouthful of coffee. 'Go on then. What do you think you know?'

'Kelsey Winters, a fifteen-year-old girl, took her own life. She overdosed on sleeping pills.'

'Yes,' Riddick said, sitting back in his chair and crossing his arms. 'Can't argue with that. An absolute fact. In fact, Hugo

Sands did the post-mortem, and we know he doesn't get things wrong. So, what other facts did you glean from these newspaper reports fuelled by the freelance journalism of Marianne Perse?'

'Well, I didn't read the reports, my husband did. I had no internet. But it seems that you went after the mother, Hannah Winters, hard, investigating her for possible murder, or manslaughter.'

'Okay,' Riddick said, waving his hand in a so-so gesture. 'Getting a little subjective now. Going in hard? I asked a few questions.'

'Everyone, apart from you, thought it was suicide. There were no suspicious circumstances.'

He raised an eyebrow. 'No suspicious circumstances? The father, Tom Winters, told me that the mother had been giving her these sleeping pills to help her sleep. If anyone but a doctor is giving a young girl sleeping pills, shouldn't we ask questions?'

Gardner nodded. 'That wasn't in the report.'

'No, it wasn't. Because after Tom told me this, and I spoke to Hannah, he denied ever saying it. Obviously, that worked to Marianne Perse's advantage.'

'How so?'

'Well, she wanted to destroy me.' He slumped back in his chair, suddenly looking exhausted. 'Almost did too.'

'But why?'

'To sell her story. To make a lot of money.'

Gardner nodded. She could sympathise with him here. She'd seen many good coppers fall foul of the media's insatiable appetite for controversies. 'So, you didn't actually accuse Hannah of giving her daughter an overdose?'

'Of course not. I can be hot-headed, but bloody hell, what do you take me for? I simply asked Hannah if it was true that she'd given her daughter these pills in the past. Then, she accused me of suspecting her when I never actually did. After that, she clammed up…' He grunted. 'Well, at least until she spoke to the press from her hospital bed. There was no clamming up then!'

'Hospital bed? After her own suicide attempt?'

'Yes. But that was rather half-hearted. She only took a small handful. It was a cry for help. But, as you now know, the story became a big one. Big, bad and nasty DI Paul Riddick drives bereaved mother to suicide by accusing her of murder.'

'And that's it? That's all that happened? You quizzed Hannah on something Tom told you?'

'Yes. And I was suspended, investigated and my reputation around these pastures was forever destroyed.'

'Shit, Paul. Why didn't you just talk to the press yourself?'

'Why would I whine to the press? It's my word against Tom Winters. They'd probably have hung me out again for lashing out at the bereaved dad! No, boss, there was no evidence that he'd ever said it, so I had to take my medicine. Big, bad and nasty DI Paul Riddick. End of. Considered leaving Knaresborough, but sod them, I did nothing wrong.'

'I see. I believe you.' And she did. Something about the tone of his voice. Something in his eyes. Something in the gentle side of him she'd come to recognise over the last couple of days. Something told her he was telling the truth. 'Why didn't you just tell me?'

'Thought it would be interesting for you to read Marianne's take on it first. So you can see what a complete and utter snake we're dealing with.'

She didn't need an experience like this to know what a nightmare the press could be, but she nodded anyway. 'Still, next time, just confide in me. Keeps things smoother between us, you know?'

'There was a reason I didn't go back to the press with my side of the story, and just took the slap on the wrist at work,' Riddick said.

Was this it? Was Paul about to confide the 'other truth' in her? Now the closet was open, was everything going to come spilling out?

'By all accounts, Kelsey Winters was a lovely girl. Kind and studious. Quite the contrast from our current victim, it seems—'

'We've talked about this,' Gardner said, giving him an irritated expression.

'I didn't want to put their family through any more turmoil. So, I just let it be.'

'That's good of you, Paul. Very sacrificial. I'm glad you kept your job.'

'But not my reputation?'

'You'll get that back.'

'I doubt it.'

'We'll work it out,' Gardner said.

'Anyway, we better finish up and get cracking,' Riddick said.

It seems the 'other truth' wasn't forthcoming.

She took a large mouthful of coffee and steeled herself again. Her heart thrashed in her chest. 'Paul?'

'Yes, boss.' Riddick put down his empty cup.

'My husband found out something else last night when he was online.'

Paul's eyes widened.

Gardner gulped. 'Sorry, this is none of my business, but—'

'You're right,' Riddick said, his eyes still wide. 'It isn't.'

She could taste the coffee working its way back up her throat. 'Still—'

'No, leave it there. Seriously. I had a late night.' His eyes finally relaxed, and he lowered them.

She tried to force back her tears but felt them spring up in the corners of her eyes. 'I'm so sorry for your loss, Paul.'

Riddick nodded and there was a silence before he gathered himself to speak. 'We need to speak with Cherish, boss. We need to confirm this baby belongs to Bradley, and whether she was with him by the keep.'

Gardner wiped at the corners of her eyes with her sleeves, glad that Riddick was now looking down and not at her. 'Not sure Cherish would have bothered insisting on a condom.'

Riddick stood. 'Let's go and rule her out then, boss.'

As Gardner followed Riddick from the café, the same thought ran through her mind over and over.

You poor, poor man.

18

On the way out of Caffè Nero, Gardner received a phone call.

After the call ended, she turned to Riddick. 'An engineer. He wants access to my house so he can thread a fibre optics cable through the wall. Good of admin to share these appointment details with me!'

'Go, boss. I'll meet you at Mandy Spencer's house.'

'I'll be quick.'

Throughout the journey to Mandy's house, Riddick felt on edge. He chewed hard on some gum, but that didn't help ease his anxiety. He was no idiot and knew that the excessive drinking was no small part of this agitation, as was the earlier conversation with Gardner.

I'm so sorry for your loss, Paul.

What did *she* understand about loss of this magnitude?

What did *anyone* who ever said this to him understand about it?

His therapist had tried to push him into joining groups with others who'd had similar, traumatic experiences. So far, he'd pushed back.

However, he wondered now, if maybe they wouldn't be such a bad idea after all.

Would hearing those words, *I'm so sorry for your loss*, mean anything different when issued from the lips of someone who had an inkling as to what colossal emptiness felt like?

He pulled up outside Mandy's home on the Hay-A-Park estate and reached into his glove compartment. After taking out a Sprite bottle, he took two large swigs of vodka, and then took two extra-strong mints from the pocket in his door. He chewed them as he exited the car, feeling the alcohol ridding him of agitation.

Eyeing up the front door, he wondered if he should wait for Gardner. He turned around to see if he could see her car driving up on the estate. He couldn't.

Impatient, he headed down the path and knocked on the door. Mandy's daughter, Cherish, and the person Riddick and Gardner most wanted to talk to, opened it. She was wearing far baggier clothes than yesterday, but this did little to hide her pregnancy.

'Morning, Ms Spencer. I'm DI Paul Riddick. We met yesterday.'

'I remember. Cherish, please.' She wiped at her eyes.

'Are you okay?'

'Not really. I haven't stopped crying in... well, not since—'

'Enough.' Neil stepped up behind Cherish. 'Go upstairs.'

'Actually, Mr Taylor, I'm here to speak to Cherish,' Riddick said.

'You're not,' Neil said. 'And enough of this Mr Taylor bullshit – we were in the same year at school for Christ's sake:'

'Cherish is eighteen, *Neil*. She can make her own decision on that—'

Neil leaned over and hissed in her ear. 'Tell him you've nothing to say.'

Cherish's eyes filled with tears. 'I've nothing to say.'

'Now, go upstairs,' Neil said.

Cherish walked away. Riddick gritted his teeth. 'Sounds like intimidation to—'

'Can I help you, Paul?' Neil said. 'I thought we chatted yesterday?'

'We did. About your son. The one you lost. *Tragically*.'

Neil smirked, nodded and regarded Riddick for a moment. 'Do you empathise with me, Paul?'

'What does that mean?' Riddick asked.

'I think you know what that means,' Neil said, and then chewed his bottom lip.

Riddick clenched his right fist, desperately forcing back a wave of anger.

Don't take the bait... refocus...

'We *need* Cherish to help us with our inquiries,' Riddick said. 'And if we must force the issue – we will. But, you know, that really would be detrimental to everyone.'

'What's she done anyway?'

'I think you know that she's carrying your son's baby?'

Neil's smiled dropped. 'No flies on you, Paul. What gave it away?' He gestured over his shoulder. 'The fact that she's a slut, and my boy wasn't exactly a discerning gentleman?'

Riddick now had both fists clenched.

'Angry, Paul?' Neil said.

'Can we continue this conversation inside? Longer I stand here, longer the neighbours see you chatting with the constabulary. Not the best thing for you considering your line of work.'

'I break cars down for parts – I'm legit.'

'Break lives more like,' Riddick said, narrowing his eyes.

'There's only one broken life here, Paul.' Neil stepped aside. 'Let's just get this over with.'

Riddick glared at him as he passed. His heart was thrashing in his chest, and the urge to lash out was overwhelming.

Neil closed the door.

Riddick walked through into the lounge and saw Mandy sitting on the sofa nursing a cup of tea. She was wearing the pink, frilly dressing gown which Neil had been wearing the previous day.

She turned her head. Her eye was black, and her cheek was swollen.

A fire kicked up in Riddick's veins. 'What happened Mrs Spencer?'

'I—'

'The door happened,' Neil said, coming alongside him. 'Fell into it. Didn't you, love?'

Mandy nodded.

'Could you please go upstairs, Mrs Spencer?' Riddick felt every nerve in his body quivering, 'I just need a word with Neil alone.'

Mandy nodded, rose to her feet and left the lounge. She closed the door behind her.

Neil snorted. 'Such a clumsy one, that one—'

Riddick grabbed Neil by the throat, thrusting him back into the door. The air came out of Neil in one burst.

Riddick kept a tight grip. Neil's lips drew back over his teeth, and his eyes widened. Neil dug his nails into Riddick's wrists, but he continued regardless. Eventually, the bastard's colour started to change—

There was a knock at the lounge door. 'Everything all right?' Mandy asked.

Riddick released Neil, who slipped down the door into a squat, rubbing at his neck.

'Fine, Mrs Spencer.' He nudged Neil with his foot. 'Tell her,' he hissed.

'Everything's okay, love,' Neil said. He sounded croaky.

'Okay,' Mandy said.

'Get up,' Riddick said.

Still rubbing his neck, Neil stood, sneering at Riddick. 'Now there's the boy I remember from school. Always swinging. I used to have you pegged as a psycho, and it seems I wasn't wrong.'

'I was polite. I asked you nicely. Now, I'm telling you. We're talking to Cherish.'

'You do realise if anyone else had just done that to me, they'd not be long for the Earth?'

'I don't care.'

'You can hide behind a badge though, can't you? What can I do against Detective Inspector Paul Riddick?'

Riddick shrugged.

Neil walked towards his sofa, still rubbing his neck. 'You're one damaged cookie, Paul Riddick. Always said that... Tell you what, go and talk to her. I'm past giving a shit. Not like she can tell you anything you don't already know.'

Riddick noticed his hand was shaking from the adrenaline when he reached for the door handle. He paused and looked at Neil again. 'If I find out that you've hit her, I won't stop squeezing next time.'

Neil shrugged. 'Well, I guess that'll take public enemy number one off the street.' He pointed back at Riddick. 'And public enemy number two as well when he goes down for murder. Two birds with one stone and all that.'

There was a knock at the door. Riddick went to open it. It was Gardner.

'Oh,' Gardner said. 'You spoken to her, yet?'

'No, just about to. Come in. Neil was just being very welcoming.'

Gardner stepped in and eyed up Neil suspiciously.

'And Paul was being his usual enigmatic self.' Neil reached for the remote control and switched on the news. 'Now get on with it, will you? So, I can get on with my bastard day.'

19

Cherish sat on her bed, her legs crossed. She was propped against her headboard, stroking her rounded stomach as she regarded the two invaders in her bedroom.

Riddick leaned against a chest of drawers beneath a poster of Billie Eilish, creased in the middle from having been plucked from a magazine. Gardner sat on the edge of the bed, sideways on with the broken young lady.

Cherish dabbed at her eyes with a tissue in her hand. 'Sorry,' she said. 'Every time I think it isn't possible to cry any more, I start to cry again.'

Gardner smiled. 'Being pregnant is an emotional time. I remember it well.'

'It's nothing to do with that... Actually, it's *everything* to do with that! My baby's father is dead!'

Gardner exchanged a glance with Riddick. Hardly a revelation, but at least it was finally out in the open. Now, to feign surprise. 'Oh, Cherish... I'm so sorry for your loss.'

Cherish stared at the closed bedroom door and her expression darkened.

'Don't worry about Neil,' Riddick said. 'He won't be disturbing us.'

'Oh,' she said.

'And helping us with our inquiries is the best thing you can do,' Gardner said. 'So, could you tell me about your relationship with Bradley?'

'We'd split up,' Cherish said. 'I don't think we were ever going to get back together. I should be able to deal with this better.'

'He's the father of your child, Cherish,' Gardner said. 'Don't underestimate the feelings you had for him.'

'Neil will be choking on his coffee now that I'm talking to you,' Cherish said.

'We kind of got that impression,' Riddick said. 'Why do you think that is?'

Cherish shrugged. 'Because he never cared about Bradley, and he treats my mother like shit. Two things he'd like to keep quiet.'

'What do you know about Neil?' Riddick asked. 'About what he does?'

'It's not breaking cars,' Cherish said and snorted. 'You know what he does. *Everybody* knows what he does. That's why he doesn't want me talking to you, and why he doesn't want you in his house.'

'So, it's his house now?' Riddick asked.

'Might as well be,' Cherish said. 'Me mam would never throw him out. But I've had enough of him. He hits her, you know?'

Gardner heard the chest of drawers rattle as Riddick stood up straight. 'Have you seen it happen?'

'No. He's careful,' Cherish replied. 'Does it when I'm not there. She'll never hang him out though. He's well and truly in her head. If I didn't have *this* to worry about' – she rubbed her stomach – 'I'd be out of here by now.'

'When did you and Bradley first meet?' Gardner asked.

'I met Bradley before Mam met Neil. That monster was still locked up at that point. Bradley used to knock about by the community centre. I sometimes headed up there with the girls. One thing led to another. He was sweet.'

'Sweet?' Riddick said.

Gardner glared at him. She hoped her eyes delivered the message: *hold that tone. Don't even think about it.*

'Yeah,' Cherish said. 'Out of all of his friends, he was the nicest. Used to say some right kind things to me. He was quite shy actually.' She sighed. 'It was my fault his dad and my mam hooked up. I used to stay over at Bradley's house. Honey didn't mind so much. She was quite sweet too. Some nights, after he was released, Neil was around there, downstairs with Honey. I don't know why, I thought they'd split. I noticed they didn't argue, but they didn't get on well either. Kind of a cold thing, if you know what I mean. One night, my mam phoned me up pissed and acting all crazy. She has these moments. She just loses it completely, and she threatens to do all sorts of crazy shit to herself. She says it's depression and she takes pills that the doctor gives her. Don't seem to do nowt though. So, Neil drives me home one night from Bradley's, and then chats Mam up on the doorstep. Can you believe it? Mam comes out of this depression for a few months, and before I know it, the prick's living here, and acting like my bloody dad!'

Poor girl, Gardner thought. This wasn't a unique tale, and she'd heard it many times before, but it never got any easier to stomach. If anything, it became harder each time as the evidence that the world remained broken for so many young people grew.

'Where's your real father, Cherish?' Gardner asked.

'Don't know. Never met him. Can't be as bad as this prick though... so, there you have it. Another reason I stick around in this hell hole. It's all my fault he's here, and I can't leave my mam. What if he really hurts her?'

'You shouldn't blame yourself, Cherish,' Gardner said. 'She's a grown woman. She's responsible for her own decisions.'

Cherish shrugged. 'I guess.' She looked at Gardner. 'Do you know who killed Bradley?'

'Not yet, no,' Gardner said.

'I hope you find him.'

'We will,' Riddick said.

Gardner looked up at Riddick. Was that real confidence she detected in his voice? She wished she felt the same.

'I want to help,' Cherish said.

'You are doing,' Gardner said. 'Do you have any idea who could have done something like this to Bradley?'

Cherish thought and then shook her head. 'No. Like I said, Bradley was kind. Yeah, he acted all cocky sometimes, but it was all show. He was sensitive. Proper sensitive. Maybe someone from a rival gang outside the area. There was fighting, sometimes. Never heard of anyone dying though.'

Gardner made a note. She already had several officers investigating these gangs from other local areas.

'Did you know of any of these boys from rival gangs?'

'Not really. Me and the girls only ever hung with the local lads.'

'How about Neil?' Riddick asked.

Again, Cherish thought about it. 'I just can't see it. He didn't give a shit about him, but they never really argued. Every now and again, they chatted about Leeds United, but it was brief... No, I can't see it.'

'The night that Bradley died, where were you Cherish?'

'Here. In bed. I get knackered. Usually asleep by half ten.'

'Neil claims he was here all night with your mother, and your mother backed him up.'

'That's crap,' Cherish said. 'He's out nearly every night. And he was definitely out that night because Mam brought me a cup of tea before bed. She'd been watching *Bridgerton* alone.'

'What time was that?' Riddick asked.

'About half ten,' Cherish replied.

Again, Gardner and Riddick exchanged a glance.

'Do you think he could have come home between ten thirty and midnight?'

Cherish thought. 'He didn't. I remember now. I heard Mam crying late, so I went in to see her. She was having one of her moments.'

'What time was that?'

'It was definitely after midnight.'

So, Neil Taylor's alibi was bullshit, and he was now fully in the frame for his kid's murder.

'But still, he wouldn't. A father wouldn't do that to a son. Would he?' Cherish said.

Well, it's happened before, Gardner thought. 'It's rare. Tell me more about Bradley. I'll be honest, Cherish. The persona he presented to the world was full of aggression, and he had a record of poor behaviour. But you say he was different. Tell me how.'

'He was emotional, you know. Nothing like his friends. At least when he was alone with me he was nothing like that.' She sighed and looked down at her bump.

'Emotional how?' Gardner asked.

'He used to cry a lot.'

Really? That doesn't fit with the persona he was trying to portray. 'I see. About?'

'Mainly Kelsey Winters.'

Gardner felt as if she'd been winded. She took a deep inhalation through her nose and glanced up at her deputy.

Riddick looked as if he'd been winded too. No longer standing rigid, he eased himself back onto the chest of drawers, and was hunched over, clutching his knees, and staring down. He looked as if he was about to throw up.

'Sorry,' Cherish said, 'have I said something—'

'What the *hell* does Kelsey Winters have to do with this?' Riddick snapped.

'DI Riddick, enough!' Gardner said, glaring back at him.

He'd lifted his head, and his eyes were wide.

He caught Gardner's look, and managed to rein it in. The expression of fury seemed to settle. He lowered his head again.

Gardner moved quick. She turned back to Cherish, who also looked surprised. 'Sorry for DI Riddick's response. The Kelsey Winters case was a sensitive one for the police. Can you tell me Bradley's involvement with her please?'

'He blamed himself for her suicide.'

'Why?'

'They were in the same year at school. He told me he said some unkind things to her.'

This wasn't good, Riddick was unhinged at the best of times. She noticed her hand was trembling slightly, so she pressed her pencil hard into her pad as she wrote, to try and control it. 'Specifically?'

'He never said.'

'Kelsey was subjected to a lot of bullying,' Riddick said. Fortunately, he sounded calmer now. 'Throughout most of her final year – Year 11.'

'About what?' Cherish asked.

'The usual. A shy, sensitive girl, high achieving, attracting the attention of angry individuals wanting an easy target,' Riddick said.

'But Bradley wasn't like that...' Cherish said. 'And he regretted whatever he said.'

Riddick shrugged. 'He *still* did it though.'

Gardner glared at him again. She was about to ask if it was better that he waited outside, but, after potentially reading her intention, he raised a hand to signal he was okay.

'A couple of his friends were far worse,' Cherish said. 'Dan, in particular.'

'Dan Lotus?' Gardner asked.

Cherish nodded. 'He was like their leader. They always did what Dan told them to do. After Kelsey had died, Bradley tried approaching her mum and dad to apologise, but they wouldn't talk to him. None of the others, including Dan, ever bothered trying to do that.'

Gardner made notes. This would need looking into. Her heart sank. More pain and anguish for the broken Winters family. And Riddick too, of course. She glanced up at her deputy SIO, who appeared lost to his own thoughts. With these cases potentially linked, would he be even more of a liability?

'I know you don't believe me,' Cherish said, crying again, 'but he was a good person.'

Gardner looked at Riddick, ready to move if necessary. Fortunately, he remained quiet.

'Again, I'm sorry for your loss,' Gardner said, turning her attention back to Cherish. 'May I ask why you and Bradley split up?'

She touched her bump. 'After this, he just grew more and more distant. We split up, but we were still close friends. He told me everything... but then... then... he started shagging Mrs Harrison.'

'Mrs Harrison?' Gardner asked, not really liking the sound of this at all.

'You know, Mrs Harrison?' Cherish said. Her voice was full of surprise.

'I'm not from around here, Cherish—'

'A maths teacher at the local secondary,' Riddick said.

'A maths teacher?' Gardner echoed, unable to keep the surprise out of her voice. 'Are you sure, Cherish?'

'Positive. He admitted it to me. Swore me to secrecy. Like I said, we were best friends. I was still hoping he'd come back to me. I knew it would never last with a teacher, so I just listened, and *promised...*' Her eyes filled with tears again. 'I guess it doesn't matter any more, does it?'

Oh it matters very much!

Gardner looked up at Riddick. 'She still working there?'

Riddick nodded.

Gardner looked back at Cherish. 'How did this happen? Did he tell you?'

'Not all the details... no. She used to teach him maths in Year 11. Then, when he failed, he came back to retake in Year 12, and again in Year 13. He just told me that he was in love with her, and she felt the same. Again, I was just waiting for it to fall to pieces, so he would come back to me.'

'When did the affair actually start?' Gardner asked.

'Only six months ago. So, he was old enough, I guess. It's not against the law, is it?'

'She had a duty of care to Bradley,' Gardner said, feeling the investigation becoming messier with every revelation. Did they have a case of professional misconduct here? Had the schoolteacher's fear of exposure led her to murder?

Cherish welled up again. 'No, please, I don't want to be the one to get her into trouble.'

'Again, if this turns out to be the case, you're in no way responsible!' Gardner said. 'And, ultimately, we can't find out what happened to Bradley without all the details. So, what you are doing is right and proper. Did you ever approach Mrs Harrison?'

'No.'

'Do you think she knew that he'd told you?'

'No. He'd promised not to tell anyone. He was in love with her. But I still believed he loved me too, which is why he confided in me.'

Gardner looked at Riddick, who was pale, and appeared as if he needed some fresh air. She decided to move the interview to its conclusion.

Following several more questions, Gardner reached over and patted Cherish on the knee. She handed her a card with her phone number on it. 'Phone me day or night.'

'I think I've told you everything I know,' Cherish said.

'Not just about Bradley,' Gardner said. 'Day or night phone me if you want to talk or need anything at all.'

Cherish wiped her tears away and smiled. 'Thanks. You're nice.'

Gardner stood. 'There're a lot of nice people in the world, Cherish. It's just sometimes, when things aren't going great, it can seem like the opposite. You're not alone, Cherish.' She looked at Riddick. 'And what's more, none of us have to be alone.'

20

Despite having driven separately, the two of them sat together in Gardner's car to consider the revelations.

Riddick remained pale. He stared out of the window, clearly waiting for Gardner to spark the conversation.

She offered him a peppermint tic tac. He shook his head. 'Don't do peppermint.' He reached into his pocket and produced half a packet of extra-strong mints.

'Did you know Bradley was one of the bullies, Riddick?' Gardner asked.

He sighed. 'No. Thinking about it now though, I do remember the best friend Dan Lotus posting something on Facebook. But there were a lot of nasty comments online. I didn't trawl through them all, personally. I was pulled from the case very early on, remember?'

'It's probably just a coincidence, Paul, but we're going to have to revisit the Winters case. But you know that already, don't you?'

Riddick continued to stare out of the passenger window. 'It's a problem, boss.'

'Yes,' Gardner said. 'But I think we can keep you separate from this angle until we rule it out.'

She glanced at him to gauge his response. She knew it would be best to just contact Marsh and have him pulled, at least temporarily. That would be the safer option. However, she couldn't help but follow her gut instinct. Riddick was a major asset on this case. He knew and understood the people involved. Without him, she may just put the investigation at a disadvantage. She wouldn't exactly be lost at sea, but she would be weaker for his absence.

Riddick turned and met her eyes. 'Maybe it's just best if—'

'Do *you* want off the case?'

'No, of course not. But don't put your head on the block for me.'

'I'm not putting my head on the block for anyone. I will put the Winters angle out to someone else in the team. Meanwhile, you and I can follow up on this Mrs Harrison.'

'*Susan* Harrison.'

'Susan Harrison. Please tell me that you don't have any history there too, do you?'

'Apart from going to that school, no. I don't know her personally.'

'What do you know about her?'

'She's a maths teacher. Late twenties, possibly early thirties. Married with children. She always seems to be involved in community events. Her name pops up a lot at organised events, such as the FEVA arts festival every August.'

'Well, if Cherish is telling the truth, that woman's life is about to come crashing down.'

Riddick nodded. 'Deservedly so.'

'Listen, I'm going to check in with the chief now and organise someone to speak to Kelsey Winters' parents. Give me fifteen minutes, and we'll head to the school together to speak to Susan.'

Riddick nodded again. 'We've also got another problem.'

'Go on.'

'Have you forgotten Neil Taylor's false alibi? He was out, God-knows-where, the night his son was killed.'

'Oh, I haven't forgotten, Paul. I was going to brief the chief constable on that too and arrange for someone else to come and take him to the station for a detailed statement. It's time we got this eel on record.'

'Let me have another quick word with him, first,' Riddick said, eying up Mandy's house.

'Is that a good idea, Paul? You look like you took quite a shock in there. Let's just wait for his detailed statement—'

'Boss,' Riddick said, looking back at Gardner. 'I know this prick. I know what makes him tick. Let me have a quick run at him. I promise there'll be no fireworks.'

He had a point. If she was going to retain Riddick's services due to his knowledge of the locals, she might as well let him use that knowledge to their advantage.

'Okay. No longer than twenty minutes unless you unearth a gold nugget. And if you do, you open that door and wave me straight in.'

Riddick crossed his heart.

'And no scrapping,' Gardner said. 'This isn't a schoolyard.'

'You have me pegged all wrong, boss,' Riddick said, exiting the car.

'No,' Gardner said. 'I think I have you pegged all right. Which is why I want you to stay on the case.' She smiled.

Riddick looked in, returned her smile and closed the door.

* * *

Gardner checked in with a few team members for an update, and then contacted Chief Constable Marsh to brief her on the events of the day so far.

'I appreciate the update, Emma, but it is still rather early, so I'm guessing there is something else on your mind.'

'Yes, ma'am. A couple of things.'

'I'm intrigued. Where would you like to start?'

'Paul's background, ma'am.'

'What about it?'

'Surely it would have been prudent to provide me with details before I began working with him.'

Marsh laughed. 'Prudent? We'd only just met, Emma, and we'd a murder case. I wanted you focused, and not full of doubt over your deputy SIO. This sudden link to the Kelsey Winters case is completely out of the blue, and hopefully nothing more than a nasty little coincidence.'

'But how about what happened to him personally, ma'am?'

There was a stony silence.

'The poor man... how could anyone—'

'Precisely,' Marsh said. 'Do you think I wanted you drowning Paul in sympathy the first time you met over Bradley's body.'

An exaggeration, Gardner thought, *but, yes, I cannot deny it would have been on my mind.* 'Obviously, I'd have been discreet.'

'I don't doubt it. You come highly recommended after all. However, how'd you feel when you found out?'

'Bad. Awful, in fact.'

'I assume you told him you knew?'

'Yes.' *And I struggled to keep the tears out of my eyes.*

'Uncomfortable?'

'Yes.' *But I haven't let that get in the way of my job.* She thought about the decision she'd made to keep him on the case following

Cherish's revelation around the Winters case. *At least, I don't think I have...*

'Look, I wasn't trying to play games, Emma. I just wanted you both focused when you met the first time at the crime scene. As you've probably noticed, Paul isn't the easiest with people at the best of times; I didn't want to muddy the situation. I knew you'd find out on your own and process it in your own way. I trusted you to handle it professionally. Which I believe you have.'

'Maybe it would have been best for you to assign me a different deputy SIO, at least until, you know, I'd got to know him—'

'What are your impressions of Riddick so far?'

'Abrasive. Somewhat aggressive. Astute... extremely observant.'

'He's the best I've ever worked with, Emma. And, if not for his history, he'd be already standing where you're standing.'

Gardner thought about the other officers in her briefing. Some of them looked capable, but none of them had presented themselves with the same fire as Riddick had done so far. The man was clearly carrying demons around with him. Sacksful of them to be honest. But still... there was a sense that nothing would stop him until he had the truth. And with a brutal murder on their hands, this was a very welcome characteristic.

'Would you like a different deputy, Emma? Is that why you're phoning?'

'No, of course not, ma'am. He's clearly driven, and it would be counterproductive to take him off now, but I just worry.'

'Leave the worrying to me. I'll carry the can if anything goes wrong.'

Really? Easy for you to say that now... Wouldn't be the first time a superior had delivered a false promise.

'He may seem broken, Emma – and to a certain extent, he is – but you'll never find a better person to rely on.'

'Okay, ma'am,' – *mind not at ease* – 'but speaking of relying on. I don't know my team very well at the moment, and I need to put someone on the Winters angle while I head to the school. It'll be very sensitive. Do you have any suggestions?'

'DS Ray Barnett.'

'Yes, he seems capable, but I have him all over the Waterside angle, and I don't want to disrupt him.'

'Someone else can handle that for a couple of hours. Use Ray. He's one of your best. He may look like he's been sculpted from rock, but he's the most sensitive officer you'll ever meet. He'll handle the Winters angle with decorum.'

'Okay… there's one more thing—'

'*The Viaduct Killer* by any chance?'

'Yes. How did you know I was going to flag that up?'

'Well, if you didn't quiz me over the leak, I'd wonder where you'd been for the last twenty-four hours.'

'Fair enough, ma'am. What can you tell me about DS Phil Rice?'

Marsh snorted. 'That he's an irritant, but it wasn't him.'

'Are you sure—'

'Positive. He's belligerent, stubborn, and as you probably discovered, oppositional. But it's all front. He's a good officer, and he wants to get the job done. He'll keep you on your toes, but he's not our leak.'

'Okay… do we have any idea who is talking to this awful journalist, Marianne Perse?'

'I have a few suspicions, and I'm following up on it myself, but I want you to focus on what you're doing, Gardner. Joe Bridge is doing a great job at keeping them at bay, but the hounds want a press conference with us. We'll hold them off today and see where we're up to tomorrow. Hopefully, by then, we'll have sealed the leak, and you'll have more tangible information to give them.'

'I hope so, ma'am.'

'I have every faith in you and your team.'

I wish I shared your faith. 'Thank you, ma'am.'

Gardner hung up and reached for her tic tacs again, disappointed to find the box empty.

She sighed, annoyed with herself for the under confidence.

She wondered what DCI Michael Yorke would say to her right now. Something along the lines of, 'A new town, a new team, and a partner with a closet bursting with skeletons – you'd be abnormal if you were chock full of confidence.'

Yes, Mike. You're right.

She contacted DS Ray Barnett to ask him to visit the parents of Kelsey Winters.

21

Neil opened the door and rolled his eyes.

Riddick forced back a smile.

'Seriously?' Neil said. 'Are you having a laugh?'

'I'll tell you what's serious, Neil. Mandy has lied. She wasn't with you between nine and midnight the day before last.'

'Really. Says who?'

'Not relevant... Now, can I come in so you can be straight with us?'

'And if I tell you to piss off?'

'Then I'll charge Mandy with obstruction of justice, and I'll apply for a warrant for your arrest.'

'For?'

'The murder of your son.'

Neil laughed. 'Behave.' He stood back to allow Riddick access. 'Can I expect more police brutality?'

Riddick waited until the door was closed behind him before answering the question. 'Depends.'

'On?'

'Whether you take your frustrations out on Mandy again.'

'She isn't the one talking to you lot. That'll be her bitch of a daughter upstairs.'

'Well, she's pregnant. So, lay a hand on her, and you'll remember the brutality as little more than a pleasant appetiser.'

They went through into the lounge and sat side by side. Neil spoke while Riddick got out his notepad. 'D'you realise what my son and that slut's mistake is going to cost me? Who do you think is going to end up footing the bill?'

'Let's get to the point, Neil. Your son is dead. The circumstances are suspicious. Did you kill him?'

'No.' He pointed at his mouth as he said it. 'Why in God's name would I do that?'

'Well, in all honesty, you don't seem that bothered that he's dead.'

'Because I'm not in tears? Give me a break. Listen, Bradley was a pain in the arse, and did he cause me problems? Yes. He was also too bloody emotional, and so he was never going to be of use to me.'

'With what? Breaking cars?' Riddick said and sneered.

'Among other things. Man's work in general. However, he was still my son, and I still loved him. I may not seem it, but I'm gutted.'

'Gutted, but you can't even shed a tear?'

'I've never been the crying type.'

'Well, at least get angry then. Shouldn't a man like you be out for revenge?'

Neil smiled. 'How do you know I'm not?'

'Well, if you are, I suggest you stop right there. It's easier to talk to us, and have it dealt with properly—'

'Properly! You're as heavy-handed as the next man, Paul. You just demonstrated that earlier.'

Riddick ran a hand over his head. 'Where were you between

nine and midnight the day before last? And, if your alibi doesn't check out this time, we're coming back for you. Guns blazing.'

Neil sighed. 'The Worlds End.'

Riddick felt his blood run cold. 'That pub's right next to the bloody river. Fifteen minutes, *if that*, from the bloody crime scene.'

'Precisely!' Neil said. 'Why do you think I didn't tell you? Better to keep it simple. I can see it in your eyes already. I'll give you two reasons why I didn't kill my boy. Number one – I've already gone down, and don't fancy it again. *Ever*. Number two – he was my boy.' His voice began to crack. 'My bloody boy for Christ's sake.'

You're a good actor, Neil. There's only one person in this room you've ever cared about, and it isn't me! 'Who were you with at the Worlds End?'

'Simon Turner and Nick Foley.'

Riddick guffawed. 'Two people that'd happily lie for you.'

Neil shrugged. 'I'm sure you've got other means. Ask the bar staff. Check the CCTV.'

'What time did you leave?'

'About eleven.'

'Who with?'

'I walked with Si down Waterside. All the way down to Abbey Road, out onto Wetherby Road. Then I headed off left to Fountains Way where Si lives.'

'Why?'

'We fancied more drinks.'

As well as the rest, Riddick thought. 'Was there anyone else there?'

'His wife. She can vouch for us. We must have been there from half eleven.'

Riddick made some notes.

'Did you and Si head up to the castle via the steps?'

'No. We never went to the bloody castle! We walked right past those steps.'

'Will you consent to a DNA sample?'

'Hardly any point when you already have it, but yes.'

'Okay, we will be speaking to Simon Turner, his wife, Nick Foley and the staff at the Worlds End. Anyone else who will be able to confirm your account of events?'

'Not that I can remember, no. I'm sure someone must have seen me through the window of one of their houses?'

He thought of the witness who'd seen someone arguing loudly on the phone. 'Were you wearing a hoodie?'

'No... a jumper.'

'Will you be happy to submit this jumper for a fibre test if required?'

'Wouldn't be great if I said no, would it?'

'Probably not. You want a suggestion, Neil?'

Neil growled. 'I'm all ears.'

'Head to the station in Harrogate and deliver a detailed statement. I'll let them know you're on your way. Get ahead of this.'

Neil shook his head. 'I've done nowt. This is precisely why I lied in the first place.'

Riddick shrugged. 'Look. It seems as if Mandy has been through a lot. What with the black eye, and everything. You get to the station, and make that detailed statement, and I'll see what I can do about the obstruction of justice charge.'

'Do you enjoy your job, Paul?'

Riddick stood. 'Beats breaking cars for a living.'

'Oh, I don't know.' Neil stood. 'I could have a use for a dogged fella such as yourself. You might even find it rewarding.'

'Rewarding how?' Riddick raised an eyebrow.

Neil winked. 'Let me know when you've finally told your superiors where they can stick their job.'

'And why would I do that?'

'They shat all over you, Paul. Have you forgotten?'

No, that's not something I'd forget. 'They had their reasons.'

Neil winked again. 'Loyalty. I like that in a man too... yes, you really could be so useful.'

'Are you trying to involve me in some kind of crime, Neil?'

'Whatever gave you that idea? Besides, not everyone has to be squeaky clean, do they? You could still be the hero. Your old boss, Anders, was hardly squeaky clean, and he was the toast of the town.'

For saving kids from a burning building. You could pretty much get away with anything after that. Not that Anders had been a bent copper. Old school, yes. Bent, no. 'I'm not interested in how you see things, and I'm starting to feel rather irritated.' He clenched his fists.

Neil held his palms up. 'Easy now, Paul. One beating is enough for me today. I'm just trying to help you. You've fallen. I'm simply offering to pick you back up.'

Riddick took a step forward, and Neil took a step back.

I may have fallen, but I've not hit the bottom yet.

'Go to the station,' Riddick said. 'And deliver your statement. I'll let them know you're coming.'

* * *

He delivered the results of the interview to Gardner in her car.

'Well done, Paul. What do you think?'

'I think he's an absolute dick, and guilty of many things, but murdering his son? I'm not so sure. First, let's find out if he's telling the truth this time.'

'I'm going to give it to DS Phil Rice and some of the others to look into,' Gardner said.

Riddick raised an eyebrow. 'Phil's a prat.'

'The chief thinks he's okay,' Gardner said.

'The chief told you I was okay,' Riddick said.

'Yes. And you are. Sort of,' Gardner said. 'Look, I have to start trusting people, sooner or later, Paul. We can't do all this on our own, you know.'

Riddick nodded.

'I think it's best you contact Phil with everything you just found out, in case I get anything wrong,' Gardner continued. 'Tell him to investigate this timeline of events to within an inch of its life. We are not ruling out Neil until we are 100 per cent certain that he didn't take those steps up to the castle. Phil can also take his detailed statement at the station, so if Neil lies to us again, we've got him on record.'

22

This was a sensitive situation and Barnett appreciated the trust Gardner had suddenly placed in him. As a result, on the journey to the late Kelsey Winters' home he felt assured and determined. However, sitting here now, with Hannah Winters, someone who'd experienced unimaginable loss, he felt his confidence quickly ebb away.

He avoided picking up the china teacup she'd filled for him in case she noticed his big hands tremble. He looked right at DC Lucy O'Brien, who appeared confident – *how the bloody hell was she managing that* – and then back at Hannah. 'Mrs Winters, thank you again for seeing us; we don't want to keep you long.'

'Hannah, please,' she said and smiled.

The smile seemed false to Barnett. In fact, Hannah came across as nothing more than a sculpture, cold and unmoving, lifeless even, making that smile no more than the work of an artist's hands.

'I'm aware it's been over two years since we last spoke to you regarding Kelsey.'

'Seems like yesterday, Detective Sergeant.'

And I bet it always will do, Barnett thought, his hands still shaking. 'And we're not here to discuss the circumstances around Kelsey's passing.'

'I didn't expect you were,' Hannah said and sipped from her own china cup. 'There really isn't much to discuss. And you don't need to worry about upsetting me. I'm stronger now than when I last spoke to the police. I've a support group, I've peace, and I still have Kelsey here.' She touched her chest. 'I've also forgiven you for what your colleague, DI Riddick, did. He wanted the truth behind what happened. He was only doing his job. What he went through *after*... well... that was horrendous.'

'Thank you, Hannah. I'll be sure to convey your message to DI Riddick.'

She looked at Lucy. 'You look young, dear. Do you enjoy your job?'

'Very much so, ma'am,' Lucy said.

'Hannah, I insist! What's your first name?'

'Lucy.'

'I hope they keep you safe, Lucy. There's too much waste in this world. Too much. You really have your whole life ahead of you, dear. I hope they appreciate that.'

'They do, Hannah. I'm safe, and I take good care of myself. Thank you for asking.'

'You're welcome, dear.' She looked back at Barnett. 'Are you here about Bradley?'

'What makes you ask that?'

'He was one of the boys that bullied my Kelsey. When I heard about this Viaduct Killer, I guessed that you would find your way here at some stage.'

'The Viaduct Killer is not an official name,' Barnett said. 'We haven't named anyone.'

'I see. Regardless, it was a sad affair.' She looked at Lucy again. 'More waste. He was a troubled boy.'

'How so?' Barnett asked.

'Bullies have troubled souls.'

Barnett nodded. 'When did you become aware that Bradley was one of the boys who had bullied Kelsey?'

'After she died, myself and my husband looked through all her social media. We found all the people who bullied Kelsey. She wouldn't have minded. There were never any secrets between us.' She smiled again. 'Not a single one.'

'What do you recall regarding Bradley?'

'Many children, girls and boys, simply added comments to the images that were posted. Bradley was one of the two main perpetrators who posted the images. He actually came to see me to apologise. He wasn't the worst of the two. I remember the other boy, Dan Lotus, really seemed to revel in my daughter's anguish. He posted some very colourful images, I can tell you.' She took another mouthful of tea and stared off into space.

There was no need to ask Hannah about any of these images. They were all being recovered from the database back at HQ.

'But, you know, when all is said and done, they were children. They used words to hurt my daughter. It was malicious, it was cruel, but they didn't make her take my sleeping pills. It took me years to accept this, but I *know* that now. My daughter wasn't very well. Not well at all. Now, I believe the bullying was just a catalyst – that, eventually, this may have happened regardless. It's *our* fault you see. Mine, and Tom's. We should have been there for her more. We had our problems at the time, and we neglected the warnings. She used to hurt herself. The signs were all there.' She broke off and for the first time, the sculpted smile fell away.

'I'm so sorry for your loss,' O'Brien said.

Barnett looked at O'Brien, suddenly concerned she might

start crying, but she was holding it together magnificently, and he realised it was actually him that was struggling.

'I hope Bradley found some peace before he died,' Hannah said. 'When he came to see me – must be a year back now – he was tearful and apologetic. He claimed that the bullying wasn't his idea but didn't try to use it as an excuse.' She paused, and looked off into space, recalling the incident. 'He said he'd never done anything like that before, and wouldn't again. He also mentioned his father.'

'Neil Taylor?' Barnett asked.

Hannah nodded. 'He said he hated him. That he didn't want to be like him. But, you know, I cut the conversation short. I forgave the boy, but it was still too painful, too raw then. I wanted him gone...' She stared off again. 'Maybe I should have given him more time. Maybe... I could have helped him?'

'You did more than most,' O'Brien said. 'Accepting his apology... listening to him... you were very generous.'

Hannah sighed. 'You know that when Tom found out that I'd been speaking to Bradley, he hit the roof. Our marriage was already over at that point, but we were desperately trying to cling to each other. It felt like we had to at that point. We'd lost our only daughter. If we split up, it'd be like everything had been a waste. Sixteen years of nothing... but those around me have helped me to see that it isn't like this. We're better off apart. We're both happier. We still haven't divorced, but I expect we will.'

'Where's Tom now?'

'Overseas on the rigs. He's practically worked the entire two years since. We all have our ways. His is work. Mine is forgiveness.'

'Did your husband forgive them?'

Hannah turned her head from side to side. 'I'm afraid not.

Like I said, when I forgave Bradley, and I told Tom, we didn't speak for a long time.'

'Have you spoken to your husband recently regarding Bradley?' Barnett said.

'No... why?' She shook her head more vigorously this time. 'No... you can't think? No. He wouldn't have anything to do with that. He's a gentle man.'

'We believe you, Hannah,' Barnett said. 'But still, we'd like to get in touch with him. Can you give us his details so we can do that?'

'Of course,' Hannah said, scrolling through the numbers on her phone. 'Just one moment. This is how you'd contact him on the rig.' She read out the number.

Barnett jotted it down. 'Does he still live here with you when he's not away?'

Hannah shook her head. 'No. He rents a bungalow in Harrogate.' She gave the address and Barnett wrote it down. 'But, like I said, he's definitely away. He lets me know when he's in Harrogate. We still see each other, you know. We shared so much.'

'Thank you, Hannah,' Barnett said. 'Also... this is standard procedure, Hannah, so please don't take it the wrong way. We'd just like to completely eliminate you from the inquiry. Could you tell me where you were on Monday night between 9 p.m. and 12 p.m.?'

'I was here.'

'Were you with anyone?' Barnett said.

'Nosey!' Hannah laughed. 'Yes. My new partner. Geoff McQuarrie.'

'Would it be okay for us to contact him?' Barnett asked.

'If you must. He was here, we had a takeaway and' – she smiled – 'he spent the night.'

Just as she'd done with Tom's number, Hannah scrolled

through to Geoff's number on her mobile phone and read it out. Barnett jotted it down. Checking her alibi was probably a waste of time, but Barnett had a new boss on the scene, and he was not going to be anything but thorough. He repeated the number back to her, and she nodded to confirm it was okay.

23

Gardner had called ahead to the school to spare them the surprise when she hit the buzzer and announced herself.

'If you drive to the end of the car park, DCI Gardner, we cleared two spaces for you. You'll see the orange cones.'

Her foresight had paid dividends. Schools were notoriously difficult, if not impossible, places to park in at midday.

'Thank you,' Gardner said, watching the iron gates swing back. 'We'll see you in reception.'

After parking, she received a phone call from Barnett. He filled her in on his meeting with Hannah Winters which, surprisingly, had gone smoothly despite that historical bad blood between her and the force.

'Her alibi checks out, boss,' Barnett said. 'She was with her new partner Geoff McQuarrie all night.'

'So, we move onto Tom Winters.'

'I'm trying. Overseas working on a rig, apparently. We've tried his mobile, but it's switched off. I've left a message for him to contact us. I've also left a message for HR of his company to contact us too, so we can confirm he's at work. We're about to go over to his bungalow in Harrogate to see if he's made an unannounced return.'

'Let me know, Ray, please.'

'Of course, boss.'

'And Ray?'

'Yes?'

'Great work.'

'Thanks.'

She looked through the passenger window into Riddick's car. He was drinking from a Sprite bottle. After taking a few gulps, he threw the bottle back into the glove compartment, chomped on some mints – which she assumed were extra-strong after his earlier remark – and then stepped from the car.

She joined him outside while looking the school up and down. 'Has it changed much since you came here?'

'Just a bit! They've actually got stuff now.' He pointed at an impressive Astroturf facility. 'That was just a muddy field when I was a lad. Often see Leeds United FC running training camps on it now!'

Throughout her journey here, Gardner had been visited by the memory of her last trip to a secondary school. She hadn't attempted to block it out because, as the counsellor had told her time and time again, trying to block out thoughts simply inflamed them. Surprisingly, she'd sat well with the memory, and had not felt apprehensive on her approach.

However, as they neared the glass entrance, she was seized by a sudden, familiar cold sensation, which forced her against the brick wall to steady herself.

'You okay?' Riddick said.

'Give me a second.' She clutched her chest and took several deep breaths. She must have looked as though she was having a heart attack.

Riddick raised an eyebrow. 'Shall we go back to the car?'

Gardner closed her eyes, gestured *no* with a shake of her hand, and took a few more slow, deep gulps of air. This seemed to do the trick. 'Okay, that's better... sorry, didn't expect that... old memories flaring.'

'Do you have PTSD?'

'Something like that.'

'Boss, why don't you go and—'

'I told you, I'm fine!' Gardner said, standing up straight. 'It's all under control again.'

Riddick squinted at her through narrowed eyes.

She sighed, knowing it was best to just divulge. Burying truth, as Riddick was the master of, was never a good choice. Her counsellor was very clear that when the truth wanted airtime, *it should get airtime*.

'Years ago, in Salisbury, I visited a school to speak to a headteacher. I interrupted a knife attack. I didn't fare too well in the exchange.' She touched her chest. 'Intensive care and a punctured lung.'

'Shit,' Riddick said. 'I'm sorry.'

'Shit happens,' Gardner said. 'As long as you deal with it after, you can heal. I've healed... with the occasional wobble, it seems.' She patted the school wall. 'When faced with these reminders.'

She thought back to the moment she'd witnessed the knife fight on the eighth floor of that Wiltshire high-rise. She'd had a wobble then too, hadn't she? Was that the reason she'd impulsively chased that boy, and left Willows in such a vulnerable situation?

She took another deep breath and addressed the negative thought in the manner her counsellor had trained her to. *No. I'd have gone after that boy regardless. If anything had happened as a result of me not at least trying to challenge a boy wielding a knife, that would have been impossible to come back from.*

I was doing my job, not acting impulsively.

As with many schools these days, the reception area was more in keeping with a lounge in a corporate building than a school. Gardner and Riddick signed in at a computer screen, which took their photographs, and printed out stickers with their names on.

The head came to meet them. She was a severe looking woman with her hair tied back so tightly, her forehead looked stretched. 'Paula Bradford.'

They exchanged handshakes and introductions.

'Thank you for ringing ahead. Snowed under here. The norovirus is making the rounds. *Again.* We've emptied all of the supply agencies within a fifty-mile radius!'

Gardner remembered a bug striking the team in the middle of a high-profile investigation several years back in Wiltshire. The sight of each member taking turns to flee the incident room for the toilets had been farcical! Right now, with this killer on the streets, she couldn't afford any absences. 'We'll keep our contact with people to a minimum. We're in the thick of it too.'

'I bet,' Paula said. 'Dreadful incident. I tried to send as much information on Bradley over as I could yesterday, but I assume you're here to give it another once over. I took the liberty of getting all the information together.'

'That's one reason we came,' Gardner said. *Susan Harrison, the wayward maths teacher, is the other...*

Paula led them down a long corridor with classrooms spilling out on each side. Gardner peered into a few rooms en route, content to see the students focused. There was an eerie silence in the corridor.

'How times change,' Riddick said. 'Way back when, there

were more kids in the corridors than in the classroom.'

'Some schools still encounter those problems. I've been blessed with a good leadership team. Outstanding when Ofsted visited last year.'

Gardner noticed the proud smile on Paula's face as she led them into a boardroom and she wondered, briefly, if this may one day be her daughter Anabelle's secondary school. It certainly gave off an excellent first impression.

Paula's PA prepared them all a coffee, and they assembled at a boardroom table. The head teacher already had her documentation laid out. In the age of inspections, it always paid to be completely prepared – it then, inevitably, became a habit.

Gardner nodded at the folders. 'Thank you for being prompt with this information when we contacted you yesterday. It has been properly scrutinised, so we don't expect you to go through his school history again chapter and verse. We thought we could begin by hearing your personal views regarding Bradley – have you been the headteacher throughout his entire school career?'

'Yes,' Paula said with a nod. 'From Year 7 through to Year 13.'

'It's surprising he lasted that long,' Riddick said, 'considering his profile.'

'Well, DI Riddick, we don't make a habit of shipping them out every time we have a problem with them. This isn't "way back when" any more.'

Gardner glanced at Riddick. He'd been put in his place, not that he looked in any way bothered. His expression was completely nonchalant.

'Actually, you may be about to hear something contrary to what all these facts, profiles and data are telling you,' Paula said, sitting back in the chair, no longer interested in her folders. 'He was a complicated character, Bradley. Despite his troubles, he was quite a kind boy.'

'We've heard that from others,' Gardner said, glancing at Riddick, willing him not to pass comment about the bullying.

Paula continued. 'When children come from a broken home, as Bradley did, you have to appreciate that their decision-making isn't always the best. Here, we appreciate that. We put plans in place for Bradley. Time out cards, reduced timetables and reward plans for example. We did the best we could by Bradley and, at times, when home life wasn't weighing him down, he could have a good sense of humour and a kind word for some of his peers. If anything, he was a rather quiet boy, prone to the occasional outburst. Again, as a result of his home life. When your mother is addicted to drugs, and your father goes to prison for dealing them, well, you can only imagine.'

'No need to imagine,' Riddick said. 'We live it daily too.'

'Yes, quite,' Paula said, flinching. Unlike Riddick, she did look as if she'd been put in her place.

'It may be a sensitive issue,' Gardner said, 'but important. What can you tell us about the Kelsey Winters' suicide?'

Paula flinched again. 'There really isn't much I can say. We were investigated. We were found to have acted in an appropriate manner. Most of the bullying took place online. We provide regular assemblies, and life lessons on bullying, and the dangers of the internet. All bullying that took place on site was investigated and reported to the parents. Several of the boys were suspended for chanting in the corridors. It was challenged at every angle.'

'I'm sure it was,' Gardner said, 'but please understand, Mrs Bradford, this isn't about questioning your integrity. We're here regarding Bradley. He was found to be one of the main bullies, wasn't he?'

'Yes, he was, and,' Paula said, holding her finger up defensively, 'he was suspended and considered for exclusion. But the panel decided he'd been influenced by a peer, who was subsequently excluded... permanently.'

'Dan Lotus?' Gardner asked.

'Yes. Now, he was a whole different kettle of fish to Bradley.'

'How so?'

'Not a sensitive bone in that boy's body. He was also regularly absent and a complete pain while he was in school.'

'Why was he not excluded until Year 11 then?' Riddick asked.

Paula fixed Riddick with a stare. 'I know what you're getting at. But we're not like that here. We're *inclusive* and we try our hardest to keep the students. Come what may.'

'Even if they're dangerous?' Riddick pressed on.

'Dangerous is bringing a knife into school or physically abusing staff or students.'

'How about verbal abuse? How about *bullying*?'

'Commonplace,' Paula said. 'If we excluded every student for those crimes, we'd fail in our commitment to serve the community.'

'Let me ask you.' Riddick leaned forward. 'If you'd chosen to permanently exclude Dan earlier than Year 11, would Kelsey still be alive?'

'I can't possibly answer that question, DI Riddick, and what's more, I resent it.'

Gardner touched Riddick's knee under the table. He got the message and sat back in his chair.

'Something else has come to our attention, Mrs Bradford,' Gardner said. 'Something *concerning*. We're here to speak to one of your members of staff, but I thought it was prudent to get your take on this first. It's very sensitive, and I'd like to minimise its impact if it's unfounded.'

'Go on?'

Gardner leaned forward in her chair. 'Susan Harrison.'

Paula leaned back in her chair and paled slightly.

Gardner felt her muscles tighten. *What do you know, Paula?* 'We've heard a claim that Susan Harrison was having a relationship with Bradley Taylor.'

'Nonsense!' Paula said, leaning forward again. 'We've been down this road before. The complaint is old hat.'

'I see. Please explain.'

'Last year, one of the students in Year 12 claimed to have seen them together, kissing, in a park in Leeds. Of course, it was escalated to the Local Authority Designated Officer for investigation. It came down to mistaken identity. Susan was with her mother on the day in question, and certainly wasn't conducting an affair with a student almost half her age! The poor woman went through enough. Almost destroyed her family. Surely, we're not going to drag this to the surface again?'

'This is a murder investigation, Mrs Bradford,' Riddick said. 'And our source was rather convincing on this matter. This wasn't simply a chance sighting in Leeds. Someone very close to Bradley has provided a compelling statement.'

'Who?'

Gardner raised an eyebrow.

Paula sighed. 'Well... I don't believe it... She wouldn't.'

'I thought it best we speak to her here,' Gardner said. 'Keep it as low key as possible until we establish the facts.'

'One moment please,' Paula said.

She left the boardroom to speak to her PA. When she returned, she said, 'She's teaching now. I'll ask Derek, my deputy, to step in for her. Can you please wait here while I collect her?'

Gardner nodded. 'Mrs Bradford, please don't tell her about our suspicions. It'll only cause her to panic.'

After Paula had left, Gardner turned to Riddick. 'You do like to go in hard, Paul.'

'Speeds things along, boss.'

'Listen, this situation is about to get even more sensitive. I need you to ease off. At least with this interview.'

Riddick shrugged.

Gardner felt her phone vibrating in her pocket.

'Hello Ray,' she answered.

'No sign of anyone at Tom Winters' bungalow, boss. I've still not heard back from HR at his company, either. You want me to get back on to Waterside CCTV while I wait for an update?'

'Yes, please. I also want you to scour the CCTV footage for a Susan Harrison. She's the head of maths—'

'Yes. I know who she is, ma'am.'

'If you see her on CCTV, call me straight back.'

'Will do. In fact, I'll get my team on it this second.'

'Thanks.'

After ringing off, Riddick said, 'How closely have we looked at Dan Lotus, boss?'

Gardner consulted her notebook. 'John and Lucy took a detailed statement from him yesterday. Why? What're you thinking?'

'I'm thinking Lotus is a nasty piece of work. Made Bradley look like Mother Teresa.'

'They were best friends,' Gardner said.

'Friendships turn sour,' Riddick said.

'Agreed, but nothing was flagged up following the detailed statement. You want to take another run at it?'

'I think so, boss, yes. Right now, we're sitting on two persons of interests. Neil Taylor and Susan Harrison. As much as I despise Neil, I don't fancy him for it. Also, Susan Harrison? You heard the pathologist. The assailant would have to be strong to overpower Bradley. She's a very slight woman.'

'Well, let's at least hear her story first.'

'I agree, boss. But it seems to me that if you mix with bad people, as Bradley has done, you're going to come unstuck. I fancy the gang culture in all of this, and I'm just wondering if we should move our focus more in that direction—'

Paula opened the door. She was pale and shaken. 'I'm sorry...'

Gardner rose to her feet.

Riddick said, 'Why? What's happened?'

'As I was leading her away from the classroom, I told her your suspicions.'

Riddick shook his head. 'We asked you—'

'I'm sorry. I just couldn't believe it, you know?'

'And what's happened?'

'She ran,' Paula said. 'She just turned towards reception and ran.'

Riddick stood and stared at Gardner. Gardner's phone rang. 'Yes, Ray?'

'Boss. Two things. ANPR picked up Susan Harrison's vehicle in the car park opposite Waterside, behind the Ugly Duckling, at five past eleven on the night Bradley was killed.'

Gardner felt her heart rate increase. 'Christ. And the second thing?'

'CCTV has picked her up on Waterside,' Barnett said. 'She would have reached the steps up to the castle at eleven fifteen. She was also filmed returning to her vehicle via Waterside at ten to twelve. It fits, boss. Right place, right time.'

Had Susan Harrison killed Bradley to hide the truth of their relationship?

Unfortunately, the person that needed to answer this question had just slipped through their fingers. 'She's done a runner, Ray. *Shit!*'

'I'll get an APW out now, boss.'

24

Cherish listened for the roar of Neil's car engine, and then peered out her bedroom window. With her heart fluttering in her chest, she watched him drive out of Hay-A-Park estate. She'd no idea where he was going. Best case scenario: she may not see him again until tomorrow. Worst case scenario: she'd see him again in ten minutes after he'd picked up a fresh batch of rolling tobacco.

Best to be quick, despite nothing being quick when heavily pregnant.

Her mother was taking a nap in her bedroom. Mandy was a heavy sleeper at the best of times, but her afternoon gin and tonic gave Cherish an extra layer of security. This was good, as there was no point in creeping on tiptoes when she was like a small elephant. She flinched as every floorboard creaked but stayed confident that her mother was dead to the world.

The previous day, she'd heard Neil gloating over his mobile. He'd hurt someone in some way, although the details remained unclear. She'd briefly considered the possibility that it may have been Bradley, but she was unable to buy into that. Fathers, even ones as bad as Neil, just didn't kill their children. Surely?

However, whatever Neil had done, he'd pay. And paying might see her mother freed from his control.

At the end of the conversation Neil had talked about cleaning up, 'just in case'. He'd also said, 'I bloody loved that jumper!'

Cherish went out the back door and over to the bin. The lid had been left off, leaving the flies in their element, hovering, exploring, *eating*. She waved them away and looked down at the heap of bloated bin liners. The top one had been torn open– a cat, or a fox, she suspected. A chicken carcass poked through the gap. She squirmed, plunged her hands in and began to search.

A couple of bags later, she recovered Neil's jumper.

Despite being crammed in with other waste, it was relatively clean. Her hands weren't though, so she held the garment between her two fingers so as not to contaminate it any more.

She gulped.

Red stains.

Got you.

As she approached the house, the fear that was chewing through her already overburdened insides was replaced by a burst of excitement.

Could this be the way to free both her and her mother?

Inside, she placed the jumper on the kitchen table and washed her hands thoroughly, scrunching her face up over the thought of that chicken carcass. Afterwards, she retrieved a plastic bag from under the sink and slipped the jumper into it—

She heard Neil's car.

Clutching both the plastic bag and her stomach, she marched across the kitchen, and into the lounge but, before she made it to the stairs, he was through the front door.

She froze. She could sense him lingering behind her.

'Oi,' he said.

She turned, slipping the plastic bag down from her stomach

to her hip.

He had a roll-up hanging from the corner of his mouth, and a four-pack of Stella in his hand. 'They're watching me, you know,' he said. 'Because of *you*, they're watching me.'

'I'm sorry,' Cherish said. She started to back away through the open lounge door towards the first step. The plastic bag crackled as she pressed it forcefully against herself.

'Well, you're going to have to prove that to me.' His eyes ran the length of her body. 'Can you do that?'

She felt the urge to vomit, but she forced it back. 'I'm eight months pregnant... we... it wouldn't be right.'

Neil guffawed. 'Jesus, girl! What do you think I was asking for? Just because you're a slut, doesn't mean that everyone is wired the same way!' His eyes moved to the bag. 'What's in there, anyway?'

It felt as if her heart was going to explode. She opened her mouth to speak, but nothing came out.

'I asked you a question.' He opened his hand towards her, gesturing that she give the bag to him—

Think, Cherish. Please God, think! 'A maternity dress. Katie brought one round for me.'

Neil brought his hand back and then pulled the roll-up from his mouth. 'Katie, eh? Now there's one good looking lass.' He winked. 'And not heavily pregnant. Maybe you'd like me to go around and say thank you?'

'You're disgusting.'

Neil laughed. 'Watch your mouth.' He nodded at her stomach. 'Remember who's footing the bill for your little bastard after it makes its appearance.'

Cherish took another step back. She wondered if the sweat she could feel springing up all over her body was visible on her face. Would he see it? Would he know what she was doing?

'Wait!'

She stopped. 'Why?'

'*Why?* Because I need a favour from you, that's why! Your way of apologising for talking to the pigs. I need you to drop something off for me tonight. I can't do it, because they're watching me, because of you.'

'What?'

'Never you mind. I just need it done at eleven.'

'Eleven!' She shook her head. 'I'm eight months pregnant...'

'Eleven o'clock,' he said and then told her where.

'That's far...'

'I'll leave the money for a taxi,' Neil said. 'I'll also leave a rucksack on the sofa for you. Get it there by eleven. Someone will be there to collect it. And, another thing?'

She chanced another step. 'Yes?'

'If you know what's good for you, then you won't look in the rucksack.'

She nodded, turned to the stairs and climbed them, her heart still thrashing.

When she reached the top, she was sweating profusely, and she realised she was gripping the bag so hard that she'd actually broken through the plastic.

'Cherish?'

She felt her stomach sink. Was this it? Was he about to ask her for the bag. 'Yes?' she asked, just turning her head slightly but not her body.

'You need to get used to this. You and that little bastard are going to put a burden on this family. Time you earned your keep.'

Then, he was gone.

She managed to get into her room before she shed tears of relief.

25

Chewing on half a box of tic tacs, Gardner reversed from her spot in the secondary school car park. Following Riddick's car towards the opening gate, she caught the wail of an ambulance in the distance.

After Riddick passed through the gate, he stopped his vehicle. Gardner paused behind him and saw, to her annoyance, that the lane of the road they planned to turn right onto was packed. A peculiar place for a traffic jam.

The sound of the ambulance intensified.

When it was clear that the traffic was not moving for love nor money, and that the ominous sound of the emergency services was coming this way, Gardner exited her vehicle. She knocked on Riddick's window.

He rolled down his window. 'An accident?'

'My thoughts... Let me check.'

The jammed cars on the road just ahead of her had concluded it was time to leave. One by one, they reversed into the car park of a leisure centre, so they were able to turn, and drive away in the opposite direction. She could hear the ambulance full blast now, and she could also hear the sound of an approaching fire engine.

She turned the corner.

A beige Fiat 500 had mounted the kerb at the end of the road, just before the busy A59, and ploughed into a pedestrian guardrail. Gardner couldn't see the front of the vehicle clearly, but the smoke rising from its bonnet suggested the damage may be terminal. A fire engine had already pulled to the side of the A59 adjacent to the front of the Fiat whereas the ambulance had turned onto the road and was alongside the accident.

'Jesus,' Riddick said, coming up alongside her. 'Someone must have been going at some speed to lose control and clip that.'

The emergency services went to work. It looked as if they were preparing to cut someone from the smoking vehicle.

Her phone rang. It was Barnett again. 'APW out, boss.'

'Susan Harrison doesn't drive a Fiat 500, does she?' She gave the registration on the back of the vehicle.

'Yes... how did you... You've got her, boss?'

'I wish I had. No, Ray, she got herself. She slammed into a guardrail getting away from us.'

'Good God. Is she okay?'

'I'm about to find out. I'll call you back.' She pulled her badge from her pocket and approached the emergency services with Riddick.

* * *

Gardner and Riddick followed the ambulance to the hospital where they were provided with a private room while they waited for a doctor to speak to them. Susan Harrison's next of kin would be on their way, and Gardner wanted to avoid any awkward moments with an emotional husband.

Details as to Susan's condition were at a premium right now. In the end, the fire service hadn't needed to cut her loose, but she hadn't looked in the best state when she'd been removed from the Fiat, unconscious with a bloody head. However, it always looked bad when someone was strapped to a stretcher with a neck brace on, so Gardner tried to stay positive.

'We've no idea how long this will take, Paul,' Gardner said. 'Your instincts are with the friends and the gangs. Why don't you go and probe Dan Lotus and then run the briefing? Draw the day's findings together for us?'

Riddick nodded. 'You sure you want to hand me that responsibility knowing what a liability I am?'

'If a lass from the alien lands of the south can handle that bunch of middle-aged northern men, then I'm sure you'll be fine.'

'I'm more concerned about the press,' Riddick said, 'I can think of one journalist who will love the fact we scared a suspect into a major RTA.'

'Well, keep schtum and order everyone else to keep quiet too. Joe Bridge can handle it unless our bloody leak gets there first.'

After Riddick had left, Gardner sat and used the internet to scroll through old news stories on Knaresborough and Harrogate, focusing specifically on county lines, and gang culture. Unsurprisingly, being rural and middle-class, it wasn't a hive of villainy, but it did have its moments. The history of Neil Taylor and his enterprises was there in black and white. Dan Lotus got a few mentions, and it seemed a lad called Michael Sanderson had spent some time in a juvenile centre for dealing ecstasy tablets that caused the death of a young lady from Wetherby. Gardner was interrupted by a phone call from an anonymous number.

'DCI Gardner speaking.'

'Hi… sorry… it's Cherish.' She sounded as though she was whispering.

Gardner stood. 'No need to apologise, Cherish. I told you to call me anytime, and I meant it. Are you okay?'

'Yes… I think so.'

Gardner started to pace. 'Where are you?'

'I'm in my room. I've *found* something. I want to give it to you.'

'What?'

'Something big, I think…' She went silent.

'Cherish?'

A really quiet whisper. 'He's outside my room.'

'Who? Neil?'

'Yes. Just wait…'

Gardner paced some more, her heart rate picking up. She couldn't bear it any longer. 'Cherish?'

'I'm okay, he's going back down.'

Gardner sighed.

'Can you come now?' Cherish asked.

'Are you in danger?'

'No… I don't think so.'

'Can I send someone, Cherish? I'm—'

'No, just you. I'll only give it to you.'

The door to the waiting room opened and a woman wearing spectacles and a surgeon's gown stepped in.

'Okay. I will get there as soon as I can, Cherish. Sorry, what is it you want to give me?'

The phone was already dead.

Gardner put the phone in her pocket and shook the surgeon's hand. 'DCI Emma Gardner.'

'Doctor Fiona Marshall.'

'How's Susan Harrison?'

'Indebted to an airbag. As many are in this day and age.

Susan is bruised and sore, but she's awake and communicative. We've taken x-rays, and nothing seems broken or damaged. However, she did lose consciousness a couple of times, and is clearly suffering from concussion. So, she won't be going anywhere for the moment. Strict observation.'

'But I'm free to go and talk to her?'

The doctor eyed her warily. 'I won't ask you how important it is because it obviously is. A DCI wouldn't be standing in the waiting room otherwise. But, can I ask you to go as easy as you can? She's had a shock and won't be thinking clearly from the concussion anyway.'

'Message received. However, she is a person of interest in a major crime. So, I will have to keep an officer here while she's in hospital.'

'Are you going to arrest her?' the doctor asked.

'She tried to run from us, and some of the evidence we have against her is compelling. Like I said, at the very least, she'll have to be guarded.'

'I understand. It won't be the first time this has happened.'

'Can you take me to her then please?'

26

Susan Harrison had taken quite a knock. She had a blood-stained bandage over her forehead, and one of her eyes was already blackening. She was propped up against a pillow with a drip in her arm when Doctor Marshall showed Gardner into the hospital room.

As soon as Gardner neared the bed, a tear formed in Susan's unhurt eye.

'Mrs Harrison,' Gardner said offering her badge, 'I'm DCI Emma Gardner—'

'You came to school,' Susan said.

'Yes.'

Susan sobbed and winced. 'You're going to ruin my life!'

Gardner took a deep breath. 'I'm here regarding a major crime.'

'You're here about Bradley?'

'Yes. What can you tell me about that?'

She let her head fall to the side, and she stared at the machines measuring her vitals. 'Not much.'

Gardner nodded. 'Why did you run then, Susan?'

'Because the last time the authorities spoke to me about this, my life was torn to pieces.'

'You were cleared.'

Susan glared back at Gardner. 'Do you think it stopped my husband looking at me with suspicion? Or people passing comments in the street?' She groaned. 'These painkillers are shit!'

'I'm sorry you suffered, Susan; however, this is an extremely serious incident – running was never going to solve anything.'

'I can't explain it... it was a moment of madness. I've been sad about his death – he was one of my students after all.'

'I see,' Gardner said. 'Could you describe your relationship with Bradley?'

'*Strictly* platonic.'

'When did you last see him?'

'A couple of weeks ago. He hasn't been in school in a while.'

'And where were you between nine and twelve the night before last?'

'I was at a friend's house until midnight drinking cocktails. Marcie Bright. Phone her.'

Gardner wrote it down. *Marcie Bright, eh? Someone else willing to lie to the police.* 'We will.'

Gardner pulled up a chair and sat beside the bed. 'Listen, Susan. I know you're concussed. Doctor Marshall has warned me of this. So, I can understand why your memory may be letting you down here. Otherwise, it could be obstruction of justice, and I know a good-natured citizen of Knaresborough wouldn't possess such intentions. So, let me help your memory out. We have evidence that your now written-off Fiat 500 was in the car park behind the Ugly Duckling Tearoom at five past eleven on the night Bradley was murdered. We also have CCTV footage of you walking down Waterside—'

She started to cry again.

'—towards the steps that lead up to the castle. Bradley was murdered sometime between eleven and midnight, which means—'

'Okay… stop!' She reached up to her split lip and groaned.

'Now, that I've refreshed your memory, please tell me Susan, did you meet Bradley that night?'

She paused, clearly thinking about it. Surely, at this point, she must realise that the game was up? Gardner didn't know how much longer she could remain calm, especially if she went down that route of *it's a coincidence*.

'Do I need a solicitor?' Susan said.

'Of course, that's your right.'

Susan didn't reply.

'Did you meet with Bradley?'

Susan nodded. 'But it isn't what you think.'

'I think meeting students socially outside the classroom is inappropriate.'

'We weren't having a relationship.'

'Really? Then why meet? Why risk your reputation?'

'I think it's safer to wait for a solicitor.'

A solicitor wouldn't help the situation and waiting for one would slow down the investigation. It was better to talk her out of this. 'If you've done nothing wrong, Susan, you've nothing to worry about. Delaying talking to us is just delaying the investigation. You said before you were sad that Bradley had died, surely you want to help us find whoever was responsible?'

She looked away. 'I met with him to tell him that he needed to leave me alone.'

'Leave you alone?'

'He was phoning me and texting me. He was *obsessed* with me. I met with him to ask him to stop.'

'At quarter past eleven at night?'

Susan closed her good eye and sighed. 'He texted me that night and I reached the end of my tether. I was meeting with him to threaten him with the police.'

'I see,' Gardner said, recalling Bradley reading a text message on CCTV by the Blind Jack sculpture. 'Can I see that text message please?'

'I've deleted it.'

'Okay,' Gardner said, knowing this was most certainly a lie. She made a note of it. 'Don't worry, we can recover it.'

Susan sighed and let her head fall back. She stared up at the ceiling this time.

'So, how did he take your threat to go to the police?'

'He was upset, but I think he saw sense in the end. I was never going to have a relationship with him.'

'And then?'

'And then? Nothing. I went back down those steps and went home.'

'What time?'

'Close to twelve?'

Gardner nodded. 'The CCTV camera shows you returning to your car via Waterside at ten to twelve.'

'Sounds right.'

'Bradley died sometime before twelve.'

Susan fixed Gardner with an angry stare. 'It wasn't me.'

'Will you consent to a DNA test to help rule you out?' Gardner asked.

'Of course. Yes. But I may have touched him, you know? I think he hugged me when he agreed to let it go. A farewell.'

'I see. Strange thing to do with someone who was intimidating you.' Gardner made a note. 'Did you have sex?'

'No, of course not!'

'I see. We found a used condom, but I guess your DNA will rule—'

'Oh God!' Susan cried.

Here it comes...

'I'm screwed, aren't I?'

Yes.

'Susan,' Gardner said. 'A large part of what went on that night will be pieced together from the evidence. The text message, the DNA, the CCTV footage. You can wait for a solicitor, but facts are facts, I'm afraid.'

'What is going to happen to me?'

'Did you kill him?'

'No! I really bloody liked him!'

'Well, if that's true, I don't think you'll go to jail.'

'But what will happen to me? I've had a relationship with a pupil.'

'He was eighteen... so it'll be up to the relevant parties to decide.'

'They'll throw duty of care at me. They'll say I abused my position!'

That's the truth of it though, Susan, isn't it?

Despite the tears forming in Susan's eyes, Gardner forced back her feelings of sympathy. Susan may have loved this boy, but she *should* have stopped it before it got out of hand. She'd had a duty of care to Bradley. Gardner understood all too well the frailty of the human condition, but when it came to people exploiting their positions of power, her sympathy was in short supply. 'The most important thing you can do right now is convince me that you're innocent of murdering him. So, start by telling me in detail what happened.'

27

Susan Harrison wasn't the murderer. Gardner's intuition couldn't scream it any louder. However, Gardner was no mug. She ensured that an officer was stationed outside Susan's room before departing the hospital.

On her way to see Cherish to collect this mysterious item, she contacted Riddick.

After she'd explained what she'd learned, Riddick said, 'It seems everyone is a sucker for this sensitive side of Bradley.'

'It seems so. Cherish, Paula and now Susan, really saw the positives in him. It seems we have enough to challenge the negativity over him in our incident room.'

Riddick grunted. 'He was part of what happened to Kelsey! Everyone feels sorry for him because the guilt was tearing him up. Good, I say. The guilt should have been tearing him up!'

Gardner sighed. The fact that Riddick's life had been turned upside down by the Winters case had him blinkered. Bradley had been a child when he upset Kelsey. Children make a lot of mistakes – it was part of growing up and learning. However, she knew Riddick wouldn't want to hear that right now.

'So, how long was this relationship going on between them?' Riddick asked.

'I suspect since he was sixteen, but don't think she'll admit to it.'

'The sighting of them in Leeds was real then?'

'Probably. But whatever she does or doesn't admit to, we have her bang to rights on the fact she had sex with him during Bradley's final hour. But did she kill him? I don't think so. Not only does she not fit the size profile, but she had strong feelings for him. She said they'd planned another meet for the weekend. She was going to tell her husband she was at the movies with her friend, Marcie Bright. Marcie is obviously happy to cover for her, God knows why. Bring it up at the briefing. Assign someone to speak to this Marcie in the morning.'

'The briefing is starting in a moment, boss, I'd best go.'

'Okay. I'm following up on something, and I'll try and get there for the end.'

'See you then, boss.'

As she drove into Hay-A-Park estate again, she couldn't help but feel she'd spent most of the investigation at Mandy Spencer's house. Was this indicative of Neil's guilt, and if so, would it not prove embarrassing that it was taking so many visits to pin him down?

She parked up in a spot that was starting to feel like her own and approached the front door.

Cherish opened it before she'd had chance to knock. The young woman looked pale and worn out. This wasn't down to pregnancy. Gardner recognised the expression and facial language. It was fear.

Cherish thrust a plastic bag into Gardner's hands.

'Sorry, what's—'

'Just take it. *Please.*'

'I will, but Cherish—'

Neil stepped into the doorway behind Cherish. 'You must be having a laugh... Hang on, what's that?' He pointed over Cherish's shoulder at the plastic bag in Gardner's hands.

'If it's relevant to you, Mr Taylor, I'll be sure to let you know.'

'A maternity dress? How would that be relevant to me, exactly?' He creased his brow. 'In fact, how is it relevant to you?'

Cherish regarded her with wide eyes. Her pale face was now glowing red.

Gardner had no idea what was in the bag, and she had no idea why Neil was talking about maternity dresses, but she did know this – Cherish had put herself in harm's way by doing this, and lying was the least she could do.

'I don't know anything about maternity dresses,' Gardner said. 'However, these are some of the clothes Bradley left in Cherish's possession. I requested them for forensic analysis.'

'So, you lied to me?' Neil said, putting his hand on Cherish's shoulder.

Cherish flinched. 'Yes... I didn't want you to get annoyed. I told them I had some of his clothing earlier, and I would dig them out.'

Neil narrowed his eyes and regarded Gardner. 'Why would I have been annoyed?' He pulled his hand away from Cherish.

Gardner smiled. 'Well, if that's everything, Cherish, thank you for these.'

Neil stepped alongside Cherish. 'Hang on. Why would you need to do some forensic analysis of some old clothes anyhow?'

Gardner took a step back on the chance that Neil might just suddenly spring forward to retrieve the mysterious evidence. 'I'm sorry, Mr Taylor, I can't divulge all the details of—'

'Bradley was *my* son.'

'I understand that and, you can rest assured, we are doing

everything we can, while being as prudent as we can. The press can be ravenous at such times. We prefer to keep the more sensitive details on a need-to-know basis.' Gardner nodded at Cherish, hoping she'd done enough to protect her, smiled at Neil, turned and walked away. Her hand trembled. *What was in this bag? Was the whole case about to be blown wide open?*

* * *

Gardner drove around the corner before opening the plastic bag. The smell of rotting vegetables made her retch.

She stared at the cream jumper inside. *What?*

If this was evidence of a crime, she didn't wish to contaminate it any further, so she didn't reach in. Instead, she switched on the car light and held the bag directly under it.

And then her heart leapt when she saw the bloodstains. *Neil's... this has to be Neil's jumper.*

Her phoned beeped. It was a message from Cherish.

He threw it in the bin. I think he hurt someone.

Gardner thought of the two-inch letter *E* carved into the small of Bradley's back. Had the blood transferred to Neil's clothing as he worked the knife?

Knowing the briefing would be in full flow, she contacted Marsh directly. Gardner explained what Cherish had just given her.

'There's a good shout here for fast-tracking the DNA testing, despite the fact that it will take a wrecking ball to my budget. However, it won't be tonight, Emma. No chance. It's past six. Only clowns like us work this late. But I'll be all over it, first thing. Rest assured. Please drop it in.'

After the phone call ended, Gardner drummed her fingers on the steering wheel. *Neil? Motive?*

Well, he didn't like his son that much, that was clear to see, but kill him? Why? Why?

She racked her brains.

Neil had said that Bradley had been asking for handouts. Had his kid gathered dirt on him? Had he developed the balls to blackmail him? And rather than pay for Bradley's silence, Neil had opted to shut him down completely.

It seemed reasonable, and it was the best she had, except when you considered the carving. *What the hell did the letter E have to do with the price of tea in China?*

She looked back at the entrance to Hay-A-Park. Maybe she should just march in there now and put Neil to the sword. But, if he had done it, would he really cough under her pressure? The man was a hardened criminal. She wouldn't be able to arrest him until she matched that blood to Bradley, and she'd be giving him the heads up that they suspected him.

Then what? Cherish in danger? A lovely way to reward her for the biggest development in the investigation yet.

No. Tomorrow morning. It would wait.

Knowing she'd miss the briefing, she opted to simply drive the evidence in, and update Riddick on it.

Then, despite promising her sore head all day that she wouldn't, she'd pick up a bottle of wine from the Co-op.

28

Riddick took a large mouthful of Rooster's Yankee pale ale. He closed his eyes, savouring the citrus bite.

He then looked at the glass of Diet Coke in Anders' hand and shook his head.

Anders snorted. 'Take note, Padawan.'

'Of what?'

'Of the fact that a lifetime of heavy drinking can lead to a retirement of perpetual boredom.'

'Only because you stopped. I fully intend to continue.'

'You'll stop!'

'Because?'

'Because people like us have to stop. Or… eventually… we die.'

'Bollocks,' Riddick said. 'My old man drank until he was eighty.'

'So, he drank at breakfast?'

'No, not exactly.'

Anders gave a smug grin and took a mouthful of Coke.

'He could have done,' protested Riddick. 'He was a secretive bugger. I didn't follow him about the place.'

'Well, if he drank as much as you do, he wouldn't have made it to eighty. I know.'

'Jesus, is there anything you don't know?'

'No. Not the last time I checked anyway.' He winked.

Riddick rolled his eyes and took another large mouthful. He knew full well that Anders was right. That this couldn't continue. That he was drinking himself into unemployment or, worse still, a painful death from cirrhosis of the liver. However, at this point in his life, he was struggling to summon up the willpower to begin the battle against his addiction.

He heard the squeaking of the steep staircase that led up to the first floor of Blind Jack's. A young couple, unrecognisable to Riddick, and so unlikely to be local, reached the top of the stairs, commenting on and admiring the poky Georgian building.

Riddick waited until they'd entered the second room upstairs, so he could continue his conversation with Anders.

'When will the DNA results on the jumper be back?' Anders asked.

'Harsh Marsh told Emma that it would be first thing.'

'Shit,' Anders grunted. 'I don't remember her ever fast-tracking something like that for me! Emma must have struck up quite an impression.'

'Maybe. I think it's more the fact that it could put the investigation to bed sooner rather than later,' Riddick said.

'You think?' Anders smiled. 'Neil Taylor is a lot of things, but the killer of his boy? Nah. I don't see it. People like that can hate their families all they want, but they never turn on them.'

'Anders knows?' Riddick said, rolling his eyes.

'Anders knows.' He smiled again. 'These are the rules of the street.'

Riddick finished his pint. 'You can't breathe a word of this to anyone.'

Anders looked offended. 'How could you even think such a thing?'

'Well, someone has been blabbing to Marianne Perse. Don't know what they were smoking though. *The Viaduct Killer!* Give me a break.'

'Honestly, I trained you, nurtured you, Padawan, and you believe I would cough to the press. And not just the press, mind. But Marianne *bloody* Perse!'

'Of course I don't think it's you. I need another pint,' Riddick said, rising to his feet. 'Another Coke?'

Anders looked up at him. 'Seriously though, buddy, I do appreciate you keeping me in the loop.'

'Well, it's that or have you nagging all day. Personally, when I'm done, *I'm done*. I won't need updating on anything.'

Anders said, 'Let's see how you really feel. When you live for it, like we do' – he moved a finger between them – 'you can never switch it off. Yeah to the Coke by the way.'

Before turning, Riddick looked out of the window onto the town square. 'What the—?'

Cherish, wearing a winter jacket despite the warm spring weather, was passing through the town square. She had a yellow backpack on.

'What time is it?'

'Coming up to half ten,' Anders said. 'What's got you spooked?'

'Wait here.'

Riddick spun and flew down the wooden stairs, two at a time, using the brick walls to steady himself. It was cramped downstairs, so he apologised to the punters as he weaved past them. Unbelievably, nobody seemed to lose a drop of beer. At least, no one complained of doing so.

He burst outside into the town square.

Only a few public houses and a fish and chip shop were open at this this time of night, so the square, as was often the case on a weeknight, was quiet. He ran over to the benches in the centre and stood by the sculpture of Blind Jack and turned.

His heart skipped a beat when he thought he saw someone alongside Stomp, the children's shoe shop, beside Blind Jack's, before quickly realising it was his own reflection.

He shuffled to his left so he could see down Market Place. A drunk couple was embracing outside Castlegate Books, but there was no sign of Cherish.

Where have you gone?

He did another turn. She can't just have disappeared!

Riddick opened his mouth to call out for her when Anders appeared in the doorway of Blind Jack's.

Not now, you daft apeth! Go back inside...

Using his new walking stick, his ex-boss made his way towards him. Riddick used his hand to wave him back inside, but the inquisitive old man was having none of it—

'Get off!'

Cherish.

'I said get off!'

Riddick turned towards the source of the sound. Directly opposite him, between two shops, was a dark covered passageway. She had to be in there. He ran.

As he neared the entrance, he could see two people tussling in the passageway. When he was at the entrance, he identified Cherish, pregnant and squat, and a taller person, fighting over the yellow backpack. At this point, he won the tug of war. She gasped and fell to her knees.

'Please, I'm pregnant—'

Cherish's assailant took a step back and then kicked her.

29

Gardner was woken on the sofa by her mobile.

Unbelievably, she was still holding a glass of wine. She must have only just drifted off or that would be all over her!

Disorientated, she put the glass on the coffee table, glanced at her watch – *almost eleven* – and reached for her mobile. She'd been expecting a call from Yorke this evening and was disappointed to see it wasn't him. The number was unknown.

'Hello?'

'Emma.'

She bolted upright, no longer disorientated. She opened her mouth, but nothing came out.

'Emma, are you there?'

Her stomach turned somersaults. She took the phone from her ear and looked down at it with widening eyes, tempted to throw it at the wall.

'Emma, are you there?'

She could still hear him.

'It's Jack... Emma... it's—'

'I know who it is,' she said, putting the phone to her ear. 'How did you get this number?'

'You gave it me. Years ago. *Before.*'

She nodded, realising she must have had this number for over ten years. Time flew.

She rose to her feet. 'What do you want, Jack?'

'To see you.'

'Why?'

'You're my family. My *only* family.'

'You never cared about family.' *You never cared about anything, actually. Anything at all.*

He didn't reply. Did her words hurt? *No, don't be ridiculous.*

'I've changed,' he said, eventually.

Impossible. You can't change. 'I'm not interested.'

'Please, Emma, I'm your brother—'

'You're a murderer.'

Another long pause. 'It was an accident. I've paid my debt. I'm different now.'

Bollocks. 'Look, Jack, if this is true, I'm happy for you. Nothing would give me greater pleasure than you finding some peace. But I'm busy right now, with work, something big.'

'What're you saying, Emma?'

'I can't do this right now.' *Or ever to be honest.*

'Surely we owe it to Mum and Dad, to put this behind us, to move on—'

You never gave a shit about them! 'Jack, I'm going to go now.'

'Aren't you even going to ask me where I am? What I'm doing?'

You're in a halfway house – Yorke has already told me. 'Good-night, Jack.'

'How's my niece? How's Anabelle?'

Gardner hung up. She could feel her heartbeat through her

entire body. She stared at the phone as if it was a dangerous weapon. With trembling hands, she blocked the number.

It wouldn't make any difference. If he wanted to call again, he'd use another phone.

She'd have to change her number.

How's my niece?

How's Anabelle?

She threw the phone down on the table as if it was contaminated and reached for the glass of wine that had almost ended up down her front.

She drank it back and emptied the rest of the bottle into the glass.

How's my niece?

She stared at the mobile phone, lost in disbelief.

How's Anabelle?

She reached over and grabbed her mobile. She switched it off. She drank the rest of the glass and slumped back.

How's my niece?

She dreamed about Malcolm's Maze of Mirrors and a fractured skull.

And, all the while, in the background, in a deep, grating voice:

How's my niece?

How's Anabelle?

30

Cherish pleaded for her assailant to stop. The bastard responded by ploughing her with more kicks.

'She's pregnant, you animal,' Riddick called, diving into the alleyway.

The balaclava-wearing mugger was gripping the yellow backpack. Riddick was almost certain the tall, lanky individual was male.

Prize in hand, the mugger turned to run. Riddick skipped around the prone figure of Cherish and managed to kick out at his ankles, sending him stumbling into the brick wall and down to his knees.

Riddick reached for him—

Cherish screamed in agony.

Riddick swung. Cherish was doubled over on the floor, clutching her stomach. She screamed again, and Riddick fell to his knees.

'Blood,' she gasped.

'Okay... I got you,' Riddick said, seeing that there was lots of blood. He cradled her head—

He felt a sudden blow to the back of his skull, and everything flashed white. As he slumped sideways against the brick wall, he desperately tried to keep hold of the young woman's head.

Riddick heard footsteps alongside him. 'What the bloody hell are you doing?'

Anders!

Then, came the sound of scuffling.

Despite the pain in the back of his skull, Riddick could feel clarity returning, and he turned his face up to see what was happening.

Anders had his walking stick across the mugger's throat, pinning him to the wall.

The big man may have had a bad back, but that was no barrier here. Adrenaline could be funny like that. While holding the walking stick against the mugger's throat with one hand, he slammed his fist repeatedly into his stomach.

Riddick lowered Cherish's head and rose to support his friend—

Anders backed away suddenly, crashing into Riddick. With the brick wall behind him, Riddick managed to keep his footing, but the wind was knocked from him. He desperately tried to catch his breath.

'Put it down,' Anders shouted. 'Now!'

Riddick looked back up to see the mugger slicing the air with a knife. He'd already had some success with it, judging by the way Anders was clutching his shoulder.

Anders darted forward but jolted back again when the mugger jabbed the knife in his direction.

'I'm going to break your bloody neck, son,' Anders said.

The mugger slid along the brick wall, still holding the knife out to ward Anders off. When he'd opened enough space between them, he turned and sprinted away down the alley.

'I'll find you!' Anders shouted after him, his voice laced with frustration. With his back issues, he'd not be able to chase down any youngster, so Riddick staggered forward to give chase instead, nearly losing his footing. It seemed he hadn't actually recovered full control of his senses following the blow to his head.

'Paul... stop,' Anders said. He pointed down at a brick with his walking stick. 'He clocked you quite hard.'

Riddick touched the back of his throbbing head and looked at his bloody fingers. A sudden wave of nausea followed.

Cherish was moaning in pain on the floor, still clutching her stomach. 'Don't worry, lassie,' Anders said. 'It'll be okay.' He hoisted out his mobile. 'I'll get us help.'

31

Dan Lotus tore off the balaclava and shoved it into his jacket pocket. Then, with the backpack bouncing off his shoulder, he sprinted through the car park behind Sainsbury's. There weren't many cars at this hour, so there were no obstacles to slow him.

Shit! The contents of his stomach were rising up his throat. *He'd just stabbed a sodding copper!*

He managed to get to Gracious Street before vomiting on the pavement.

Coppers hadn't been part of the deal.

Not at all!

He caught his breath and reduced his speed to a quick march. He heard the wail of an ambulance, before seeing it fly past. The paramedics were going to have their work cut out up there. He'd dealt all three of them a good seeing to. The coppers would need stitches, and Cherish, well, she'd been taught good and proper... He may have just done that little bastard in her belly a favour. Imagine having that bitch as your mother. It'd never been the same between him and Bradley after she'd shown up. The way she'd led him astray had been disgusting. He wouldn't be surprised if she'd been involved with his death.

Realising that being out on a main road with the emergency services burning a route to that bloodbath was an act of stupidity, he took a right onto Cheapside, and started to run again. He crossed over to avoid a drunk couple that were using the entirety of the pavement to keep their footing and burst onto Castle Yard.

Up ahead, he sighted the imposing solid towers in the castle's enclosure wall. He felt the sting of doubt when he considered what'd happened to his best friend here but decided this was his best option. Through the castle grounds, down the steps and to the river Nidd offered his best route out of this danger zone.

He ran between two large patches of grass, past the bowling green. It was impossible not to take in the largely ruined keep, behind which, Bradley – *Jesus, how he missed his bro* – had been left like a piece of meat; however, he kept his focus mainly on the dominating Knaresborough viaduct, because once he was down the steps, and beneath that, then he would feel as if he'd reached sanctuary.

Fearful of taking a tumble, Dan was more careful on the steps leading down to Waterside, but he was still going at a brisk pace. He was surprised at how well he was running, having smoked and drank himself senseless these past days following his best mate's death.

At the bottom of the steps, he tore down Waterside towards the viaduct. Despite his concern over what he'd done to a copper, he couldn't resist a smirk. He'd certainly given them the slip.

He'd run well, but he was long overdue a breather. He descended some steps onto the Viaduct Terrace: a small platform where you could either throw bread to the ducks, despite the signs telling you not to; or stare up in wonder at the jewels in Knaresborough's crown – the four arches of the viaduct.

Completely spent, he hoisted the yellow backpack off, dropped it on the floor, and leaned against the railing. Despite feeling certain that he'd dropped his flick knife in his jacket pocket, he reached in to double check, and was reassured. His fingerprints would be all over it, so dropping that during his escape would have been a disaster. His next task, once his senses had recovered, was to get rid of the bloody thing.

He winced over the pain in his damaged cheek. It had been a painful couple of days, and there was no getting used to that constant throbbing! He decided to grab some cider and paracetamol on the way home.

He picked up the backpack and unzipped it. It was stuffed full of newspapers to give it a bit of bulk and weight. Of course, it hadn't been important what was actually in the bag. It had simply been a ruse to get Cherish there. As if anyone would trust that stupid girl with a real bag of drugs. He laughed, sealed the bag up and chucked it back on the floor.

Dan reached into his pocket for his vape pen, and looked out over the river for a time, recovering from his exertions, knowing he'd done enough now to make amends for his recent discretions. He'd be firmly back in the good books—

He felt a tight grip around his throat.

Dan dropped the vape pen, seized the arm around his neck and tried to yank it free. Useless. This was one strong bastard.

He tried to plead, but no sound passed through his throat; it was being crushed. He tried, and failed, to draw in breath—

Dan was yanked back. His arse landed on the floor. He dared to hope, briefly, that the sudden impact would jar his aggressor's grip loose. It didn't. The bastard was unrelenting, and he was now being dragged backwards across the concrete. He kicked his legs out, but there was nothing there to hit but air and his discarded backpack.

Help! His head was pulsing.

I don't want to die! He watched as the distance between himself and the railing he'd been leaning on expanded.

He heard a train streak over the viaduct.

Please!

He looked up at the four arches and the colour disappeared from everything.

32

'So, the noggin is fine?' Riddick asked.

'Yes... well... it's not fractured,' Dr Sally Fisher said. 'However, I recommend—'

'That's okay,' Riddick said, swinging his legs off the hospital bed. 'That won't be necessary.'

She flushed red. 'I haven't even made my recommendation yet.'

He smiled. 'I'm a mind reader. You're worried about concussion. You want to keep me in. I'm not concussed. I feel great.' He wandered over to a chair in the corner on which his jacket lay.

'I'm surprised you can read any mind after today. You were hit with a brick.'

'He should've taken a run up. I was still standing – in a fashion.' He hoisted on his jacket.

'Be aware that this goes against my advice – you need to be supervised.'

'I've had my stitches; I appreciate it. I need to find out what's going on with Cherish – the girl I came in with. Do you know anything?'

'I'm afraid not.'

As he exited the hospital room, Sally called out, 'And Paul?'

He turned back. 'Yes?'

'When are you calling me by the way?'

'Calling?'

'Are you sure he didn't take that run up when he hit you? We chatted all night, and you said you were going to call me?'

'Oh yes.' His face reddened slightly. 'I was... I mean, I *will*... it's just been a crazy couple of weeks.'

'You still got my number?'

Riddick hoisted his phone from his pocket and held it in the air. 'Yes.' He must have looked a plonker – what did having a mobile prove! 'I'll call.'

He turned around and made a quick exit. When he was a suitable distance away, he tried calling Gardner on her mobile. He was sent straight through to voicemail.

'Call me, boss. I'm in hospital... I'm fine. It's all gone off here, and I'm not sure Cherish is okay... You have to phone me!'

Anders was in the A&E waiting room. He was holding a bandage to his shoulder. Riddick sat down beside him.

'You still not been seen?'

'It seems retired coppers aren't afforded the same priority as active ones.'

'They clearly haven't heard of us. You'd have moved to the top of the list, and I'd have hit the bottom.'

'How it should be! You got a bump on the bloody head, while I took a knife to the shoulder.'

'You told me it was a scratch.'

'Aye, yes. A painful one, mind... So, what the bloody hell was that all about then?'

'Not a clue, but I need to thank you. If you hadn't been there, well, he'd probably have finished the job.'

'Are you telling me you owe me one?'

'Shit... here we go.'

'I'll make that appointment for you.'

'I'm not talking to anyone about my drinking.'

'Yet, you owe me...'

Riddick stood, shaking his head. 'Let's talk about this another time.'

'Aye, let's.'

Riddick showed his badge and enquired at reception after Cherish. The receptionist made a few phone calls and then reported that Cherish had gone into labour and given birth. 'Baby and mother doing well.'

Riddick sighed. *Thank God.*

He nodded over at where Anders was sitting. 'Get this old man looked at for me, please. He's a miserable sod at the best of times, you don't want to get him even more cranky.'

The receptionist smiled.

Riddick headed out of the ward, followed the appropriately coloured lane around the maze of a hospital, took the lift and arrived at the maternity ward.

As he entered the waiting room, he heard a baby wailing in the distance, and for a moment he was catapulted back to the day his twins were born. Molly and Lucy had been in immediate competition with each other to prove themselves the loudest – unfortunately, that competition had not settled down for the best part of the year. He caught himself smiling in a glass door.

Neil and Mandy were sitting in the waiting room.

You have to be kidding me.

He considered giving the irritant a swerve, but found himself, on autopilot, marching in his direction.

Neil rose to his feet before Riddick reached him.

Riddick opened his mouth to speak when a memory of something Neil had said earlier in the day hit him like a tonne of bricks.

'D'you realise what my son and that slut's mistake is going to cost me? Who do you think is going to end up footing the bill?'

Surely not?

'Something wrong, Paul?' Neil asked.

'Why're you here?'

Neil looked at Mandy, whose eyes and cheeks were red from crying. 'Take a guess.'

Riddick took a step back and sighed. 'Do either of you know why she was out at almost eleven o'clock?'

'No, it makes no sense,' Mandy said.

Neil shrugged. 'However, it's all turned out okay. The lassie was a little premature, but she'll be just fine.'

'Turned out okay?' Riddick said with raised eyebrows. 'She was mugged by an armed nutter! He could have very easily killed her and her baby...'

Mandy sobbed. Neil put an arm around her shoulders. 'Please, Paul, tact.'

Riddick could feel his blood boil. 'We'll get him though. Rest assured.'

'You've a lead?' Neil asked.

Was that concern on the bastard's face?

'I got a good look at him,' Riddick said.

'Cherish told her mother that he wore a balaclava.'

Riddick backed away, nodding his head slightly. 'Yes, but I'm confident. We'll have him before the night's through.'

So, chew on that, prick, Riddick thought. *And if you were involved, Neil, we'll have you too.*

He approached reception, showed his badge and requested permission to see Cherish.

He was led into her room. She was sitting up against several cushions, staring at the incubator beside her. Riddick looked inside at the tiny, bluish figure. 'Beautiful.'

'Yes,' Cherish said. 'What a shitty start for her...'

'Yes, but it's not your fault, and the doctors here are great and have it all in hand. I've spoken to them. You're both going to be fine.'

'Thanks to you.'

Riddick shrugged. 'I was just there... Did what anybody would have done.'

'Thanks though.'

'Don't mention it.' Riddick looked down at the baby, who was sucking at her lips. 'Have you got a name yet?'

'Ariah.'

'I like it.' Riddick looked up at Cherish. She looked worse for wear. She'd caught a blow on her cheek, and it had swollen.

'I'm leaving, you know,' Cherish said with a smile.

'What do you mean?'

'As soon as we're both well enough, I'm getting out of here. Away from my mum. Away from *that* man.'

Wise decision. 'Do you know where you'll go?'

'I have a friend in Starbeck. She's going to put us up until I get myself sorted.'

Riddick nodded again. 'I hope it works out for you. I really mean that... Cherish, what were you doing out at almost eleven?'

Cherish looked away. 'I couldn't sleep. I went for a long walk. It helps.'

A lie.

'I see. It's quite a way from your home, but I guess when you're restless, you're restless.'

She looked back at him and nodded.

'What was in the yellow backpack he stole?'

She looked away again. 'Just some snacks. I get hungry. All the time...'

Another lie.

She looked at the incubator. 'Hopefully not any more. Food is going to be expensive. Especially now there's two of us.'

Riddick looked at the bruised mother and premature baby. He was desperate to press her further on what had really happened, but the situation was sensitive. He also kept thinking about his own wife, holding their two newborn babies. It was the most exciting, if not the most exhausting moment in your entire life. For the first time in as long as Riddick remembered, he held back.

Neil appeared at the door. 'Just checking in. The nurse told me you really need to rest up, Cherish.' He glanced at Riddick. 'The nurse is actually quite worried out there.' He threw a thumb over his shoulder. 'Maybe you should leave, Paul?'

Riddick scowled at him.

'What is your problem, anyway?' Neil asked. 'Your pal, Anders, never used to give me this much grief!'

'What does that mean?'

'What do you think it means?'

'Please,' Cherish said. 'Don't argue in front of Ariah.'

Riddick looked back at Cherish. 'I was just leaving anyway.'

'Good,' Neil said.

'Thanks again, Paul,' Cherish said.

'No need to thank me, Cherish, just get yourself rested up.' He looked down at Ariah. 'This one here looks like she's going to be quite the handful.'

33

After DI Riddick had left, Cherish avoided eye contact with the dangerous bastard in the room with her.

'Everything all right?' Neil asked.

She stared straight ahead, ignoring him.

'You always had a bad attitude, Cherish.'

Out of the corner of her eye, Cherish watched Neil approach the incubator.

She turned her head to glare at him. 'Get the hell away from her you dickhead!'

Neil widened his eyes and put a hand on the incubator. 'Big words for a little girl.'

'I swear to God if you touch Ariah, I'll kill you.'

Neil shook his head, incredulous. 'Bloody hell, it's a good job Paul has left. Threats like that will get you in trouble.'

'It was you, wasn't it? You lied to me. You didn't send me there to deliver something. You sent me there to... to...' She couldn't get the words out. Her face reddened. She paused for a deep breath.

'Me?' Neil touched his chest. 'How could you think such a thing? I've done nothing but care—'

'You've cared for no one since you walked into Mum's house! And you've made a mess of everything, haven't you? But I'm fine. Ariah is fine. We're both fine. None of us need you any more.'

'You're crazy,' Neil said, stepping around the incubator. 'Delusional.'

'You're done. I know what you did. You need to leave.'

'Know what I did? Really? Why would I send you out to be assaulted? Who's going to believe that?'

'Doesn't matter about me. It's what you did to Bradley, *your own son*, that's going to catch up with you.'

Neil rolled his eyes. 'You're traumatised.'

'I want you to leave our house tonight, Neil. I don't want Mam by your side as they drag you through the courts. You can run now and spare her that.'

'Jail? Are you sure you didn't get hit on the head?'

'I found the jumper, Neil.'

The colour drained from his face. His mouth opened, but nothing came out.

'There was blood on it. Your own son; how could you?'

He shook his head. 'You don't understand! Where is it?'

'In that plastic bag, Neil.'

He staggered backwards, and only stopped because there was a chair in his way. 'You stupid bitch. You stupid, stupid bitch.'

'It's over Neil. The police have it. Run. Go away. Leave us alone.'

Neil shook his head. Then, his eyes widened. He clenched his fist, and red-faced, stormed forward—

'Is everything all right here?' It was the nurse.

Neil steadied himself against the bed, took a few deep breaths and stared into Cherish's eyes. 'This isn't over.'

'It is,' she hissed.

He stood, turned and barged past the nurse. Cherish smiled and looked over at her beautiful newborn.

34

Another day, another hangover.

Gardner reached over from the sofa and switched on her mobile phone.

It had a buzzing, beeping fit.

Five voicemail messages.

My sociopathic brother?

With her stomach doing somersaults, she listened.

They weren't from her brother.

The first three messages were from Riddick. All sent throughout the night.

Anders stabbed... Riddick and Cherish assaulted... baby born, premature, but alive.

The fourth and fifth messages were hours old. They were from Chief Constable Marsh. 'Where're you? There's been another murder.' *Shit...* She listened to the details of where the crime was. 'See you ASAP, Emma.'

The next message was less than complimentary. 'Where the hell are you, Emma? It's been over an hour. Paul isn't even picking up his goddamn phone either!'

Gardner looked at the empty bottle of wine on the table and then ran to the toilet to be sick.

35

Riddick opened the fridge to get the milk for his Weetabix. He looked at the row of Brewdog Punk IPA on the top shelf. He considered it, but then decided he couldn't face a beer this morning. He turned back to the breakfast table, where his usual breakfast drink awaited him – vodka and lime. Rachel was looking at him with a raised eyebrow from the head of the table.

'Morning,' Riddick said.

She didn't respond.

'Don't be like that.'

'You keep promising to cut down.'

He sighed. 'I probably shouldn't keep making that promise.'

'Surely at some point, you have to mean it?'

Riddick sat down beside her.

'You don't want to die, do you?'

He looked at her. He wasn't about to grace that with an answer. The easiest option was to take a mouthful of lime vodka. He then poured the milk onto his Weetabix. 'I will stop, Rachel, but not today, not after last night. Besides, my head is throbbing where the bastard hit me. I'll be good for nothing until I numb the pain.'

'Daddy swore!' Molly said.

Riddick looked up, opposite him, where his daughter was now sitting. 'Sorry, honey...'

'Daddy's cool!' Lucy said from the chair beside him.

'Daddy is *not* cool,' Rachel said.

Riddick smiled at Lucy. 'It's the language that's not cool. You were right about Daddy though.' He winked.

He'd only slept for two hours last night, and in his clothes. He reached into his suit pocket for his mobile phone and saw that the battery had given out on him. He bit his lip to stop himself swearing again.

'Excuse me, I need to plug this in,' he said, standing.

'You like her, don't you?' Rachel said.

'Who?'

'Emma Gardner, your new partner.'

'New boss, actually... Anyway, what makes you say that?'

'I can just tell.'

There was a charger by the toaster, so Riddick plugged it in.

'She's married. Besides, she really isn't my type.'

'I didn't mean it like that!'

'Ah... okay, so how did you mean it?' he asked, walking back to the table.

'I mean in the way she's got you juiced up again.'

He paused halfway to the table with raised eyebrows. 'Not quite sure what juiced up means?'

'It means she's woken something up in you. This is the first time in years I've seen you like this.'

Riddick shook his head. 'No, you've completely lost me.'

'Tell her. Tell Emma about us. Talk to her. She's your way out—'

There was a knock at the door.

Riddick stared at his wife a moment longer, her words hitting him harder than any brick ever could. Then, he went to answer the front door.

It was Anders. 'I hope you got some sleep... I didn't get a minute.'

'You're retired; you can sleep all day.'

'Forget that,' Anders said, closing the door behind him, following Riddick into the kitchen. 'We can sleep when we're dead.'

Riddick sat down and continued with his breakfast. He pointed at his vodka lime. 'You want one?'

'One bad night, a knife wound, and you think I'll turn back to drink? I'm stronger than that, and you will be one day too.' He sat down where Rachel had been sitting moments ago.

'What relationship did you used to have with Neil?' Riddick asked, not looking up at his former boss.

'Why do you ask that?'

'Something the prick said last night.'

'What did he say?'

'Something along the lines of you never used to give him this much grief.'

Anders guffawed. Riddick eyed him.

'What're you saying here?'

'Just answer the bloody question.'

Anders sighed. 'It's not anything untoward. How long you known me? Jesus. Neil has always been a problem, but he's part of the ecosystem around here. It's a delicate ecosystem. I just kept my eye on him. I always knew what he was up to, so I could keep him on a short leash.'

'I'm pretty sure the job description states you should just bust him?'

Anders said, 'I did, if you remember!'

'Eventually… but why not years before?'

'Because, as I said, better the devil you know. There were plenty more people ready to step up and do what that idiot was doing. He knew I was watching, and things never got out of hand.'

Riddick drank his vodka lime. He'd always known that Anders was old school. That his associations with the less savoury locals could often go beyond what was considered appropriate for a member of the constabulary. However, Riddick had always believed that his old friend was simply keeping his enemies close in order to shut them down when the opportunity presented itself. It was distressing to learn now that Anders had allowed some lowlifes to continue unrestricted in their careers of exploitation. 'I can't believe I'm hearing this.'

'No one was ever murdered on my watch, Padawan, you remember that.'

'Don't call me that… and, also, what's that supposed to mean?'

'That wasn't aimed at you, Paul. It's just a fact. Since I've retired, things have slipped. That's not just down to you—'

'You know it was Neil that put that mugger in that alley, don't you?' Riddick pointed at him.

'I don't doubt it.'

'It's a mystery to me how you ever thought you could control a man like that?'

'I imagine he's different now he's been inside. Hardened, perhaps? Anyway, I've no doubt you'll hold him to account for what he's done.'

Riddick's phone beeped. He sighed and went over to it by the toaster. He saw that he had voicemails.

His face paled as he listened to the voicemails from Marsh and Gardner.

He put the phone down. 'The boy who attacked Cherish last night...'

'What about him?'

'He's dead.'

36

The bruised sky looked ready to burst, so despite the insane humidity, Gardner zipped up her yellow raincoat. She was putting on her white overalls by the cordon which had sealed off the first set of steps leading down to the Viaduct Terrace. Up ahead, the steps that took you down to the other side of the terrace had also been cordoned off.

She looked up at the striking eighty-foot viaduct that she'd paused by for a good look at the previous day on her run. She'd been dubious of the glorified railway bridge then, but now with a swift nod, she concluded once and for all that it was indeed an eyesore over a beautiful river. She would leave others to believe that it was something of breathtaking magnificence. Yes, she admitted to herself, she was biased. However, how could you not be when the majority of your experience with this location was down to its backdrop to two brutal murders? No, it was going to be hard to build fond memories of the place, and she was going to have to take side with the small minority who didn't enjoy this stately structure.

She looked down at the body, which was central on the

terrace, just in front of a wooden bench. Without much space to erect a tent, the SOCOs worked quickly before the rain joined the party.

The rest of Waterside was quiet; not simply because it was a crime scene and people were asked to stay back, but because it was still very early. Of course, the press were gathering again; fortunately, this time, Marsh had ensured more officers to keep them further back. She thought she could spy Marianne Perse in the crowd and felt a surge of anger in the pit of her stomach.

'Better late than never, Emma,' Marsh said, coming up alongside her.

'Apologies, ma'am. The connector on my phone charger is temperamental. How certain are we that the victim is Dan Lotus?'

'Certain. We've his driver's licence from his pocket, and, like Bradley, he's been recognised by several officers too. Like his best friend, he'd spent many of his teenage years on our radar.'

'Who found him?'

'The Cook family. Which is a shame really. They have an autistic boy that rises at half past four every morning. They always take him to look at the ducks when he wakes, regardless of the weather. Theo is obsessed with ducks. Poor kid. He ran down and discovered Dan first. I saw the family before they left. The lad was inconsolable.'

Gardner shook her head. 'That's awful.'

'It is... I see the yellow raincoat made another appearance.'

Gardner gestured up at the dark clouds looming over the viaduct.

Marsh smirked. 'Going to take more than that flimsy coat if that comes down.'

Gardner watched forensic pathologist, Dr Hugo Sands,

circling the body. He was regarding it from different angles, kneeling regularly to inspect something that took his interest.

'He's bloody irritating,' Marsh said. 'Inspects for God knows how long and then tells you sod all.'

Gardner nodded. 'What've we got so far, ma'am?'

'Same killer it seems. Same MO and another scabby letter on the lower back.'

'Which one?'

'Not sure. Sands will fill you in. Do you know what happened to Paul and Anders last night?'

Gardner nodded. 'Yes, ma'am. And Cherish. Poor girl.'

'Well, whoever killed Dan has saved you one job.' She pointed to the yellow bag which was being examined by a SOCO. 'That's the bag stolen from Cherish. We also recovered the flick knife used on Anders, and the balaclava he disguised himself with.'

'Planted?'

Marsh shook her head. 'Unlikely. He's wearing the same clothes that Anders and Paul saw him wearing in that alleyway off the town square.'

'What was in the bag?'

'Shredded paper. At the hospital, Cherish told Paul it was full of snacks. She also told him that she was out walking. Eight months pregnant, miles from home, at eleven at night.'

Gardner thought about this. She recalled the danger Cherish might have been in with Neil regarding the evidence she gave her. Had Neil tried to get rid of her? Forced the poor girl to make a delivery to put her in harm's way? That way, there was no need to put anything real in the bag, if Neil was just trying to get her to a certain place.

'I should try to get in touch with Paul again, he may know more—'

'Leave that to me, Emma. I want you to speak to Hugo Sands, and then get to HQ to run your briefing.'

'Yes, ma'am.'

Marsh took a deep breath through her nose. It sounded as if she was inhaling everything in. She then blew the breath out in a long sigh. 'Bradley and Dan were best friends with criminal history. Are we dealing with a rival gang? Or someone unhappy about something they've done together in the past, perhaps?'

Kelsey Winters? Gardner thought. 'I've a feeling we're close.'

'I hope so, Emma. I just postponed the press conference scheduled today. The bastards are incensed. But, finding out what happened here is more pressing. Two murders are unacceptable… a third, well, you know, that is one catastrophe we must avoid. The worst thing is both murders were committed under the watchful eye of our viaduct. That's going to give weight to the idea of the "Viaduct Killer" and is going to turn Waterside into a ghost town for the foreseeable.'

Suited, Gardner headed into the crime scene. She nodded greetings at several SOCOs en route and met with Sands next to the body.

She looked down at Dan Lotus. His eyes were open but looking at nothing. He had a large cut down his right cheek glued together with butterfly stitches.

She expected Sands to be his usual tentative self, but he spoke without hesitation this time. 'Killed in exactly the same way. Choke hold.' He knelt and, with a gloved hand, pointed at the neck. 'This time the bruising has made an earlier appearance.'

'The gash on his face?'

'Almost five inches that! I'd approximate about two days ago. It's a clean slice – a knife wound. He could have done with getting it looked at in the hospital, instead of attempting to dress it himself. This would have ended up infected, I bet.'

'The letter carved into his back?' Gardner said.

'L.'

She heard a groan from the swollen sky.

'What is this bastard spelling?' Gardner asked.

Sands shrugged.

Gardner nodded. 'Time of death?'

'Well, he was last sighted at just before eleven, I believe. So, between then and about two in the morning.'

There was suddenly an eruption of noise from the press.

Gardner turned to see Knaresborough's most infamous copper, Riddick, approaching Marsh at the cordon.

'Excuse me, Dr Sands,' Gardner apologised. She turned and headed back up the steps to the cordon. Out of the corner of her eye, she could see Marianne Perse who, having evaded the police line, had worked her way up the road so she was level with the terrace and was shouting.

'DI Riddick, can we ask you a few questions please?'

Gardner couldn't help herself. She marched over to Marianne.

'DCI Gardner, are you able to tell us anything about the Viaduct Killer's second victim—'

'You're crossing a line, Marianne.'

'Sorry, what do you mean?'

'Exactly what I say. You're crossing a line. You're also being fed incorrect information. We never used the name the Viaduct Killer, and never will. The viaduct is irrelevant in this investigation. So, if I were you, I'd be very careful to sell accuracy from this point on. I intend to hold the press to account following the conclusion of this case. Unless you want to deal your earning potential a severe blow, I suggest you spend a lot more time researching, and a lot less time hounding.'

At that point, one of the officers who'd been part of the breached line, came back and addressed Marianne. 'Ma'am, can you step back over here, please?'

Marianne nodded. As she was led away, she maintained eye contact with Gardner.

Was that a smile? Smug bitch.

Gardner turned and went over to join Riddick and Marsh.

'What was all that about?' Marsh asked.

'Just asking her to move back.' She looked at Riddick. 'How're you feeling?'

'Nothing a few painkillers won't handle.'

Gardner filled him in. 'I'm going to head in and kick off the briefing.'

'I'll take a quick look at the body, and then join you,' Riddick said.

'Two bodies in three days,' Marsh said, looking over at the press. 'Is it any surprise they're so hungry?'

37

On the way to HQ in Harrogate, the sky made a horrendous belching sound, but held.

Gardner pulled into a Starbucks drive-through for the largest Americano she could get her hands on, and a Danish. After arriving at HQ, she grabbed another strong coffee, so she was suitably wired as she prepared for the briefing.

On the *Operation Eden* whiteboard, she pinned up a picture of Dan Lotus. This was taken from his Facebook page. Like Bradley, he strived for an aggressive aura; the only noticeable difference was that he'd hacked at both eyebrows rather than just the one.

She made the mistake of having a *third* coffee before everyone filed into the room. She felt as if she was talking at 100 mph as she briefed everyone on the events of the previous evening with Cherish and Riddick, as well as the Dan Lotus crime scene. When she finished, she looked at all their bemused faces, wondering if they'd made any sense of what she'd just said.

'County lines,' Rice said. 'Has to be.'

Gardner nodded. 'Thanks, Phil. It's now a line of enquiry with real weight and one we'll continue to pursue, *rabidly*.' She looked over at Riddick and nodded. 'Before the incident yesterday, DI Riddick was following up on the rival gang angle, and has been talking to Neil Taylor, regularly, so he will update us momentarily. First, though, I want to run through what we *know* for certain.'

She turned to the board. *Start with the murder.* She jabbed at the picture of Bradley and ran through the main details of the crime again. When she hit on the used condom, she pointed at the image of Susan Harrison. 'I've had confirmation from the officer watching at hospital that she was in her hospital bed all last night, which means she cannot be responsible for Dan's murder. It doesn't necessarily rule her out of Bradley's murder, but Dr Sands is adamant that it's the same killer. And when Sands is adamant about something, it's worth a listen.' She continued to revisit the timeline they'd already built – the drinking in The Crown Inn, the argument outside the pizza takeaway. She handed it over to Barnett. 'Ray?'

'Thank you, boss. Obviously, we are in the process of acquiring Waterside CCTV from last night. I know the Viaduct Terrace itself won't be covered, but some of the area leading from the bottom of the steps to the terrace is. We should be able to find footage of the victim Dan Lotus and whoever followed him. In terms of the CCTV from the night of Bradley's murder, we've accounted for everyone now in the footage... apart from one. The hooded figure, who was witnessed arguing on the phone. I'm afraid we're still no closer to pinning him down.'

'No closer, but not giving up,' Gardner said. 'There was an E carved into Bradley's back.' She pointed at a blown-up photograph of the grizzly carving. 'There was an L in Dan's back.'

She wrote LE on the board in big letters. 'Mean anything to anyone?'

They all looked at the letters. People murmured different words including the two letters. Gardner herself said a few: puzzle, blue etc.

'Swap them around please, boss,' Riddick said.

Gardner obliged. *EL.*

Another minute's thought. You could almost hear the hum of brain cells – like electricity at a pylon.

'Add a K at the beginning…' Riddick said.

KEL.

Bloody hell, of course.

KELSEY.

Unsure as to whether it was the caffeine, or the revelation, Gardner felt a wallop of adrenaline the likes of which she'd never felt before.

She turned to the audience, forcing herself not to shake, but not quite sure whether she was succeeding or not.

She met Riddick's eyes, which were wide and unflinching.

Matthew Blanks, the HOLMES 2 operative, had stopped typing for the moment which gave the room an eerie, silent atmosphere.

KEL.

KELSEY.

She turned back to the board and thrust her finger at the picture of Kelsey. With her heart thrashing in her chest, she ran through the Kelsey suicide narrative again with the team.

Could it be a coincidence, or was the motive lying here, plain as day?

'If someone is writing her name out, that could mean four more murders?' Rice asked.

Gardner's blood ran cold. Four more murders! On her first case, in Knaresborough? She wouldn't be long for this job!

'We won't let it get to three, never mind six,' Riddick said. 'We need to dig out every scrap of evidence from the Winters case.'

'Evidence, because you *made* that an investigation, sir,' Rice sneered. 'The poor family.'

Riddick glowered and inched in Rice's direction.

Gardner pointed a finger at Riddick. He stopped. She then turned her finger on Rice. 'Watch how you speak to your superiors in my incident room, Detective Sergeant Rice – especially if you want to stay in it.'

Rice scowled and looked down.

'I'm suddenly very appreciative you collated that evidence now, DI; what're you thinking?'

'I'm thinking we identify every bully on those Facebook posts. *Every one.* And we get to them as quickly as we can.'

She turned back to Rice, who was still looking down. *Throw the sulky bastard a carrot.*

'How about it, Phil? Can you handle that?'

He looked up. A glow moved over his face. He'd just been given a huge responsibility. 'Yes, boss.'

'And Ray, how are things progressing with Tom Winters, Kelsey's father? Have you confirmed his whereabouts?'

'No, boss. HR from his company have still not been in touch. I'm getting on to them again straight after this meeting.'

Gardner nodded.

She turned back to the board. The Kelsey angle was more than promising, but all eggs were not going in one basket. This board was full of angles.

She ran through them all with the team. *What was Cherish doing out at that time with a bag of shredded paper? Why had Dan Lotus been waiting for her, wearing a balaclava? Had he meant to kill her or scare her?*

She shared her theory that someone, potentially Neil Taylor, had set up Cherish. That she was unaware the bag held nothing of value and was being sent to meet an unthinkable fate.

Gardner moved around the board drawing lines as her team discussed in depth the range of evidence and people involved. She drew lines between many of these angles and Neil.

'Phil, could you run us through Neil's detailed statement again from yesterday? Run through his timeline of events.'

Gardner listened intently. They had Neil on CCTV footage with his friend, Simon Turner walking as far as the castle steps – which meant everything hinged on the truth of the next point. *Did Neil and Simon continue, as Neil claimed, to Simon's house for drinks?*

Rice looked at his notes. 'We have spoken to Simon Turner's wife, and she is adamant they were there, drinking.'

'Could they have had time to murder Bradley before going on for this drink, perhaps?'

'The timeline wouldn't add up,' Barnett said. 'We considered all variations. They would have encountered Bradley and Susan having sex.'

Gardner sighed. 'So, we need to take another run at Simon and his wife. Neil's name is coming up far too often – *far too often*.'

The door to the incident room opened. Marsh stood there, staring in at Gardner. She waved her out of the room.

'Excuse me a moment,' Gardner said. 'DI Riddick, can you take over please?'

Riddick rose and approached the front.

Gardner exited and stood in the corridor with Marsh. 'I've heard back from forensics on Neil's jumper, Emma.'

Not for the first time this morning, Gardner felt her heart rate jump. 'Bradley's blood?'

'No.'

Gardner felt her heart sink.

'Dan Lotus'.'

* * *

Gardner stepped back into the incident room, her head reeling.

Riddick was in full flow. He looked over at her, but she held her hand and shook her head to indicate that he continue.

'Thank you, Lucy and John for notifying Dan Lotus' next of kin. Dan lived with his aunt, Mary Thompson,' Riddick said. 'His father died when he was a baby, and his mother ran off abroad when he was a toddler. Anything you'd like to say on that, Lucy?'

O'Brien nodded. 'As you can imagine, she was distraught. She'd cared for him most of his life and considered herself his mother.'

Rice snorted. 'He could've at least paid her back by staying out of trouble.'

Gardner shook her head but bit her lip. She was always astounded by people who believed that life could be so straightforward. That people were only ever faced with one clear choice, and that any deviation was unforgivable.

'Anyway,' O'Brien said. 'She's accepted an FLO, and we're going back for a more detailed statement later. I can tell you now that she won't be a suspect. She had a stroke a number of years back and can't move her left arm, but she can certainly help build a picture of who Dan was.'

Not just another little shit, Gardner thought, her eyes boring into the back of Rice's head.

'So, we need the usual. CCTV, door to door. The assignments are at the front.'

'Before we finish,' Gardner said from the side of the room.

'There's more. And it's *significant*. It won't affect your current assignments. Both DI Riddick and I will follow up on it.'

The tension was palpable. Blanks had stopped typing again and was staring at her through a curtain of hair. Although not an investigator, he would be just as enthralled by the unravelling mystery.

'We've heard back from forensics about the jumper Cherish gave to us.'

Eyes widened.

'The blood belonged to Dan Lotus.'

Brows furrowed.

They'd all expected, and hoped, it would be Bradley's, potentially hurtling this whole investigation towards a tidy conclusion.

Gardner said, 'Dr Sands believed that Dan Lotus sustained a knife wound to the face several days ago – potentially around the time Bradley was murdered. We already know from our investigations that Dan ran some drugs for Neil, or at least used to, before Neil was sent down. So, has Dan been working for Neil again since he was released? And if Neil cut Dan's face – why?'

'Let's not forget that Dan could have been sent by Neil to assault Cherish, or worse,' Riddick said.

'It's not looking good for Neil,' Gardner said. 'But I don't want us to reach any solid conclusion. We have evidence that he hurt Dan, badly, and so motive of some kind must exist, but that's as far as it goes. So, DI Riddick and I will do the honours of speaking to him and finding out what he was up to during that window of opportunity last night. I am also going to apply for a warrant to search his premises.' She looked over at Riddick, and felt her heart quicken.

She couldn't deny that Riddick had an uncanny talent of drawing important information from the likes of Neil, but it didn't come without its risks. Those two had been particularly antagonistic towards each other on their last meeting – could she be inviting more of the same? Additionally, since the Kelsey Winters link, Riddick was coming across as a ticking timebomb. However, despite her concerns, her gut still told her Riddick was important to this investigation. Central, almost. Things seemed to move on at a rapid pace in his presence.

'Everyone else continue with your area of investigation and we will reconvene at six,' she concluded.

38

The front door of Neil's house opened. Mandy stood there. Her face was blotchy from crying.

Gardner gave her a sympathetic look. 'Mrs Spencer—'

'He's gone.'

Gardner and Riddick exchanged a look.

'Where?' Riddick asked.

'I've no idea. The bastard packed his stuff, and said he was done.'

Shit, Gardner thought. *You may not realise it yet, Mandy, but that's great news for you. For us, however... Unless...* Again, she looked at Riddick. He gave a little shake of his head. He didn't think Neil was hiding in the house.

Shit times two.

'When exactly did this happen?' Gardner asked.

'He went in to talk to Cherish and came out in a foul mood. He was silent the whole way back, and every time I tried to speak to him, he told me to shut up.'

The jumper. Bloody hell, Cherish, you didn't tell him about the jumper, did you?

'Then, he packed and left. Last thing he said to me was, *"If you want to blame anyone, blame that slut of a daughter."*'

'Did he take a car?' Riddick asked.

She nodded.

Good. ANPR will collar him.

'Where did Neil go before the hospital last night?' Gardner asked.

'Nowhere. We watched the latest James Bond film together. *Honestly.* I know I lied for him before, but why would I lie now? We watched the film from about nine thirty until close to midnight, and then the hospital rang. We were there until about four in the morning.'

'Okay,' Gardner said. 'I believe you.'

'Are you safe?' Riddick said, raising an eyebrow. 'Are you really alone in there?'

Mandy stepped to one side. 'Yes, of course. Check if you want.'

'If that's okay?'

Mandy nodded.

Riddick looked at Gardner. 'Wait here, I'll be a minute.'

While Riddick used Mandy's permission to look around the house, Gardner tried to engage Mandy in further discussions about Neil. She was too emotional though, and the tears were coming thicker and faster now.

When Riddick re-emerged, he shook his head to indicate that Neil wasn't here.

Outside on the doorstep, Gardner said, 'We've applied for a warrant to search these premises thoroughly, Mandy. Would you grant us permission to save us time?'

Mandy rubbed at her tears and nodded. 'Yes. Sod him.'

'Thanks. I'll make the call.'

Back in the car, Gardner put out the APW on Neil Taylor. She also contacted HQ to request forensics come and search Neil's premises immediately.

Riddick popped his head in. He looked uncomfortable and didn't make eye contact with her. 'I want to show you something… sooner rather than later.'

'To do with the case?'

'No.'

Gardner raised an eyebrow. She thought back to her earlier concerns that he was a ticking timebomb, and now this peculiar request. 'It probably isn't the time, Paul.'

'No, it *definitely* isn't the time.' He looked at her, briefly, but then looked away. 'However, I'd like – sorry – *need* to do this before I change my mind.'

Even though it wasn't linked to the case, she felt compelled to accept. Anything that Riddick was willing to share should not be taken lightly. He'd not been an easy nut to crack so far, that was for sure – and she shouldn't be passing up opportunities like this. Also, Gardner could be a slave to curiosity, especially when it involved someone as enigmatic as Paul Riddick! 'Okay, where're we going?'

'Follow me.'

In her rear-view mirror, she watched him climb into his vehicle and drink from his Sprite bottle. He was forever drinking Sprite!

Well, she thought, reaching into her pocket for her tic tacs, *we all have our vices, I guess.*

39

As Riddick led Gardner through the chapel, she broke out in a cold sweat. *This is it, he's about to open up to me.*

Outside the back, Riddick led her down a path between rows of gravestones. Some of the stones were crumbling, and many were worn to the point of being unreadable, but that simply added to the beauty of the scene. Vines crawled up the stone walls that enclosed the resting place, while daffodils waved in the gentle breeze, and purple crocuses rested in the enduring quiet.

'It's beautiful,' Gardner said.

Riddick, who was ahead of her, didn't reply.

She inwardly sighed. *Keep your mouth closed, girl.*

They reached the last of the gravestones, and the end of the path. Ahead were several rows of planted trees, all still in their infancy. Each tree came with a small golden plaque. Gardner was too far back to read what was written on any of them.

There was a bench to their right, and Riddick sat down. He shuffled along to make space for Gardner.

She looked out over the trees, each one representing a life lived and a life lost and felt a lump in her throat.

You owe this poor man your composure.

She sat beside him.

Riddick pointed at the trees. 'Second row back, furthest right. That's Rachel. My wife. She was long-suffering as you can imagine. She was also the most beautiful woman I ever met.'

Gardner swallowed.

'Next to her, are my two little scoundrels, Molly and Lucy…'

Gardner turned her head away from him, worried she was going to break.

'Don't be fooled by the quiet. They were anything but.'

She broke. Gardner reached up and wiped a tear away. She turned to look at Riddick's profile. He was staring at the trees, smiling.

'I'm sorry,' she said, wiping her other eye with the back of her hand.

Riddick shook his head. 'There's no need for you to be sorry. That's not why I brought you here, boss.'

'Don't call me boss, Paul. Now of all times, please don't call me boss.'

Riddick nodded. 'As you wish.'

She stared at his profile. He looked so relaxed… *so calm*. She couldn't even imagine being in this situation, never mind handling it as stoically as he was doing. 'Thank you for bringing me here, Paul. I… I—'

'Want to know why?'

'No,' Gardner said, feeling flustered. 'I mean, yes—'

'Relax, Emma.' Riddick looked at her for the first time in a while. 'Rachel asked me to.'

Gardner nodded, paused and then said, 'I don't understand.'

Riddick stared off over the trees again. 'I still talk to Rachel. In fact, I still talk to all three of them.'

Gardner opened her mouth to respond, but then realised she had no idea what to say to that.

Riddick smiled again. 'Don't worry, I'm not mad... well, not completely. I know they're not there. Not really.'

Gardner nodded. She searched hard for a response. The best she could come up with was, 'They'll always be with you.'

Riddick shook his head. 'Yes... that's what they say... but I don't believe that.'

'Oh,' Gardner said, suddenly feeling foolish.

'They're not there, Emma. They're gone. *Completely.* I'm not religious, nor do I believe in ghosts. I see them because I want to.'

Gardner nodded. 'I understand.'

'Do you?' Riddick asked, looking at her with a raised eyebrow.

I don't know. 'I think so.'

'You don't think it's insane?'

'No... however, I'm not the best person to ask. Have you spoken to anyone about this—'

'Why would I do that? I want to see them. I like to see them.'

Gardner nodded. She felt her face reddening. 'Of course.'

'So, you don't have to worry, Emma. This is all based on choice. But, I understand, this way, this *life*, it isn't sustainable.'

Gardner opened her mouth to agree but managed to hold back.

'I can't believe I'm telling you this. I haven't even told Anders. Mind you, he's a pompous prick at the best of times, I don't know if I could cope with his patronising response. I already know that if I want any chance at a life, I have to start letting go.'

Gardner nodded, glad she'd not told him what he already knew.

'Rachel, or at least my version of Rachel, believes you can help me with that.'

Me? Jesus wept. I hardly know you, Paul. Yes, I have experience of being the shoulder to cry on, but never something as heart-wrenchingly tragic as this.

'Don't look so flabbergasted, Emma.'

'Am I the right person for this, Paul?'

'My wife... sorry... *I* think you are. You must have seen my enthusiasm for the job. I've not felt that in years. I've not felt that since... since... well, *you*... I think?'

Gardner took a deep breath and shook her head. This wasn't down to her. I mean, how could it be? 'Paul, maybe you're just ready. I didn't put the body there! I think you found this enthusiasm all on your own.'

'No.' Riddick emphasised this with a shake of his head. 'I saw the way you looked at Bradley. I saw the way you *felt* for the victim, how you championed him. I've seen the passion in your eyes, Emma, for justice.'

'And I've seen those things in you too, Paul.'

'You made me remember what they were.'

Gardner nodded. 'I'm just glad that you're feeling better, Paul.'

'So, I want to tell you the story now of how my life was ruined. I want to tell you it – at least, the part that matters, then, afterwards, I want us to leave and find this bastard who killed Bradley and Dan. I want us to do that so badly.'

'I understand. I'm honoured that you're confiding in me.'

'So here it is.' He looked over at the trees as he told his story. 'Ronnie Haller was a drug dealer, not unlike Neil Taylor, using youngsters to run drugs. County lines. One of the big fish. Ronnie had taken it too far. He'd killed two young men who'd skimmed from him. We had him bang to rights. He was going to spend his life in jail, and I craved one last interview. I got what I wanted...'

40

Ronnie Haller bared his teeth. Some were missing; some were rotten and hanging on for dear life.

Riddick stifled a yawn. Not because he was bored by Ronnie's aggression, but rather because he was exhausted. The last two weeks had been full of late nights and legwork, arguments with Rachel and limited time to watch Lucy and Molly grow.

But it'd been worth it.

He looked at the beast opposite him. All tattoos, scar tissue, sweat and anger. Off the street.

God, had it been worth it.

'This is the last time I'm going to ask, Ronnie.' Riddick leaned forward. He could smell Ronnie's body odour. These last few weeks of poor personal hygiene had seen Riddick grow accustomed to his own odour, but it was nothing like this. Ronnie smelled of earth and mud. 'Your DNA is on Oliver's body. Oliver's DNA is on your clothing. We've the CCTV footage, the murder weapon, the eyewitness statement. We've built a case so strong that no lawyer can break it.'

Riddick looked at Nathan Rose. The oily lawyer sneered. He knew he was beaten too.

This really was a day to remember.

'We've also strong evidence that it was you that sent a photograph of Jimmy's bludgeoned body to his mother. We actually have footage of you pushing the envelope into the letterbox. You see, we left no stone unturned, Ronnie. You'll get two life sentences. I've never heard the CPS sound so convinced. Tell him Nathan.'

The sneering lawyer shrugged. 'My client's aware of his situation. He has chosen to refrain from helping you further with your inquiries—'

Riddick slammed his hand on the table. 'Help? This isn't help! It's decorum. A modicum of respect! You've nothing left to lose, Ronnie. Jimmy is dead. You killed him – no jury will fail to convict. For Christ's sake, give up the body for his mother. How would you feel if it was your mother, desperate to bury you?'

Ronnie leaned forward. The nerves in his eyelids quivered. 'My mother? I buried her a long time ago. Cancer. What sodding decorum or modicum of respect did that disease show?'

'You're moving off subject, Ronnie—'

'I'm very much on subject. You know how I work, how I operate, don't you, DI? You've been sniffing around me, crawling inside my life, for two weeks now. You think I didn't know? You think I didn't sense you every time I walked around a damn corner?'

'It wasn't just me. I can't take full credit.'

'Credit! Ha. Spoken like a true leader. You can take full credit... In fact, you will take full credit...'

Riddick stood. 'I knew this was a waste of time. We've played this game long enough. I'm terminating this interview—'

'What time is it, Paul?' Ronnie asked.

Riddick ignored him and pushed his chair under the table.

'What time is it?' Ronnie looked sideways at Nathan.

Nathan looked at a watch which must have cost the same as Riddick earned in a month.

'Ten to five.'

'Ah... not long off, then.' Ronnie smirked.

Holding the back of his chair, Riddick succumbed to curiosity. 'Long off what?'

Ronnie bounced his head from one shoulder to the other. 'Patience.'

'You're pathetic. This interview is terminated.'

Riddick turned towards the exit.

'Tick tock. Tick tock,' Ronnie said. 'When you were crawling around my business, building up a report on me, I was doing something very similar. Returning the favour, shall we say. You have an interesting life, Detective Inspector Riddick.'

Riddick swung around. 'Are you admitting to another crime?'

Ronnie gave a quick shrug of his shoulders. 'I'm just saying I prepared a dossier on you, just like you did on me.'

Riddick felt the adrenaline bubbling in his stomach. 'What've you done?'

'Rachel is a pretty woman, Paul, and those two twin daughters are heart breakers—'

Riddick launched over the table to grab at Ronnie. He took him by the prison shirt. 'If you've touched my family, I'll kill you.'

'But I'm dead already, Paul, don't you see that. You've already made it clear that I've nothing left to lose.'

Riddick dragged Ronnie forward onto the desk. 'What've you done?'

He heard the door to the interview room swing open behind him, but he carried on dragging until Ronnie had come right the way off the desk and onto the floor—

Riddick felt hands under his armpits. 'Get off me!' He was pulled towards the exit. He tried to yank back, but whichever colleague had him, had him good. 'Let me go!'

He watched Ronnie rise to his feet, dusting off his prison shirt. 'What time is it now?' He looked at Nathan.

Nathan, who was trembling, looked at his watch. 'Five to five.'

Ronnie smiled at Riddick.

'What time does Rachel leave to take the children swimming, Detective Inspector?' Ronnie asked.

Riddick felt the world collapse around him.

'What time?'

Five to five... five to five... five to five... The answer ran through his head again, and again.

'My wife.' Riddick fell limp in his colleague's arms. 'Phone my wife. Phone Rachel.'

41

'It was too late,' Riddick said.

Gardner was gripping one hand with the other. She could see the white of her knuckles.

'A car bomb,' Riddick said.

Jesus. She felt a tear running down her cheek.

'They didn't suffer... At least, they told me they hadn't.'

You poor, poor man. She opened her mouth, but quickly closed it again. He'd already made it clear that he'd no time for anyone saying that they were sorry.

Riddick rose to his feet and stepped forward. He gazed out over the fledgling trees.

Gardner took a few deep breaths, adjusting to the gravity of Riddick's tragedy.

She watched a squirrel scurry over the vine-covered stone walls.

After a minute of silence, Riddick turned. 'We should get going.'

Gardner could barely move. 'Ronnie Haller? What happened to him?'

'He's inside. He won't ever get out.'

Gardner almost said *good* but thought better of it. There was nothing positive in this situation. Absolutely nothing.

'Who planted the bomb?' Gardner asked.

'Two youngsters. Manipulated by Ronnie. They were easy enough for us to find.'

Yes, Gardner thought, *as if anybody was walking away from a crime that vicious.*

'Ronnie threw them to the wolves,' Riddick said. He turned around. 'Dan and Bradley were old enough to know better too, but they were also young and thrown to the wolves. No one was there to show them the right way.'

Yes, she thought, nodding, *you do get it, don't you? All that hot air when I first met you was bravado.* 'I agree.'

'Ronnie and Neil,' Riddick continued. 'Evil, manipulative bastards. These are the real monsters.'

Exactly. You're one of the good guys, Paul. You can find yourself again. I'll help you.

Riddick stood up. 'I want to stop them. I want to stop them all.'

'Me too,' Gardner said, feeling a warmth for Riddick swelling inside her. 'Me too.'

42

By their vehicles, at the entrance to the chapel, Gardner received several updates by phone. She then fed back to Riddick. 'Firstly, Neil Taylor ditched his car in town and then went on foot.'

Riddick slammed his hand down on the bonnet of his car, then turned to lean against it. 'He's no dummy. Who doesn't know about ANPR these days?'

'Everybody has eyes out for him,' Gardner said. 'We'll get him. However, Mandy's statement suggests Neil isn't Dan Lotus' killer. Also, Ray has recovered CCTV footage of Dan running into the castle grounds, and recordings of him sprinting down Waterside. The cameras have picked up someone following at speed.'

'Who?'

'Someone with a hoodie, who does a good job of hiding his face. It could be the same person seen on the night Bradley died – you know, the one arguing on his phone?'

'It's a shame Viaduct Terrace isn't covered. We'd have the murder recorded.'

Gardner's phone rang again. It was DS Ross.

'What do you have for me, John?'

'Simon Turner crumbled, boss. And I mean crumbled. As soon as we told Simon that there was concrete evidence proving that Neil used a knife on Dan, he blamed the entire assault on Neil. He claims that after they left the Worlds End pub at last orders the night Bradley died, they walked all of Waterside to his home as originally claimed, but then, this is where the story changes from the original... Neil took a phone call from another lad that worked for him, claiming he had evidence that Dan had been skimming money from the drugs he was selling for Neil. I'll read from Simon's detailed statement, boss. "*Neil just lost it. He'd that wild look about him he sometimes gets. You know to stay out of his way. He phoned Dan and asked him to meet him near the cricket club. I was glad when he left... there was no chance I was going with him. He looked ready to kill a man, and I didn't want anything to do with that... you have to believe me. I was relieved when I saw Dan the next day, and he'd only a cut face... Boy got off lightly considering what Neil is capable of.*"'

Gardner thanked Ross for the information and then told Riddick. 'The cut face from two days back was the warning then... Maybe Dan skimmed again, and Neil went to finish the job? It would mean that Mandy has lied to us about Neil being home last night.'

'Possibly. But that assumes Bradley *was* killed by someone other than Neil, because he would have been preoccupied slicing Dan's face. Aren't we convinced that we're dealing with the same killer?'

'Unless Neil purposely made Dan's murder look like it was the same killer?'

'Canny,' Riddick said. 'However, how would he have known about the carving in Bradley's back in order to duplicate the MO? The press never printed that information.'

'True. For some reason, that information was never leaked. I thought at the time that it was a peculiar detail for our traitor to omit. Either way, we need Neil in custody. Killer, or not, that bastard holds his fair share of the answers.'

Another phone call. This time, the belligerent DS Rice. 'Phil?'

'Shit.' Rice sighed. 'That lass, Kelsey, got one heck of a hard time. Are you sitting down, boss? I think I'm really onto something here.'

Come on you smug plonker, crack on! We've a bleeding murderer out there.

'I started by looking through all the Facebook posts targeting Kelsey. It happened over a four-month period. Dan was the worst, by a country mile. He photoshopped all sorts of images using Kelsey – some real offensive stuff. Nothing pornographic, or it would have been taken down, but nasty shit just the same. He made her look like some grovelling animal and put captions on her, trying to make her look like a teacher's pet. The problem with these posts is that they pick up a lot of likes and comments. It keeps the posts alive. I guess the targeted individual can only ignore it for so long before it becomes overwhelming...'

'Thanks, Phil. I'm aware that social media is a shithouse. Can we get to it, please?'

'Well, Bradley chipped in with a few posts, making him public enemy number two, but that was it, really. No one else posted a nasty image. Everyone else just liked or commented.'

No more ringleaders? Maybe the letters EL weren't spelling KELSEY? Maybe, there won't be more victims? And maybe, this is all unconnected to Kelsey after all?

'So, I spent some time reading through all the comments, and making notes of everyone who wrote anything nasty. A few people stuck up for her, but very few, unfortunately – most people opted to bat for the nasty team. People are pricks, huh?'

In a lot of ways, people are sheep, Gardner thought. It was a sad reality, especially in cases such as these.

Rice sighed. 'There're a lot of names. We're talking over a hundred.'

'He's going to struggle to target a hundred people,' Gardner said. 'It'll also be a needle in a haystack as to who's next.' *Was the Kelsey angle falling flat on its face?*

'Wait, boss. I did tell you I was on to something. There were a number of names in these comments that stuck out. Names that were more frequent. So, I tallied up the most regular names and narrowed it down to five.'

Now this is getting interesting, Gardner thought, enjoying a sudden rush of blood.

'I ran those names through our system. The first four got me nowhere, but the fifth... well, the fifth flagged up a report...'

Gardner stopped leaning on the bonnet and stood up straight. She saw Riddick raise an eyebrow at her, eager to know what was happening.

'His name's Richard Hill. His parents reported him missing last night...'

The rush of blood intensified... In fact, it was suddenly like a tidal wave.

'He's eighteen years old, and it's not even been twenty-four hours, so it's not glowing on anyone's radar yet...'

It is now.

'He was in the same year group as Bradley, Dan and Kelsey.'

She could hear her heart thump. 'Okay... wow, Phil. This is unbelievable—'

'Woah, boss – I haven't finished yet.'

Haven't finished yet? Wow – maybe Phil was the second coming.

'I accessed Kelsey's email and found correspondence between

Kelsey and Richard *before* the bullying began. Are you ready, boss? This is the kicker…'

God, you've a right to be smug now…

'Kelsey and Richard dated, and they broke it off before the bullying began…'

Gardner looked at Riddick with wide eyes. Despite not overhearing the conversation, he smiled.

Her excitement was contagious.

43

Richard Hill's parents both answered the door. Gardner and Riddick showed their badges.

'Finally...' David Hill puffed out his cheeks. 'We thought no one was listening.'

Joanne Hill, red and flustered, looked as if she'd been going all out on a treadmill. 'I've lost count of the amount of phone calls I've made.'

Once they were all installed in a spectacularly unfurnished, albeit very tidy living room, Gardner came clean. 'Your son is eighteen. Your concerns were noted at the station, but he's not a minor, and he's not been off the radar a particularly long time—'

'But there's *something* wrong,' Joanne said.

Gardner nodded. *Which is why I'm in your living room...*

David wagged his finger. 'Our son doesn't go a day, sorry, strike that, an hour, without letting us know where he is.'

'So, you see,' continued Joanne, 'he's missing. There can be no doubt.'

'We're listening, and we'll do whatever we can,' Riddick said.

Gardner nodded in agreement with Riddick, thinking, *when did you become the sensitive one?*

'When was the last time you saw Richard?' Gardner said, opening her notebook, and turning back to the parents.

'We've been through this already,' Joanne said.

'In the countless calls!' David said.

'I understand,' Gardner said with a reassuring nod. 'But it's still best if the information is delivered face to face.'

'It was yesterday at six o'clock... after dinner. He grabbed his football and went to the park,' David said.

'Alone?' Riddick asked

'I'm not sure. He just headed out. He sometimes meets friends there, but we don't know many of them. He's a private boy, our son. Never really brings anyone back.'

'I see,' Gardner said. 'Which park?'

'Stockwell Community Centre,' Joanne said.

'Okay, when did you realise there was a problem?' Gardner asked.

'When the sun went down. It was almost ten, and there was still no sign of him. Then, by eleven, we were going out of our minds.'

'So, you started to phone the police?' Riddick asked.

'Yes, of course,' David said. 'As I mentioned before, this is completely out of character. And now, here we are, in the afternoon of the following day and we haven't heard a word.'

Joanne started to cry.

'Neither of us could go to work,' David said. 'Not with this weighing on us.'

'Was your son friends with Bradley Taylor and Dan Lotus?' Gardner asked.

The colour drained from David's face. 'The dead boys! *No*, of course not.'

Joanne shook her head, suddenly looking terrified. 'Please… not that… no…'

Gardner held up her hands. 'There's nothing to suggest that he has—'

'Apart from the fact that he is missing, and now you're here talking about murdered boys that were in his school year?' David said. He looked angry. He drew closer to his wife and put his arm around her shoulder.

'Could this be anything to do with that Viaduct Killer?' Joanne said with a trembling voice.

'Again, we have not made any such connections,' Gardner said.

'Was Richard *ever friends* with these two boys, as far as you know?' Riddick asked.

'Absolutely not!' David said. 'Those two lads were criminals – everyone knows that! I don't buy into this serial killer, viaduct nonsense. They messed about with bad crowds, and when you mess about with bad crowds, bad things happen.'

Gardner made a note. 'What do you know about your son's relationship with Kelsey Winters?'

She looked up in time to see David and Joanne exchange a look.

'Did you know they were together?' Gardner asked.

'It was brief,' Joanne said. 'You're talking a month, if that.'

'Again, what has this got to do with anything?' David hissed.

'Do you know what Richard and Kelsey's relationship was like?' Gardner asked.

'*Brief!* What more is there to say?'

'Mr Hill, I know you're frustrated, but we all want the same thing here – to find your son,' Riddick said.

'What does a girl who committed suicide two years ago have to do with my son?' Joanne said.

Gardner and Riddick exchanged a glance – they'd have to be very cautious how much they revealed here.

'I'm sorry to tell you this,' Riddick said, 'but it seems your son was involved in the bullying that caused Kelsey to take her own life.'

Gardner inwardly sighed. *Hardly patient!*

'Nonsense,' David said, pulling his arm back from his wife's shoulder and sitting forward. 'He's a great lad.'

'I'm afraid there is evidence that your son passed a few comments on some inappropriate images on Facebook regarding Kelsey just prior to her suicide.' Gardner paused for a deep breath. 'Images posted by Bradley and Dan.'

Stunned silence.

Joanne was shaking her head; David's face was reddening.

'But,' Gardner said, 'lots of her peers commented. *Lots.* Your son was one of many. So, there may be little in this.'

'Has this killer got my son?' Joanne asked, with tears in her eyes.

'As I keep saying, there is nothing to suggest that,' Gardner said. 'But the only thing I do know is that Richard had a connection to Kelsey that the other peers didn't have – in that he dated her.'

'Honestly,' Joanne said, tears streaming down her face. 'There was nothing in that relationship... it could never have lasted. It ended for a good reason.'

'Which was?' Riddick asked.

The parents exchanged a glance. David seemed to redden even more. Joanne said, 'Because Richard is gay.'

Gardner made a note, wondering how Kelsey would have responded to this. Bitterly, perhaps? Encouraging Richard in turn to respond by bullying her? She looked back up at Joanne.

'He felt dreadful at the time about breaking it off with her. He told me he thought he was gay – and asked me what he should do. I told him he should do the right thing. He was the perfect gentleman.'

Gardner forced back a guffaw. *Perfect gentleman! He joined in the bullying!*

David had gone very quiet and was looking down at the ground. Had Richard's father been unhappy with all of this?

'How did you feel about this, Mr Hill?'

He glared at Gardner. 'Fine. This is the twenty-first century. Why do you ask?'

Clearly a sensitive issue then.

'Just trying to gather as much information as I can,' Gardner said.

'I was perfectly all right with his sexuality,' David continued. 'It was his choice in partner that had me concerned.'

'He liked the rogues,' Joanne said.

Rogues. Gardner hadn't heard that word in a very long time.

'He told me he found that boy who died – Bradley – attractive!' Joanne said.

'So, he did *know* Bradley?' Riddick asked.

David's eyes widened. 'Knew, yes. You asked me if they were friends, which they certainly weren't!'

'How did you respond when you found out about Richard's feelings for Bradley, Mr Hill?' Gardner asked.

David was shaking his head. 'I told him that liking people such as him was a one-way ticket to disaster!'

Joanne said, 'Richard became adamant that Bradley was misunderstood, and that he actually had a sensitive side.'

'So they *were* friends?' Riddick asked.

David scowled, crossed his arms and sat back.

Gardner glanced at Riddick. *Down, boy!*

'As far as you know, did anything ever happen between Bradley and your son?' Gardner asked Joanne.

'No. He would have told me. Besides, my son was shy, he was never about to admit his sexuality to a dangerous boy such as Bradley!'

Was this why Richard joined in the bullying then? Gardner thought. *Was he trying to impress Bradley?*

Gardner ripped a page from the back of her notebook and handed it over to Joanne. 'Can you please write down the full names of all of Richard's friends?'

'Of course, but there aren't many, and we've already rung around them.'

'No harm in double checking,' Riddick said.

'Also, Joanne, could you draw us a map of the route your son would have taken to the football field?' Gardner said.

Because we need to find Richard, we really do.

44

Back in the car, Gardner contacted O'Brien first. 'Lucy, I'm going to give you a list of names. I want you to contact all of them and find out when they last saw Richard Hill...'

After O'Brien, she phoned Rice. Rice had proven himself by bringing them to this point. He'd be a good fit for what came next. 'Phil?'

'Boss, what did the parents say?'

She explained. 'So Richard is a potential victim.' She gave him the details of the route to the park. 'He left his house at six. He was expected back around nine. You have a three-hour window.'

'I'm on it.'

She left her car, walked over to Riddick's and tapped on the window. He wound it down. 'I'm going to drive the route to the park—'

Her phone rang again. It was Barnett.

'Ray?'

'Boss. I finally heard back from Tom Winters' company. *He's not there.*'

'Come again?'

'He quit over a month ago. He phoned up HR and told them he was done, and he was not returning to the rig. They've not heard from him since.'

'Jesus.'

'I also checked with the Home Office. He's in the country. He flew into Leeds from work over two months back and hasn't taken another flight out.'

Tom Winters – the broken father.

'We need to find him now. If he's killing these boys, he could have Richard.'

'Already on it. APW out. I stopped by his bungalow the other day in Harrogate – I assumed he was away, but what if he was in there?'

'Precisely why I'm getting a warrant to go in. Tom Winters is now a significant person of interest.' She said this on purpose, so Riddick could catch the revelation.

Riddick nodded as if it all suddenly made sense.

'I'm heading to the bungalow now with DI Riddick. Text me the address.'

'Will do, boss.'

Gardner felt a cold chill at the bottom of the spine as she ended the call to Barnett. Had the killer been this obvious the whole time? Had the belief that Tom Winters had been out of the country delayed the resolution of the case?

She put a hand to her mouth. Could they have prevented Dan's death if they'd been more thorough with this angle?

'Boss?' Riddick said. 'Are you okay?'

'Change of plan.' She told Riddick what she'd learned. 'En route, I'll contact Marsh to get us that warrant organised.'

'It won't be that quick.'

'No, it won't, but if I even suspect someone is in that

bungalow when I get there – we're going in. We've reason to believe someone's life is in danger.'

She looked up. Framed by a black sky, Joanne Hill was looking out the window at them.

* * *

Gardner and Riddick stood in front of Tom Winters' bungalow. Marsh had already told them the warrant would happen, but late afternoon was the best they could hope for.

If Richard was still alive, did he have until late afternoon?

Gardner surveyed the property, over its dormer, up to its gable roof.

The answer to everything could be within these walls, but if she went in without a warrant, then the CPS would have a fit, and Tom Winters' defence lawyer, a field day.

They tried the front door, achieving the same lack of success that Barnett had done the previous day.

Riddick prowled the front garden from one high hedge to the other, looking over at the adjacent bungalows – then he returned to Gardner. 'Let's try the neighbours... find out about any comings and goings.'

'Yes... one moment,' Gardner said, peering in through the front window. 'Come here, Paul. Do you see that?'

Riddick peered into the lounge. 'See what?'

'The open kitchen door, behind the sofa; you see it?'

Riddick squinted. 'Yes... Smashed glass?'

'Does it look like there's been a struggle to you?'

'Well, it's possible – more likely someone just dropped a glass...'

'And didn't sweep it up? I think it warrants further investigation.'

Riddick nodded. 'Agree, boss.'

They went through the side gate and down a stone path. The back garden was tiny and had very little going for it in the way of floral decoration.

Gardner went straight for the kitchen window, and her heart almost leapt from her chest. 'Bloody hell! *Paul!*'

Paul joined her and looked through the window. 'Christ on a bike.'

A man was curled up to the side of the open kitchen door. He was unmoving and faced towards the rear kitchen wall rather than the window, so Gardner had no idea who this was, or if he was alive. There was also a small pool of blood around the upper half of the victim.

'Phone an ambulance,' Riddick said, looking around the ground. Ornamental rocks lined the small patch of grass that made up the garden and she watched Riddick swoop for the biggest rock he could find.

Gardner phoned an ambulance, and gave the details while Riddick ploughed through the glass in the centre of the back door. He reached in. 'Key's in the lock!' He proclaimed excitedly.

She watched him fumble around through the broken glass. 'Careful!' she called, holding the mic on her phone so as not to deafen the person on the other end.

Riddick went through the door, knelt and put a finger to the man's neck, while she confirmed the emergency services were coming.

She rang off and started to jog to where Riddick knelt. 'Ambulance is coming!'

Riddick looked back at her. 'Too late for that. He's ice cold.'

* * *

Tom Winters' left eye remained open, but his right eye was glued shut with blood. His forehead and cheek on that side of his face were also badly damaged, while his jaw was clearly offset.

Gardner stood alongside Riddick. Both looked down as Dr Hugo Sands inspected the body, holding back on questions as he formulated his preliminary findings.

Gardner looked around the kitchen as the SOCOs worked. Apart from the smashed glass that had alerted their suspicions initially, there was very little sign of a struggle. Whoever had killed Tom had done so quickly, and without warning. More than likely, Tom would have known the killer and let him into his bungalow with him; although, the possibility that an intruder had been waiting here to ambush him could not be ruled out at this stage.

Sands stood up, sighed and looked down at the body a moment longer, before looking at Gardner. 'The deceased is a man in his early to mid-forties—'

'Yes. We know. It's Tom Winters,' Riddick said. 'Even with half his face caved in, I can see that. Look at the photographs in his lounge.'

Sands looked long and hard at Riddick.

'Let Dr Sands talk, Paul,' Gardner said.

'I suspect the cause of death is the trauma to the forehead, but confirmation will come when he's on my slab.'

'Time of death?'

'I'm suspecting a couple of days but, again, there are tests that I can do back at the hospital to confirm and then narrow down.'

'Was he struck from the front?' Gardner asked. 'It looks that way.'

'Correct,' Sands said. 'He'd have seen it coming.'

'Why did he not put up more of a fight?' Riddick said.

Sands looked at the broken glass. 'Again, this is just theory. I suspect he was having a drink with his killer. The killer surprised him with the first strike from some kind of blunt object. The victim dropped the glass, and then fell. Then, when he hit the floor, the assailant made sure he wasn't getting up again.' Sands pointed over to the kitchen table where a SOCO was dusting a glass. 'The killer's drink?'

Gardner called over to the SOCO. 'Fingerprints?'

The SOCO nodded. 'Yes, ma'am.'

'Great.' She tried not to get too excited. In the past, she'd been involved in an investigation in which a victim had shared a drink with their killer. The victim's fingerprints were on the glass because they'd provided the drink; the killer, however, had worn gloves.

Gardner looked up at Riddick. He had a glazed look in his eyes. It wasn't the first time she'd noticed this. Sometimes, he looked alert, other times, like now, he looked as if he was off in his own world. More than likely this was grief, but the possibility of substance abuse suddenly darkened her mind.

'Stay here and help, Paul; I'm going to make a few calls.'

'Yes, boss.'

Outside, Gardner looked up into the bruised sky. She was surprised by how long it was holding out.

Tom Winters had looked a dead cert. The victims were all connected to the bullying of his deceased daughter, the opportunity due to his presence in the country had been there, the letters on the victim's backs, potentially spelling her name...

And yet, it hadn't been Tom Winters.

It couldn't have been him because he'd been dead for two days.

So, if not Tom Winters, did that put them straight back in camp Neil?

She sighed.

Considering the glazed look again, she made her way straight to Riddick's car. She looked over her shoulder and checked that no one was watching. Riding a sudden wave of adrenaline, she tried his door. He'd left it unlocked.

Quickly, before she was sighted by one of the forensic team, or worse still, Riddick himself, she scurried over the seats and popped open the glove compartment.

She pulled out the bottle of Sprite.

There was about a third left.

She unscrewed the lid and smelled it.

'Shit.'

A large drop of rain smashed into the window screen.

* * *

Not wanting to confront Riddick about this just yet, Gardner simply informed him that she was going to notify Hannah Winters of Tom's death.

'You fancy her for it now?' Riddick said. He looked nervous. 'She's been through enough, you know.'

There's that hidden sensitive side making a rare appearance again.

'Right now, with Richard missing, I fancy everyone. Best way. We can't afford to miss anything.'

'Let me come with you… I'm ready to see her again.'

Ready! You're not ready for anything, Paul. Pissed is what you are!

'No, I want you to stay here. One of us has to liaise with Marsh. I also need to ensure this forensic team swells – we need this house scoured top to bottom. Even if it means taking SOCOs off Neil's house. There's something here in Tom's bungalow – I just know it.'

Gardner drove quickly to the Winters' residence. The raindrops were getting bigger, and heavier, but were still sporadic.

There was an almighty downpour on the horizon. Her mobile rang. It was Rice. She answered on the handsfree.

'Phil, go on.'

'Boss. We've got footage outside the primary school near the community centre. At quarter past six, Richard met with another boy. They did not head into the park. We've been unable to determine where they went next, but we do have an identification on the other boy. His name is Andrew Langsdale. He's two years younger than Richard, and still attending school.

'Address?'

Rice gave her the address. 'And you may want to tread lightly with this one boss. He's in care.'

'I always tread lightly,' Gardner said. 'Once again, good work, Phil.'

'Thanks, boss. And...'

'Go on?'

'Actually, it doesn't matter.'

'No, seriously, go on Phil!'

'Sorry for being a prick that always speaks his mind.'

Gardner smiled. *Seems I was wrong about you, and Marsh was right.*

'Sometimes, it's best to speak your mind.' *And sorry for ever thinking you were the leak.*

'Thanks boss.'

'Only sometimes, mind.'

'Heard loud and clear.'

After ending the call to Rice, she contacted Barnett. 'I need you to break the news to Hannah Winters about Tom.'

'Okay, boss.'

'Press for her movements over the last couple of days. We're running out of people with motive, and we've no idea where Neil is. If she raises your eyebrow even a fraction, call me immediately.'

'Will do, boss.'

Gardner hung up.

The situation felt desperate. The bodies were piling up, and they seemed to be bouncing from one suspect to another with no real joy.

She reached into her pocket for her tic tacs.

* * *

Expecting Andrew Langsdale to be in school, Gardner was taken aback when a young man answered the door.

She showed her badge. 'Andrew Langsdale?'

'Yes... Andy please.' He pushed his lank hair back over one ear.

'I'm DCI Emma Gardner; are either of your carers in?'

'No,' he said. 'They're both at work.'

She inwardly sighed. She had to be careful here.

She couldn't go interviewing a minor without an adult or solicitor present. 'That's a shame, I really need to talk to them. No school today?'

'Stomach's off.'

Gardner nodded. 'Know how that feels. Got a young daughter; she's forever bringing home stomach bugs.'

Andy nodded.

'Are you able to give me one of your carer's numbers – save me time?'

'Sure,' Andy said, reaching into his pocket for his phone. 'What's this about anyway?'

'Just need to talk to them. They're not in trouble or anything.'

Andy held out his phone, so Gardner could see the number of Helen Tibbot. She wrote it down in her notebook.

She looked up at Andy; he had a pale face, a dusting of acne and an athletic look about him.

'Is this about the Viaduct Killer?' Andy asked.

Gardner slipped her notebook in her pocket. 'Why do you ask?'

'It's all anyone ever talks about round here, and now the police are on my doorstep.'

'There are a million and one other reasons I could be on your doorstep, Andy – I wouldn't sweat it. What do you think about' – Gardner made quotation marks with her fingers – 'the Viaduct Killer?'

'Well, my boyfriend reckons it's all a lie.'

Gay, too, then. Could this boyfriend be Richard?

Gardner nodded.

'He reckons that kids from different gangs are just clocking each other.'

Gardner nodded.

'Is that true?' Andy asked.

Gardner shrugged. 'I can't possibly comment.' *And I've been talking to a minor alone for far too long, here.* 'Look, I'm just going to make a phone call. Was nice talking to you Andy.'

Andy regarded her for a minute with a confused look and then closed the door.

45

After finishing off his vodka, Riddick intercepted Barnett outside the Winters' home. He wiped a couple of heavy drops of rain from his forehead.

'Change of plan, Ray,' Riddick said. 'I'm going to speak to Hannah.'

Barnett eyed him suspiciously. 'The boss only just contacted me, sir.'

'And me. She was very clear – she asked me to do it.'

Barnett nodded. 'I suppose we could do it together then?'

'She wants all hands on deck in the search for Richard and Neil – could you head back to HQ?'

Barnett furrowed his brow.

'She was very clear about this too,' Riddick said. 'Problem, Ray?'

'No, sir.'

'Good man.'

He waited until Barnett had driven away before heading down Hannah's driveway. He rested his finger on the doorbell but didn't press it. The alcohol had given him enough courage to get this far, but not enough to take the plunge. He took a deep breath.

Get a grip, Paul. This is one thing you can give her back.

He pressed the doorbell.

Hannah opened the door. Her mouth fell open. Her head turned slowly from side to side. Riddick wasn't sure if it was an expression of disbelief, or a flat-out refusal to entertain his presence.

'What do *you* want?' Hannah asked.

Riddick looked down at the ground for a moment, took another deep breath, looked up and said, 'I'm sorry... I'm sorry for what I put you through.'

He paused, letting the weight of his words sink in.

It took a long time.

Eventually, she said, 'Thank you... I appreciate it.'

Riddick saw that she had tears in her eyes, before realising he did too. He wiped them away.

'I was so sorry to hear what you went through,' Hannah said.

Riddick nodded. 'Thank you. I do also need to speak to you about something. It's not good news, I'm afraid. I felt I owed it to you to deliver it.'

'What is it exactly?'

'Can I come in first? It's better if I do.'

46

After Gardner explained the severity of the situation, Andy's carer, Helen Tibbot, agreed to return home so Gardner could interview Andy in her presence. 'Is forty minutes okay?'

'That's fine.'

'Andy won't have harmed Richard... he *loves* him.'

Well, why's he not concerned that his boyfriend has been missing for twenty-four hours then? I mean, surely, he knows. Richard's parents have Knaresborough on full alert...

She looked at her watch, judged the time she had to be back to meet Helen and Andy, and went for a coffee. Along the way, she contacted Rice and asked for a thorough breakdown of Andy's background. *Why was he in care for a start?*

While she was nursing a coffee in Nero that would put a spring in an elephant's step, her phone rang.

Barry?

He never called during the day. In fact, he rarely called, full stop!

'Jesus, Em, why didn't you at least tell me he was out?'

Gardner stood, rocking the table and spilling coffee. 'What's happened?'

Eyes were on her in the café. She realised she was talking loudly. She headed for the exit.

'Your brother happened.'

She was out in the town square now, gulping air. 'Where're you?'

'Home. Safe, don't worry. But he came here…'

Jesus… No…

She realised she was hyperventilating, so she steadied herself against a bench, and took deep breaths. 'What happened?'

'Not much. He knocked on the door, asked after you, and when I told him you were working elsewhere, he turned away.'

'Okay… good. Maybe he got the message?'

'Oh, he got the message, all right, but he wasn't happy about it.'

'How do you know?'

'He stood over the road and watched the house for the best part of ten minutes. I couldn't see his expression from the window, but he wasn't smiling. Maybe he was waiting to see if you would make an appearance.'

A wave of nausea washed over her, and it took her a few moments to respond. 'He wants to intimidate us.'

'Well, it's working!'

Gardner pushed herself away from the bench. She felt a surge of adrenaline and realised that her terror was being replaced with anger. 'Listen, Barry, I didn't tell you, because I didn't want to believe it was an issue. It was only last night, when he called me, that I realised that there was more to this. He wants to see me. Why? I don't know. And frankly, I don't care.'

'You need to do something about this, Em. The man is

dangerous. I don't want him near any of us. Ana could tell I was scared. This can't happen again.'

'It won't. I'm phoning Mike. And if he can't help, I'm coming home.'

She hung up, suddenly feeling more isolated than she'd ever felt before.

47

Hannah Winters took the news regarding her husband well. 'Did he suffer?'

'I don't think so.'

'Will I need to identify him?'

'That won't be necessary,' Riddick said. He'd seen the state of Tom. It wasn't something Hannah needed to be subjected to. Dental records would suffice.

'He had his faults,' she said, staring into the distance with tears in her eyes, 'but, he was a good father. A very good father. He adored Kelsey. Absolutely adored her. And he couldn't find any peace after.'

Riddick allowed her some time to reflect. Eventually, she asked, 'Have you found peace, DI Riddick?'

'Paul, please,' he said, fighting back tears again. 'And no... no peace, yet.'

'You will,' Hannah said. 'You must. One day, you'll realise that finding peace is the best way to honour those you've lost. Without it, you can never enjoy your memories of them. So, you need peace in order to truly find them again.'

Riddick looked down at the table. Hannah sounded as if she was reciting from a self-help book, but he did see the truth in what she was saying. He nodded to show he was listening, and then went to change the subject. 'We need to eliminate you from our enquiries, Hannah. Purely a formality. I need to make a note of all your actions and whereabouts for the last couple of days.'

'Of course,' Hannah said, smiling. 'Anything you want. I've nothing to hide.'

Riddick made notes as Hannah gave him the details. 'Would you consent to DNA and fingerprints?'

'Of course.'

'Thanks,' Riddick said. 'I'll have that arranged. Do you know of anyone who disliked Tom, anyone that could cause him harm?'

'No. Not really,' Hannah said. 'He was genuinely a likeable man. Even after we grew apart, we still had a good relationship. In fact, it was better. We never really argued any more.'

'Were you aware that he hadn't returned to his job?'

Hannah shook her head. 'If I'd have known, I'd have said when DS Barnett was here.'

'Is there anything you can think of? You must think it strange how the two victims, Bradley and Dan, were Kelsey's bullies.' He stopped short of telling her about the letters engraved on their backs.

'Or a painful coincidence? Those boys were forever up to no good – this could have happened for many reasons.'

'You told DS Barnett that Bradley came to apologise to you?'

'Yes. He was a sensitive soul. A lot of pain. I forgave him, like I forgave you. There's a lot to be said for forgiveness. It gives you the peace I spoke of earlier.'

Riddick nodded. 'Did you ever meet Richard Hill?'

'No, I didn't,' Hannah said. 'Kelsey liked to have her secrets.

Richard was one of them. He broke it off with her because he claimed to be gay, and then joined in the online bullying. Who knows? One day, he may decide to apologise too.'

'Sorry, Hannah, how did you know about Richard if Kelsey kept it secret?'

'Ah.' Hannah looked away. 'Rumbled! I read it in her diary. You know, for months after I read it, I felt guilty. Dreadfully guilty. As if she was going to walk back through the door. Obviously I realise now how irrational that was. DI are you okay?'

No, he wasn't.

Riddick was on his feet now, pacing. It was either that or scream at the top of his lungs. 'A diary? She kept a diary!'

'Yes.'

'Why didn't we know about this before? Surely, it was relevant?'

'It was only months after the investigation that we discovered it. Hidden behind her wardrobe. After everything that happened, we didn't have the appetite to drag everything up again.'

Everything that happened...

Oh God, was all this going to turn out to be his fault... again?

If there was something in that diary that could have prevented these murders, would he be able to live with that? Riddick gulped. 'Where is it?'

'Upstairs.'

'Please can I take a look?'

Hannah looked uncertain. She stared over at the fireplace where there was a picture of Kelsey. She mustn't have been more than eleven or twelve. She looked smart in her school uniform, and her smile glowed.

'Please, Hannah,' Riddick said. 'We're convinced that these murders are connected somehow.'

Hannah nodded as if she'd heard her daughter speak;

Riddick didn't find this possibility too unrealistic considering his own experiences.

'If it helps bring an end to whatever is happening in Knaresborough, then Kelsey and I would be more than happy.'

48

After finishing her phone call to her good friend, DCI Michael Yorke, in Salisbury, Gardner opted not to go in and finish the coffee.

Her mind was a mess without setting it alight with caffeine.

'Don't worry, Emma. You finish your case. I'll handle this,' had been Yorke's final words – and they'd been sincere.

She held onto them. Yorke always had a way of promising security and protection even in the most challenging circumstances. And he always delivered on his promises.

Always.

She took a deep breath and stood up straight. It'd be okay. Her brother was posturing. Yorke would put him straight.

Now, where was I in the mess that is Operation Eden?

She looked over at the statue of Blind Jack with his surveyor's wheel.

Right now, I feel as blind as you, old man. Blind as a bloody bat.

She looked at the time on her watch. She needed to head off to speak to Andy Langsdale in the presence of his carer, Helen Tibbot.

Her phone rang. It was Rice.

'Phil?'

'Boss – Andy Langsdale is Tom Winters' *biological son*.'

Gardner started to shake all over again. Rice had certainly found a talent for pumping out game-changing revelations. 'Bloody hell.'

'Yep. Two years after Kelsey was born, Andy Langsdale was born to a Ruth Langsdale in Starbeck. She put Tom Winters on the birth certificate as the father.'

'If this is true... if Tom is the father... he cheated on Hannah. Did she know? She hasn't said anything. Andy's mother, Ruth, where's she now?'

'Died of leukaemia when Andy was eight. None of his living relatives would take him in – I assume that included Tom Winters – so he was taken into care.'

Gardner could feel it all coming together in her head. She paced, her eyes wide with disbelief. 'Does Andy know who his father is?'

'I don't know. I can tell you, though, that he bounced around a few homes before landing with the Tibbots. He's been with them for five years. Good kid by all accounts. Doesn't get in any bother.'

Gardner looked through the café window. She wondered now if that coffee would have been a good idea. Her brain felt suddenly like a swamp. She needed some focus.

'Andy has a father who rejected him... a father who's now dead.' Gardner paused. 'He has a half-sister who was bullied. A half-sister who's now dead. Add to this the dead bullies...'

'There's a pattern, sure,' Rice said.

'I'm going to his house now; get me some reinforcements there.' She felt her heart thrashing in her chest. 'This is it.' After

Rice had promised her reinforcements, she hung up and marched towards her car, enjoying a feeling of optimism she'd not felt for a while.

49

'Who's this "A" Kelsey keeps referring to?' Riddick pointed at the letter and flipped the diary around so Hannah could see it.

Hannah looked. 'To be honest, I really don't know. I remember reading it at the time and having the same reaction as you.'

Riddick shook his head – something didn't add up. 'Kelsey spent time with someone she only called A – you didn't think that was secretive and strange? Why didn't you flag it up with us?'

She glared at him. 'I told you before. Your investigation was long dead. And if you remember, we never thought it needed looking into – that was all down to you.'

Riddick flinched. *Good point. However, looking at this, maybe I was right, after all, and I was just looking in the wrong place. Maybe I should have kept bloody going and saved three lives.* He continued to read through the diary.

There were many references to "A":

Only A seems to understand me…

The concentration on A's face as he listens to me. Well, it's nice. More than nice actually…

After Richard's text, I didn't even expect to get out of bed today. But, well, A happened. He just has a way about him. I love being with him…

Obviously nothing can ever happen with A, it wouldn't be right, but he just makes me feel warmer, better somehow…

Riddick looked up at Hannah. 'I suspect Kelsey wanted to keep this person's identity secret from anyone who sneaked a look at her diary – you, or Tom, perhaps? Can you think of anyone that might be connected to you or Tom – someone called A?'

Hannah thought for a moment, but then shook her head. 'Sorry.'

Riddick continued reading.

It's a place we can spend time together, a place where we can relax from all the bastards around us…

Hold on, Riddick thought. *A place?* Up to now, he'd been skim reading at lightning speed… He re-read.

Ripley… an old hut…

'Did she ever mention visiting Ripley?' Riddick asked.

'No.'

He looked at her. 'So, you had no idea she was visiting Ripley and some kind of old hut with someone called A?'

Hannah raised an eyebrow. 'Are you judging me again, Paul?'

'No… not at all. I just want to clarify it. I'm trying my best to jog your memory.'

Riddick turned the page and saw a printout from a map. *Bingo.* It zoomed into the area surrounding Ripley and its castle. A cross had been drawn onto the map – deep in the woodland, close to a farmland on an old mill he recognised.

He turned and showed her the map. 'You must have seen this?'

'She always liked Ripley... or maybe it was the ice cream she liked. We used to take her often when she was younger.'

Riddick stood. 'Can I borrow this, Hannah? I'll return it.'

She looked hesitant, but then cast another look in the direction of her daughter's photograph on the fireplace, and nodded. 'Okay... Can I ask why?'

'Well, because X marks the spot?'

'But what spot?'

'At this point, Hannah, your guess is as good as mine.'

50

Gardner arrived at the Tibbot household before any reinforcements, so she called them off.

Andy Langsdale had gone.

Helen Tibbot was shaken and pale. 'He's taken the second car. He's *never* done anything like this before.'

'When?'

'I don't know. I arrived back five minutes ago. The keys and the car were gone.'

'Type of car and registration please, Mrs Tibbot?'

'What's he done?'

'Please, ma'am, we may not have time.'

'A black Toyota Yaris,' she said, following it up with a registration number.

Gardner phoned it in, and then turned back to Helen. 'Have you any idea where he might have gone?'

Helen thought about it, and then shook her head. 'I'm sorry... He was sick this morning – his stomach. He was pale, and genuinely seemed under the weather. Look, Andy's a *good* boy.

He really is. Whatever you think he's done, you must be wrong. He hasn't a bad bone in his body.'

Realising that there was nothing she could do until she learned Andy's whereabouts, or the APW hit home, Gardner decided that now was as good a time as any to ask questions. 'Please may I come in, Mrs Tibbot?'

'Yes... of course.'

Inside, in the lounge, Gardner waved away the offer of a hot drink, and went straight into it. She gave the date and time window of Bradley's murder. 'Do you know where Andy was at this time?'

She thought for a moment. 'Yes... he was out. He was on a date with Richard. We were quite annoyed when he got back after twelve – he'd promised to come back at ten. It was out of character, but he's sixteen, you know, so grounding him seemed ridiculous. So, we had an adult discussion over it, and he promised not to do it again. He's aware of the huge responsibility we have regarding his well-being; he was apologetic. Like I said, he has a good heart.'

Gardner was making notes with a trembling hand. She was already predicting David and Joanne Hill's response when she quizzed them over Richard's whereabouts on that night – *Richard wasn't out that night, or if he was, he certainly wasn't out on a date!*

Andy Langsdale was in the frame for Bradley's murder.

'And last night?' Gardner said.

'He came back here after another date with Richard.'

'What time was that?'

'Nine-thirty. Unsurprisingly, he was very punctual this time!'

'And did he go out again?'

'No. He went to bed at around ten. He usually does on a school night.'

'And what time did you look in on him?'

'He's sixteen, we don't look in on him!'

'So, the last time you saw him was at ten?'

'Yes.'

'And what time did you and your husband go to bed?'

'Ten thirty.'

'Could he have left the house without you hearing him?'

She sighed and nodded. 'We both snore, so we wear earplugs. It's possible. Listen, if you are trying to link Andy to these horrible murders, you've got it wrong... you *really* have.'

Gardner nodded to show she appreciated Helen's concerns. 'Do you know anything about Andy's birth parents?'

'Yes... from Andy himself, actually. That information wasn't given to us by the council. His dad is Tom Winters. When he told us, we did think it strange that they placed him in a home so near to his birth father, but according to Andy, they'd never even met, so I guess that it wasn't considered a significant factor.'

'Did Andy ever attempt to contact his father?'

'Not that I'm aware of. He knew that his father never wanted anything to do with him.'

And so was very bitter towards this man? Resentful enough to kill him?

Tom's death wasn't public knowledge yet. Incredibly, they'd managed to keep this from the hounds; this wouldn't last long.

'Was Andy aware that he'd a half-sister?'

Helen flinched. She was starting to worry now. A picture was being painted of the boy in her care – it was only a matter of time before she saw the links herself.

'Yes,' Helen said. There was tremble in her voice. 'Kelsey Winters.'

'And did he try to make contact with Kelsey?'

Tears welled in Helen's eyes. She nodded. 'They were at the same school. They became friends.'

Gardner felt as if a hand had closed around her heart and started squeezing.

'Totally inappropriate, considering the situation, I know,' Helen said. 'But what can you do? Andy shouldn't have been placed so close.'

Stretched budgets, and people stretched on time – unfortunately, oversights like this were much too commonplace.

'So, they spent a lot of time together?'

'I think so. You know it broke him, don't you? Her suicide. *It broke him.*'

Yes, I know, Gardner thought. *It's clear as day now. Knowing Tom Winters was his father, he sought out his half-sister, Kelsey. They formed a bond as only siblings could.*

She thought of Jack, her own sibling. *Maybe not all siblings...*

'Do you think Tom was aware that Andy was his biological son?' Gardner asked.

'According to Andy, not a clue, even though they've met. I mean how would he? He won't know what he looks like. I suppose if he heard the name Langsdale, he could put two and two together – but he obviously never has. I know how it sounds, but what do you do? I did let the council know, but it took them ages to get back with a solution – by that point, Kelsey was gone.' She lowered her head.

There it was again. Stretched budget, and people stretched on time. The cause of many a tragedy.

'Did you know that Richard Hill was one of Kelsey's bullies?' Gardner asked.

Helen looked stunned. 'Really? He seems such a nice boy. Are you sure?'

Gardner briefly wondered if Helen was the type of person who struggled to see anything but the positive in anyone. 'I'm afraid so. Alongside the main two bullies, Dan Lotus and Bradley Hill.'

She put a hand to her mouth. 'Victims of the Viaduct Killer?' Her eyes darted left and right. 'No, surely not?' She slumped back in her chair. She now understood what Gardner understood – this was more than just a coincidence.

'Richard's missing, Helen.'

'*Oh God!* Andy wouldn't... surely, no... he *wouldn't*. He's just too tender... too sweet. You should have seen the way he cared for Kel. He looked out for her, was desperate to—'

'Sorry, what did you call her?'

'Her nickname. Kel. At least the nickname Andy had for her. Why?'

Because E was carved into Bradley Taylor's back. L was carved into Dan Lotus' back.

K was obviously reserved for Richard Hill.

51

Riddick parked near Ripley Castle. He looked up at an imposing tower while he chased down two painkillers with the dregs of his Sprite bottle. He held his hand in the air. No sign of the shakes, but he'd need a refill before the day was through.

He examined the map in the diary, solidified the route in his mind and took a photo on his mobile phone for good measure. The diary was precious to Hannah. He didn't want to risk damaging it, and so opted to keep it in the car.

It was a good decision.

As soon as he stepped from his vehicle, the sky burst. It only took the rain a couple of seconds to plaster his hair to his forehead and glue his shirt to his skin.

He looked at the boot of his car where he kept a large umbrella for such occasions. He sighed. That would be too little too late.

He marched through the torrential downpour towards the bike path that led away from the castle.

Drenched, Riddick had to trek a fair distance down the bike

path to draw level with the patch of woodland and old mill marked on Kelsey's map.

Even under the weight of heavy rain, the area was recognisable to him. Riddick had been a scout at the age of fourteen, and Ripley had been his stomping ground.

Blinded by the rain, he was proud of himself for scaling the wooden fence. Unfortunately, he only managed two steps before slipping and going arse over tit.

'Bloody hell,' he shouted at the top of his lungs. No one would hear him over the sound of heavy rain. He stood up, shaking himself off, although what he hoped to shake off, he'd no idea.

He targeted the trees ahead, sensing relief from the torrents beneath the canopy. He broke into a jog, increasing the tempo of the squelching in his shoes.

When he reached the trees, and the canopy sheltered him, he slipped his mobile from his pocket; predictably, the phone was damp, but had been spared the soaking by his trouser pocket. He went through to his photos and examined the map again, checking he was orientating himself accurately. The hut was about midway into the patch of forest, off to the left, facing towards the old mill.

He continued.

Above him, the sound of the rain on the canopy was deafening. A breeze wormed its way through the trees, sending him into a cold shiver. 'What the bloody hell am I doing?'

At least the painkillers were getting to work on the back of his head.

He must have been walking almost five minutes before the rain subsided. It was remarkable how quickly the crashing sound was replaced with a gentle pitter-patter.

Up ahead, he heard a cry of pain.

Someone's here? Really? Is it the mysterious A?

He started to run, reassured by the sound of the bracken and undergrowth crunching underfoot as that was what kept him from slipping.

He heard a second cry. Louder this time. He was getting closer.

Was this A being hurt? Or was he the one doing the hurting?

Another cry.

He tracked the sound to a small, decrepit hut.

His heart thrashed in his chest. Someone was in trouble in there.

As he approached, he reached into his pocket again, realising that he needed backup.

And then, to his everlasting shame, he went arse over tit for the second time in less than ten minutes.

This one knocked the wind right out of him. It also subjected him to a blinding flash that reminded him of the previous night when someone had taken a brick to the back of his head.

He sat upright, rubbing at his forehead, staring angrily at the trunk of a tree which had clocked him one—

'Help me!'

No time to take stock of your injuries! He rose to his feet, recalling that he was in the process of calling for backup. He looked down at the bracken and undergrowth that rose up from the ground, half-submerging his feet.

Where the hell is my phone—

'Please, help!'

Forget the phone.

Riddick sprinted to the little wooden hut, keeping a wary eye on the ground. He didn't fancy a third bang to the head. And in his experience, everything always came in threes.

He reached the side of the hut and pressed his hands against the damp wood.

There was another pained cry.

The hut was about five metres long if that, and it wasn't in the best nick. The wood was rotten, and it crumbled against his hand as he worked his way around the side.

He suspected it'd been erected by the owner of the old mill ahead, long before it went out of business. Maybe it had been used for storage?

He turned around the side of the hut, not sure if he'd meet the front or rear of the enclosure.

It was the front, and the door was missing.

Riddick put his hand to his mouth.

Inside the hut, a young man, missing his shirt, lay on his side. His hands were tied, as were his legs. The small of his back was bloody.

'Richard?'

'Yes... please, help me, before he comes back! *Help!*'

Riddick moved quickly into the empty hut and dropped to his knees behind Richard. The bottom of his back was indeed bloody, and it appeared that the letter K had been carved there.

K – E – L

Yes... it fitted...

As Riddick worked at the ropes around Richard's wrists, he looked down at his pale face. 'You're okay, Richard, I'm with the police.'

Richard's eyes were wide and full of tears, and many nerves on his face twitched. He'd had a gag in his mouth but had managed to force it out of his mouth; it clung tightly to his chin.

'Hold on, Richard, not long now, hold on for me...' The ropes were a bastard. The knot was so tight. He reached to the ropes binding the legs and identified the same problem there too. 'We need to cut through these... I need to find my phone outside and—'

'Who're you?' someone asked behind Riddick.

Riddick turned his head.

A tall, broad young man stood there, wearing a glistening yellow raincoat with the hood pulled up. He had a mallet in one hand.

Riddick narrowed his eyes. 'Police—'

The boy swung the mallet.

The world suddenly on fire, Riddick slumped to his side. He'd been right about things coming in threes. He rolled onto his back. He saw the boy was raising the mallet again.

'Stop—'

Make that four.

The mallet came crashing down and everything went black.

52

'What do you mean he went to speak to Hannah?' Gardner said, pacing around her vehicle in the Tibbot's driveway with her mobile to her ear. 'Do you have any idea how ridiculous that is, Ray? The woman accused him of ruining her life less than two years ago – why would he do that?'

She thought about earlier when Riddick had taken her to the chapel to tell her the truth about his family. Maybe today was his day for getting his affairs in order – including his apology to the Winters family.

'I'm sorry, boss. I know. He pulled the rank card though,' Barnett said.

'Why didn't you call me?'

'I thought about it, but I worried you wouldn't appreciate having your time wasted. He kept talking about how you wanted everyone focused on—'

'You could have shown some bloody common sense, Ray!'

She pulled the phone away from her ear as the frustration surged through her. After taking a deep breath, she decided that tearing apart Barnett, who'd done a stellar job up until now, was pointless. Riddick had pulled rank. It happened.

'Okay, it's done, Ray. Let's move on. *Shit. Shit.* I've rung him five times and he's not picking up. I'll go to Hannah's and get him or, at the very least, find out what bloody damage he's caused!'

* * *

Gardner parked in Hannah's driveway. The phone rang. It was the chief constable.

'ANPR has found the Tibbot's Toyota Yaris parked outside Ripley Castle,' Marsh said. 'I've got a team on its way there now. Are you certain Andy Langsdale is the killer, Emma?'

'Yes, and he's dangerous.'

'Not for much longer. Custody awaits. Well done.'

Save your thank-yous – we don't bloody have him yet, ma'am!

Gardner ended the call. Hannah opened her door and walked out. She was crossing her arms against the cold. Since the sudden rainfall moments ago, the humidity had eased, and the temperature had plummeted.

Gardner stepped from the vehicle. 'Mrs Winters. Is DI Riddick here?'

'No. He left a while back.'

Shit. Where the hell are you, Paul? 'I'm sorry that DI Riddick came here—'

'Don't be. We turned a corner.'

Gardner raised an eyebrow. *Wow – you're more forgiving than I could ever be.* 'Okay, I see. He's dropped off my radar. Could you tell me what you talked about?'

Hannah explained that Riddick had read about someone called A in the diary.

'I think A stands for Andy,' Gardner said. 'Her best friend.

And also, her half-brother.' She tried to keep the judgemental tone out of her voice, but the stare she fixed her with probably gave it away.

Hannah touched her chest. Her next breath was audible.

'You knew she had a half-brother, didn't you?' Gardner said.

'I knew he existed; I didn't know he lived around here, and I certainly didn't know my daughter was friends with him – she was secretive, you know... especially in her final months.' She looked away and shivered. 'I made some mistakes... I was a different woman back then. When my husband had that affair, Kelsey was only two. I gave Tom an ultimatum: either he turned his back on this other woman, and that child – or he'd lose me and Kelsey. Looking back, I left that boy without a father, didn't I? How monstrous of me... Am I in some way responsible for my daughter's death?' She touched her chest again, and her body wavered.

'No, I don't think so. Andy and Kelsey were best friends by all accounts.'

'Yes... and in the diary, Kelsey said he supported her when she was being bullied.'

Gardner nodded. 'Makes sense. I think what happened to your daughter had a traumatic impact on him too. He loved her.'

'Do you think Andy is this Viaduct Killer?'

'I can't comment on that—'

'And Tom! God, did he murder his father?'

'Again, I'm not in a position to comment. What else did Riddick read about in the diary?'

'He read about a hut that Hannah and A – sorry Andy – used to hang out in.'

'Where's that then?'

'Hard to describe. There was a map marked with a cross. In Ripley.'

Gardner felt as if she'd taken a heavy blow to the stomach. Andy had just abandoned his carers' Toyota Yaris in Ripley.

'Ripley? DI Riddick went to Ripley?'

'I think so. Yes.'

Gardner reached into her pocket for her mobile phone; her hand was trembling. 'Where in Ripley?'

'I'm not—'

'*Think*, Mrs Winters... please *think*.'

'Near an old mill. In a small patch of woods, I think... I don't know anything else... I'm sorry...'

'I've got to go, Mrs Winters, thanks.'

As Gardner climbed into the car, she phoned Marsh back. 'Ma'am, Paul is in danger. He discovered the location of a place Andy and Kelsey used to hang out in Ripley. An old hut. If Andy is in Ripley, chances are he's in that hut. We need to track Paul's mobile. It's switched on, because it's ringing – it's not going straight to voicemail.' Gardner reversed out of Hannah's driveway with the phone pinned between her ear and shoulder.

'Okay, leave it with me. Where're you going?'

'Up to Ripley. As soon as you have the location of his phone, text me a pin.'

53

Riddick opened his eyes, and he felt the whiplash of fear in his stomach.

He couldn't see anything.

I'm blind...

He blinked.

You've bloody blinded me...

He continued blinking... and then he could see again. It had been the blood on his forehead getting into his eyes. He was lying on his front—

Shit. He couldn't move his arms because his wrists were tied! He attempted to move his feet but had the same problem – his ankles were bound.

Richard Hill moaned in pain. Riddick turned his head towards the sound. The lad in the yellow rain jacket who'd clocked the DI was down on his haunches, looking at Richard up close.

Riddick wondered, briefly, if anyone would be able to find him before the unthinkable unfolded in this hut. His mobile phone was lying in the undergrowth outside, and his colleagues *could* track his signal. Except—

They probably had no clue he was even missing...

There was always the hope that Barnett had taken offence at being ordered away from Hannah's by an unhinged superior and complained to Gardner. It was reasonable – Riddick did have a habit of making waves.

He concluded that his best bet would be to keep the lad talking, until help arrived. And, looking at the sadness on the boy's face, sensitivity was certainly the order of the day.

Kind of shit, really, as sensitivity certainly wasn't a strong point of Riddick.

'This is over,' Riddick said.

'I know,' the lad said, looking at Riddick, before looking down at Richard. 'Almost.'

Richard, who'd been gagged again, moaned. Not surprising. His back had been carved up.

Riddick blinked more blood out of his eyes. 'Are you A?'

'Sorry?'

'A. That's what Kelsey called you. In her diary.'

At the mention of Kelsey, the lad looked down at the ground. He was wavering and looked on the verge of tears. He held it together though and, eventually, he looked back up. 'A must stand for my name – Andy. Kel was my sister, you know?'

No. I didn't know that. Riddick's head was racing. 'Sister?'

'Half-sister, actually. Tom Winters was my birth father,' Andy said with a shrug. 'We were the same, me and Kel. Never met anyone I got on with more – and I've met quite a few people. You do when you're bounced from house to house, as I've been, since my mam died.'

Tom Winters was Andy's birth father? Riddick's mind whirred.

Richard moaned again.

Riddick managed to roll onto his back, and then raised himself up into a sitting position. 'I'm sorry for your loss, Andy. Life knows how to deal out shit—'

'And what do you know about *shit*?' Andy glared at him.

Riddick raised an eyebrow, causing his head to throb all over. 'More than most, son… unfortunately. You can trust me on that.'

'I don't trust anyone. Apart from Kel… but she's gone.'

Riddick could see the tears in his eyes.

'Andy,' Riddick said, feeling as if his head was going to split open from all the recent damage it had sustained. 'I'm here to help in any way I can.'

'Help me? It's too late. You just want me back in your system. No, this ends' – he looked at Richard – 'now.'

Richard moaned.

Riddick shook his head. 'This isn't your only option—'

'Look at him.' Andy smiled at Richard. 'Look at the surprise in his pretty eyes. He loved me. He thought I loved him. Do you realise how far I've had to go to make this work?' Andy's expression changed to disgust. 'Sleeping with the enemy.'

Richard squeezed his eyes closed, and gave a quiet, pained sob.

'Crocodile tears,' Andy said. 'You don't deserve love, Richard. Not after what you did to Kel. Just like Bradley and Dan, there's only one thing you deserve.'

'Did you kill your birth father, Tom Winters?' Riddick asked.

Andy looked over at Riddick. He appeared surprised. 'He's dead?'

'Yes… and it was no accident.'

Andy looked away, shaking his head. 'I didn't know…' He sighed, and stared at the roof for a moment. 'Maybe he deserved it too… but no… I didn't kill him. I wouldn't. I hated him… yet Kel adored him, so I'd never betray her by doing *that*.'

So, if you didn't kill him, who did?

The news of Tom's death had spooked Andy. He continued to stare up at the roof, shaking his head from side to side. He also still had the mallet in one hand. Riddick didn't fancy coming up against it again – his head had already been used as a piñata enough today! He had to defuse this as soon as possible. 'You know they're coming here. My colleagues. It won't be long?'

Andy said, 'I searched you. There's no phone. How could they possibly find you?'

Riddick thought back to his phone outside in the undergrowth, and prayed to God – despite the fact that He'd never been of any use to him before – that the undergrowth, wet from rainfall, hadn't switched it off. There needed to be an active signal.

'Help me understand,' Riddick said, wanting to delay the inevitable as long as possible. 'Kelsey was your half-sister, Tom your birth father – how has all this come about?'

'You mean you don't know by now?' Andy said. 'Your colleague – that woman… DCI Gardner, I think… came to my home looking for Richard. She must have looked up my background?'

Did Gardner know? More hope flooded through him. If she'd identified this Andy, she could very well be on her way.

'Tom Winters had an affair with my mother, and then didn't want to know me when I was born.' To the backdrop of Richard's sobs, punctuated by the occasional cries of pain, Andy told Riddick of his origins: the death of his mother from leukaemia, his years in care, his return to Knaresborough… 'When I returned here, life was good for a time. I had wonderful carers. I *have* wonderful carers. I knew about Kel from my mother – she told me before she died. Kel, of course, had no idea I existed. I reached out to her… As I said before, we hit it off like a house on fire. Probably because we were both so damaged. Suffering joins people together.'

'By suffering, do you mean the bullying?' Riddick said. 'I thought that was a recent thing. Up until the bullying, Kelsey had a good life, didn't she? Her parents adored her, she was flying at school... What suffering are you actually referring to?'

'You really want to know?'

'Yes.'

'There are some things you can't unhear but wish you could.'

'Tell me.'

Afterwards, Riddick felt sick to his stomach. 'That's awful. Jesus, that's awful.'

'Yes. So, you see when she heard that Bradley and Dan *knew* of the things she'd been forced to do, and were threatening to *expose* her... well, what option did she have? She couldn't live with what was coming – so she took the only way out. Bradley, Dan and Richard were merely the final straw in a long period of suffering. Unfortunately for these boys, *I* am their final straw.'

'This happened years ago,' Riddick said. 'Why now? Why didn't you just get them back straight after it happened?'

'I wanted to, believe me. But something held me back. Maybe it was my young age. Maybe it was the hope that this was just grief, and the desire to hurt them would subside. But, if anything, it grew stronger. Recently, these bastards turned eighteen, and I watched from afar how they were beginning to enjoy adulthood. Their freedoms, the money, their girlfriends, their drug use. They chose their paths and revelled in them. Richard planned to go to Oxford University, so again, look at what adulthood has offered to him! My pain on seeing them reach this milestone, just brought all my rage bubbling back to the surface. Because do you know who else would have been eighteen and choosing a path?' He slapped Richard on the forehead. 'I couldn't cope any more.

Kelsey's path was taken from her; so, I've taken their paths from them. Especially yours, Richard. Yes. You're the worst of the lot. She loved you. *Desperately* loved you. And you couldn't find it in your heart to save her, or in the very least, support her. Instead, you chose the worst of all options.' He kicked him again. 'You joined in with those devils and tormented her.'

Andy rose from his haunches, leaned over and slipped his hands under Richard's arms. 'Stand up!'

Richard's ankles were bound, but Andy was a strong, athletic lad, and so managed to get him upright.

Andy pressed himself to the back of his trembling captive, seemingly unconcerned about the blood transferring onto his yellow raincoat.

Richard, his eyes filled with tears, looked to his right where Riddick was sitting up.

'Listen, Andy,' Riddick said. 'I know how far you've come, but it's never too late to stop. We can help—'

Andy curled his right arm around Richard's throat and placed his left hand to the back of his victim's head, making Richard's eyes widen.

'Andy, stop!' Riddick said. Knowing there was no time, he shuffled backwards until he was at the wall of the hut, and used it to work his way up to his feet.

Andy dragged Richard back towards the exit in a firm sleeper hold. Because Richard was unable to move his hands, he looked like a dangling wooden puppet in his strong assailant's headlock. The heels of his tied feet were already sliding against the hut floor.

Unable to walk because of the ropes, Riddick started to take little hops forward. He was seized by adrenaline, and desperation, so it ended, inevitably, with him down on his knees. He looked up at the young man, dubbed the Viaduct Killer, taking another life. 'Stop Andy, he doesn't deserve this.'

Andy reached the opening where the door had once stood. Richard was still trying to breathe, and keep hold of his life, but his colour was changing quickly.

'She wouldn't have wanted this.' Riddick knew this was his last chance. 'Kelsey wouldn't have wanted this.'

'How would you know? You *never* knew her,' hissed Andy, dragging his dying victim through the doorway—

Riddick's mobile phone started to ring. His eyes darted to the wooden wall, in its direction – outside in the undergrowth.

He then looked back at the surprise on Andy's face and hissed, 'They're coming.'

Andy released Richard, who collapsed to his knees, and onto his front. He was still moving, and Riddick hoped it wasn't just the twitching that accompanied death.

Andy ran outside. Riddick could hear him in the undergrowth, rustling around, shouting, 'Where is it? Where the hell is it?'

Then, Riddick sighed with relief when Richard rolled onto his back, gulping for air, before hearing Gardner's voice outside. 'Andy Langsdale, you're under arrest...'

Paul Riddick closed his eyes and sighed again.

54

Andy was cuffed and led away through the forest by two uniformed officers. The other two officers who'd accompanied Gardner were in the hut, keeping Richard company until the paramedics arrived.

Gardner showed Riddick the map on the phone, the red pin indicating this precise location.

'Thank God, I dropped the phone,' Riddick said, 'Otherwise, well, he'd have had a hat trick.'

'He was already up to three,' Gardner said. 'You're forgetting Tom?'

Riddick fixed her with a stare. 'He didn't kill Tom.'

'Did he tell you that?'

'Yes. And he was telling the truth.'

'How do you know? Tom treated his lad like shit – he left him with his mother, and after she passed, allowed him to go into care!'

'I know, but he'd never have harmed Tom. Kelsey adored their father. And everything he did was motivated by her.'

Gardner shook her head and looked away to hide her disappointment. She'd been convinced it was all over. Another killer? Not what she needed right now, not with her sociopathic brother lingering in the shadows.

'So,' Riddick said, rolling his shoulders, 'that leaves us with whatever turns up at Tom's house and Sands' post-mortem findings—'

'No,' Gardner spat. 'It leaves you getting medical attention when the paramedics arrive.'

Riddick flinched. Maybe she'd been too aggressive, but Christ, was she disappointed with this sudden lack of closure.

'I'm fine,' Riddick said. 'In fact, I'm more than fine. I'm chomping at the bit.'

'No... you're not thinking straight, Paul – your head has taken more blows than a cricket ball.'

He tapped his forehead with his knuckles, careful to avoid the bruises and cuts. 'And it's all the tougher for it.'

'You're black and blue and covered in blood. I'm not letting you do anything until you've had an x-ray—'

'Then, I'm going rogue,' he said, marching into the trees.

Gardner opened her mouth to call after him. She considered the vodka she'd found in the Sprite bottle but knew this was neither the time nor the place. However, she still needed to challenge him. 'Now, what could possibly inspire you to shatter our newly formed, albeit still rather fragile, relationship?'

Riddick turned. 'Because of something else that boy just told me in there.'

'Do share.'

Riddick paused, leaned against a trunk, looked down, took a deep breath, and then shared.

Gardner steadied herself against the trunk of an adjacent tree. 'Didn't see that coming.'

'Neither did I, and I had to hear that from a mallet-wielding psycho.'

'I mean, surely not?' She reached into her pocket for tic tacs.

Riddick shrugged. 'Can I continue going rogue please?'

'Okay, but I'm coming with you.'

55

Following the results of the search of Tom's home, and a meeting with Dr Hugo Sands regarding the body, Riddick told Gardner he was off to the hospital.

She gave that her firm seal of approval.

Then, Riddick got in a taxi and went to Anders' house instead, stopping at a Tesco en route for a half-litre bottle of vodka. An ageing taxi driver eyed him in the rear-view mirror as he swigged from it.

'Been one of those days?' The driver asked with a grin.

'Has felt like *one of those days* for over two years now.'

'Like *Groundhog Day*?'

'Good film,' Riddick said, taking another swig, trying to remember if, and how, Bill Murray got himself out of that dire situation.

The taxi driver tried to talk to him some more, but Riddick shrugged him off. The alcohol was doing a stand-up job in terms of dissipating his anxiety, but he was as far from a good mood as he could possibly get.

He left the dregs of the vodka in the taxi. 'For you, buddy. My friend has a problem with my drinking.'

'Are you okay, son?' the taxi driver asked.

'Do you know how many times I've been asked that in the last two years?' Riddick asked with a smirk.

The driver looked confused, but then said, '*Groundhog Day*?'

'Exactly,' Riddick said.

He headed up Anders' driveway and pounded on his door.

The large British-born Scandinavian opened the door, shaking his head over the sight of his former colleague. 'You should be sleeping that off.'

'The medicine has it covered,' Riddick said.

'Painkillers or alcohol?'

Riddick shrugged. 'You got a minute?'

'For you, I've always a minute, and more,' Anders said, moving to one side.

Riddick grunted as he entered Anders' home.

'Shouldn't you be in a good mood?' Anders asked from behind him. 'You've put the Viaduct Killer under lock and key.'

'Don't call him that,' Riddick said. 'He never killed on a bloody viaduct, and he was just a child for pity's sake. A mixed-up kid, not a delusional serial killer.'

'I see,' Anders said, closing the front door. 'You aren't in a playful mood, then?'

Riddick ignored him and went to sit in Anders' kitchen – he'd been here on many occasions.

'I'd offer you a drink,' his former boss said from the kitchen doorway, 'it may help with your dour mood... but you know I keep nothing here.'

'No amount of alcohol is going to cut through this mood,' Riddick said, 'but I'll take a soft drink.'

Anders walked past Riddick, using his walking stick for

support. 'Only Diet Coke, I'm afraid. You've not even got a sugar rush to look forward to.' He opened the fridge and reached in.

'Already made up my mind to knock the drinking on the head anyway,' Riddick said.

'Bloody hell,' Anders cried. 'How hard did he hit you? If I'd known sense could have been knocked into you, I'd have saved myself a lot of time trying to talk you round!'

'It's time to reassess my life.'

'God has been listening to my prayers!' Anders said, putting the can of Diet Coke down in front of Riddick.

'This is nothing to do with God, Anders. This is to do with something much closer to home,' Riddick said, opening the can.

'Well,' Anders said, propping his cane up against the table and sitting down opposite him. 'Church and God can wait. You'll come round to its virtues. Anyway, back to the reassessment of your life. Which aspects in particular?'

'I'm reassessing friendships.' Riddick reached over for Anders' cane with his right hand, and then twirled it on the floor.

Anders narrowed his eyes as he glanced between Riddick and the twirling cane.

'Feels sturdy,' Riddick said.

'Yes... cost me an arm and a leg, but it'll never break. Good wood, *treated* wood. So, friendships, you say? What do you mean?'

Riddick felt the corner of his lip twitch. 'I'm reassessing who I can trust.'

Anders nodded. 'I hear you, Padawan. I remember my days back in that place – there were a few untrustworthy souls back then too, I can tell you. Who've you got your beady eye on?'

Riddick spun the cane. He sucked in his bottom lip to stop it from shaking.

'Are you all right, Paul?'

Riddick took a deep breath. 'It seems Kelsey Winters had more of a history than we realised.'

'Kelsey?' Anders gave a brief shake of his head. 'Why're you dwelling on her? I get she was part of the case, but your days of obsessing over the girl need to be confined to the past—'

'There are things about her that her parents didn't know.' Riddick raised an eyebrow. 'Things about her she *wouldn't want* her parents to know about.'

'Well, a lot of fifteen-year-old girls have secrets.'

Riddick looked hard at Anders before finally speaking. 'Is making pornography a common secret among fifteen-year-old girls?'

Anders blanched. He placed his large hands on the table. He shook his head vigorously so his bulbous cheeks shook. 'No... I don't believe it.'

Riddick sighed. 'Shocking, eh?' He twirled the cane.

'No, I really don't believe it. Here? In Knaresborough, it's not—'

'No, it's true, all right,' Riddick said. 'Andy Langsdale told me...'

'Told you?' Anders rolled his eyes. 'Told you what? Wasn't that kid crazy?'

'She was fourteen at the time, Anders. She met someone online. *And she was groomed.*'

Anders waved him away with a big hand. 'Groomed? I knew the Winters family. No way they were letting her chat away to any chuffin' strangers online.'

Riddick took a large mouthful of Diet Coke and watched Anders.

'I don't want you buying into the rantings of a desperate kid, Paul,' Anders said.

Riddick placed the can down. 'There's more. Can I go on?'

'If you must, but I'm worried, Paul, I'm—'

'She was groomed by a nineteen-year-old man called Charlie Rigby.'

Anders took a deep breath, blanched again and looked down at the table with widened eyes.

'Do you remember Charlie Rigby?' Riddick asked.

'Is the question rhetorical?' Anders said, still looking down.

'Just answer the quest—'

'You know damn well I do!' Anders said, looking up, his cheeks now starting to flush. 'As do you Paul. What in Christ's name are you getting at here?'

Riddick glared at his former boss. 'You tell me. It seems your memory is letting you down.'

'Nicknamed "Goodtime Charlie", worked for Neil, died of a drug overdose – how's my memory doing?'

'Patchy.'

'Where are you going with this? Have you forgotten who I am? I'm your friend, not some goddamned sleazeball on the other side of your interrogation table!'

'I told you I was reassessing friendships.'

'You're *absolutely* losing your mind is what you're doing!'

'Charlie Rigby made and distributed pornography. Some of which included young girls. One of those girls was Kelsey Winters.'

Anders slumped back in his chair, shaking his head. 'I'd have known. I knew everything that was going on in Knares—'

'Because you were tight with Neil?'

Anders leaned forward and poked the table. 'Okay. I see what this is about now. You're still pissed off about the other night? However, don't you see? This is a perfect example of why I kept Neil close – it was better to know what a bastard like that was up to, rather than stumble around in the dark, clueless – like most of the bloody idiots I ever worked with.'

'So you knew about the pornography?'

'Of course not... and I don't believe it either.'

'Well believe it. I've seen some of it.' Riddick drained the can of Diet Coke. He banged it down on the table. 'On Tom Winters' computer.'

Anders' eyes widened. He opened his mouth, but no words emerged.

Riddick continued. 'It was just as Andy said. Charlie Rigby groomed her, and while he was abusing her, filmed it.'

Anders looked down, shaking his head. 'Disgusting. How could he? How could anyone? I'm sickened.'

Riddick stood, and still holding the cane, went over to the fridge. He opened it and looked back at Anders. 'May I have a Perrier?'

'Yes, of course,' Anders said.

Riddick pulled a bottle of Perrier out of the fridge and walked back to the table. He sat down, placed the Perrier in front of him, but didn't unscrew it. He was still holding the cane.

'How did Tom get hold of the pornography, I wonder?' Anders asked, scrunching up his face, signalling his disgust.

'Well, it's readily available on the internet on certain sites,' Riddick said, twirling the cane. 'Sites that charge the consumer money. I guess a man obsessed with the circumstances behind his daughter's suicide might one day find some information to send him down that path?'

'Awful,' Anders said. 'Charlie was a despicable individual... What a thing for Tom to have seen. It must have been frustrating for Tom that Charlie was no longer around to confront.'

'I doubt Charlie was the only one involved.'

Anders raised an eyebrow. 'You suspect someone else?'

'Well, someone killed Tom… and it couldn't have been Charlie. He's dead.'

'Andy, the abandoned son, killed him! I thought the case was closed!'

'We ruled Andy out of Tom's murder.'

Anders guffawed. 'On what grounds?'

'On the grounds that he couldn't have done it. He was at school, registered in his classroom.'

Anders stood. 'Shit. You've been busy. I think I'll grab a drink—'

'Please sit down, Anders,' Riddick said, pushing the bottle of Perrier over. 'I haven't touched it.'

Anders sat. His face was blotchy.

Riddick continued. 'We followed the money from the pornography websites. Guess who makes money out of selling this pornography? Who is *still* making money?'

Anders shrugged. He avoided eye contact.

'Neil.'

'Okay.' Anders nodded, but still didn't meet Riddick's eyes. 'That bastard. Stands to reason… He lacks a moral compass… I really didn't know.'

Riddick shrugged. 'So, that leaves us with a suspect – a missing suspect, mind, as no one knows where the bastard is. The motive is clear as day. He didn't want Tom Winters exposing the truth, so killed him.'

'It makes sense. God, if I'd known, I'd never have condoned it. I'd have broken him in half. You need to find him and put the animal away.'

'Except… I don't think Neil killed Tom.'

'What?' Anders looked confused. 'You just said the motive was clear as day! Who else would have a reason to—'

'Let me show you something,' Riddick said, opening the

photographs on his phone. He swivelled it around to show Anders. 'A newspaper cutting taken from Tom's drawer. A picture of the great and the good.'

Anders gulped as he looked down at a much younger version of himself standing in a group of suited individuals, alongside a fresh-faced Neil.

'A fair while ago that,' Riddick said. 'Long before I became your Padawan.'

Anders shrugged; the nerves on his face were starting to twitch. 'I don't get your point. We were involved in the opening of a youth centre together, so what? It was a bad time. Lots of kids causing problems on the streets. I wanted to be involved with helping change the direction of their lives.'

'With Neil?' Riddick said, slamming the palms of his hands down on the table.

'I believed he wanted balance. To offset some of the misery he'd caused. He had money. I wanted him to put it to use.'

'You're a liar, Anders. A bloody liar.'

Anders wagged a finger at Riddick. 'Now listen here, Paul. I won't tolerate you talking to me like that in my own home—'

'I've run the names and numbers, you pompous prick! In the three years that you "assisted" at the youth centre, do you know how many of those children were charged with misdemeanours? About twenty of them. Three years, twenty children groomed by Neil into crime.'

Anders stood again. 'That's quite enough, Paul. I want you out. Those children were living challenging lives anyway. I tried to steer them away from crime, rather than into it.'

'Maybe that's the appearance you gave, but you were just turning a blind eye to Neil, something you've continued to do for years since. How much money did you make from all this sodding misery?'

'You've no evidence of this!'

'It'll be there though, won't it? Because I'm right, aren't I? And what's more, Tom found out, didn't he?'

'Leave!' Anders said, pointing at his door. 'After everything I've ever done for you, you whining little shit. Lost in your own self-pity, while the world makes excuses for you. You should've been out of a job long—'

'Tom invited you over, didn't he?' Riddick said.

'You're talking nonsense.'

'Tom had discovered the pornography. Knowing about your connection with Neil through this photograph, he believed you would be the perfect person to expose him. Why would Tom suspect that Anders Smith, the famed figure of law and order, would actually be complicit in the crime?'

Anders shook his head.

'Except, Tom had it all wrong, didn't he?' Riddick continued. 'Because you are involved. You always have been. Did Tom grow suspicious when you tried to steer him off course? Is that what made you put down that drink he'd given you, and kill him? Was his suspicion just too much of a risk to take?'

Anders sneered. 'Give your head a wobble, why don't you? I've never heard such poppycock!'

'Before I came here, I was with the pathologist, Hugo Sands. He's completed his post-mortem. Somebody bludgeoned Tom to death. They found splinters of wood in his face.'

Riddick twirled the cane again. 'What happened to your last cane?'

Anders eyes darted left and right. Riddick could see the panic enveloping him. 'I told you, it broke, I—'

'Where is it?'

'Gone, I threw it away—'

'It's just that when I asked Sands if the injuries could have been caused by a wooden walking stick, he seemed to think that was entirely reasonable—'

'How could you?'

Having Anders raise his voice at him after his great betrayal infuriated Riddick further. He stood. 'No. How could you?' He threw the new cane to the floor at Anders' feet. 'I thought of you like a goddamn father.'

'For good reason. I've taken care of you since day one. You're letting your emotions cloud your judgement… I had Neil on a short leash… It could have been much worse without me.'

Riddick shook his head. 'No. Here's the headline. You watched as Neil ruined lives. And you knew about Kelsey, didn't you? You knew about the pornography, and the abuse. And you murdered Tom before any evidence saw the light of day.'

Anders backed away from the table. He looked left and right.

'What're you going to do, Anders, run? Where? You're an old man now with a bust back. Please. I implore you. Keep some dignity.'

Anders continued to shake his head. 'You've not got enough.'

'And you believe we won't find it? If I don't find it, Emma Gardner will. She's good, you know. Better than we ever were. Her moral compass only points one way. Not like yours. And mine… the one you damaged.'

'Damaged!' Anders snorted. 'You did that all on your own.'

'I listened to you, I looked up to you, tried to be like you, and now look… You're a monster!'

Anders knelt down slowly, and picked up his cane, groaning as he did so. He held the cane by its end, so the handle was pointing outwards, towards Riddick.

Riddick raised an eyebrow. 'Really, Anders. Have you not done enough damage to your soul already? Do you want to add the murder of someone you claim to love like a son?'

'I did...' The cane shook in his hand. 'I do... Paul. Please understand... I've had no choice. For years. No choice!'

'Save it, Anders,' Riddick said, taking a step towards him so the handle on the cane was pressed against his chest. 'Save it for your confession.'

'I can't go to jail... He made me do these things... He had enough on me to bury me... I couldn't get out *even* when I wanted to.'

'That makes it even worse. Tom Winters, Kelsey Winters, Bradley Thompson and Dan Lotus are all dead. But that's okay because you protected yourself. You're a selfish old man, Anders.'

Anders lifted the cane above his head. His arm tensed.

Riddick tapped the centre of his head. 'Go on. Life has dealt me enough blows already, and I'm not just talking about the lumps on my head. What's one more? You're done anyway, Anders, whether I die in a pool of blood in your kitchen or not. I've already emailed everything I've discovered to Emma, and if you don't confess, then at least my death is one thing they'll be able to easily convict you of.'

Anders let the cane fall to his side. There were tears in his eyes. 'I'm sorry, Paul... I'm so sorry, but I don't want to go to jail. This isn't who I am. This isn't who I wanted to be. It started, and then it just didn't stop.'

'Well, there is one good thing you could do before all this is over. Call it penance.'

Tears ran down Anders' face. He dropped his cane and sat in his chair. He stared at the table for a while, possibly considering how best to end his life as a free man. Eventually, his bloodshot eyes met Riddick's.

'What do you want me to do, Paul?'

* * *

Anders kept an old pair of handcuffs in his house. Riddick used them to cuff the ex-DCI in the back of his own Land Rover, and then, for good measure, ensured the child locks were on.

A few times on the journey, Anders tried to engage Riddick; he shut him down on every occasion. 'We're done. Just the directions now, Anders.'

Fifteen minutes into the journey, Riddick asked, 'Thirsk?'

'Yes…'

Eventually, they were heading through country roads, following signs to Thirkleby Hall.

'The caravan park?' Riddick asked.

'No. Carry on past, and past the holiday cottages too.'

'Into the middle of bloody nowhere?'

'Now… take a right here.'

The road they took wasn't fit for purpose. He heard Anders bouncing against the door in the backseat. With his hands cuffed, he had no way to steady himself.

Several bumps and groans later, the road levelled out. Thick trees rose up on their right side, blocking the already descending sun. Riddick hit his fog lights for a clearer view. There was enough roadkill dotted about the place to make him cautious, and he slowed slightly.

'Up here, on your left, follow the driveway, to the cottage.'

Riddick took the turn. He was relieved the driveway was in better nick than the road he'd just come on – he'd started to succumb to travel sickness.

No one had deemed it necessary to trim the hedges that lined the drive for a good while – years probably. They clawed at his car. 'Is this cottage all alone out here?'

'Yes… it's a dump.'

'Yeah, I'm getting that. Whose is it?'

'My father left it to me. It's not worth much, but I'd an ambition to do it up one day. During retirement. Guess that's never going to happen now!'

Riddick looked at him in the rear-view mirror. 'At least you're alive. You want me to list all those deaths you're connected to?'

Anders sighed.

Riddick hit the brakes outside the dishevelled cottage. He felt Anders head bounce off the back of his head rest.

There were no other cars in his driveway. He looked up at the cottage. Rather than sport it as a showpiece, the two-storey structure had become the victim of its ivy. The roof looked as if it was in dire need of repair. 'You should give it to charity.'

'What're you going to do?'

Riddick killed the engine and the lights, then got out of the car. He opened Anders' door and unfastened his seatbelt. 'Get out.'

Anders complied.

Riddick pointed at his open car door. 'Now, the driver's seat.'

'Why?'

'Now.'

Anders sat in the driver's seat. Riddick reached into his pocket for the key and unfastened one of Anders' handcuffs and then reconnected it to the steering wheel.

Riddick pocketed the keys to the Land Rover.

Anders stared up at him the whole time.

'What?' Riddick asked, irritated.

'Don't screw your life up, too…'

'As if you care?'

'I care, Paul, believe me, I—'

Riddick cut him off by closing the front door.

Riddick surveyed the dishevelled cottage. The curtains were drawn on the bottom floor, but not the top.

Are you watching?

A simple phone call could defuse this situation of danger, but Riddick felt the pull, the desire, to move forward himself. There was too much *wrong*, desperately wrong, with what had unfolded because of the person in there – and the bastard didn't get to do this the easy way. If anyone deserved to fear for their life, to beg for forgiveness, it was the occupant of Anders' decrepit cottage.

Riddick moved quickly down the cracked, weed-covered path and banged on an old, wooden door which almost came off its hinges.

'It's over,' Riddick shouted.

No reply. The door didn't open.

He knocked again. 'Last chance to do it with dignity.'

Again, no reply. *Except, you have no dignity, do you?*

He took a step back and prepared to run at it. The adrenaline made him shake, but it felt good. He *wanted* to do it this way—

The door opened.

The smug bastard stood there in shorts and T-shirt. He had a beer in one hand, a smirk twitching the corners of his mouth.

'It would be you,' Neil said, and nodded over at Anders' Land Rover. 'Bent old bastard finally broke under the weight of his humanity, did he?'

Riddick, pumped with adrenaline, felt like a coiled spring.

'Look at the state of you – especially your head. Like I said before, you *always* were a psycho—'

Riddick launched himself forward and drove his forehead into Neil's face.

The sharp pain in Riddick's head was far from pleasurable, but the cracking sound was satisfying.

The DI drove a fist into Neil's stomach and listened to the air come out of him in a whoosh. Enjoying his dominance, Riddick went in for another blow, but Neil evaded him this time, and darted in with the bottle in his hand.

Riddick stumbled away, clutching his ear. He steadied himself against the wall and looked at his bloody palm, and then glanced up at Neil, who was leaning against the wall by the stairs with his nose pissing blood.

In his left hand was the bottle he'd just struck Riddick with. It hadn't broken, but he pointed it at Riddick. 'Stay back, psycho.'

Riddick stood up straight. He cracked his neck which had stiffened under the surge of adrenaline. 'Drop the bottle.'

'Why would I do that? I'm going to kill you with it.'

'Be my guest.' Riddick winced. 'It'll get you off the street for the rest of your days.'

'You willing to die just to put me to the sword?' Neil smirked.

Riddick wondered if he was.

Neil had worked his way towards the bottom of the stairs. Without warning, he turned and ran up the winding staircase, still holding the bottle.

Riddick chased and, at the top of the steps, he saw a door slamming shut ahead of him. He threw himself at the door, pressed down the handle and swung inwards with it.

He was in a sparsely furnished bedroom. The bedsheets were dishevelled and there was dirty clothing on the floor.

Ahead, Neil had lifted open the window, and already had a foot outside.

Riddick charged forward, slipped his hands under his armpits and yanked him back. 'No bloody way.' He fell backwards, and the weight of Neil coming down on top of him knocked the wind from his body. Neil rolled off and crawled away.

Riddick's head fell to one side, and he saw Neil grab the bottle he'd hit him with before, and start to rise to his feet, his back to him.

Riddick sat up and worked his way to his feet. Neil turned

and swung the bottle again. The DI heard the rush of the bottle, but it missed him this time, allowing him to complete his rise.

Neil drew the bottle back again, but Riddick wasn't allowing him another chance. He threw himself forward, rugby tackling him onto the bed.

Then, he lifted himself clear and drove his fist into Neil's face. Once, twice, a third time, and then a fourth for good measure.

Riddick backed away, gulping air, as Neil moaned on the bed.

'You're a parasite,' Riddick said, clutching his ear. 'Bradley... Dan... all those children in your community centre years ago. How many young lives have you ruined?'

'Piss off,' Neil moaned.

'You targeted a pregnant girl. Are there no boundaries?'

'She was a slut, and she gave me up to—'

Riddick dragged Neil to his feet and pulled the dazed man over to the open window.

He could feel his heart thrashing in his chest, and he felt at ease with what he was about to do. He looked at Neil's bloody face. He was still laughing, despite one of his eyes being half-closed, and his nose bent out of proportion.

'What're you going to do, policeman? Really? *What're you going to do?*'

What he really wanted to do would cost him his career. But when you considered this man's lies and atrocities, was it a small price to pay? The world was better off without Neil Taylor. And if Riddick was the man to take him out of it, did that in some way even the scales after he'd failed his wife and two children?

'I'm going to do what's right,' Riddick said, spinning Neil and forcing his head out of the open window.

56

After Riddick had barged his way into the old cottage, Anders, with his one free hand, had managed to get his mobile phone from his jacket pocket.

You should have searched me Padawan... It seems I didn't teach you as well as I could've done.

Anders sighed. He was cooked. There was no way out. No doubt a nasty fate awaited him, but for the first time since Riddick had knocked on his door earlier, he felt somewhat accepting of it. Anders had made many mistakes in his life, *many*, mainly due to the devil's drink. And even after he'd done with that foul stuff, he'd been forced to continue with the mistakes. He'd got himself in far too deep to ever go back.

So, in a way, he was glad that Riddick had been the one to find the truth – it felt fitting somehow. Made it feel right. The man he thought of like a son was putting him out of his misery.

But even in this moment of relief, the sadness was unbearable.

Because their relationship was over. The stubborn bastard was far too righteous to ever accept him in his life again.

There was one more thing Anders could do though. After all, if he was truly a good father, and deep down, he felt as if he still was, then his son must come first.

He phoned Chief Constable Marsh.

She wanted an explanation. She didn't get one. What she got was this location.

Anders watched a head emerge from the top window.

'Hurry,' he shouted into the phone.

He squinted, trying to identify who was about to fall to their death, hoping, *praying*, it wasn't Paul Riddick.

57

When Chief Constable Marsh revealed the situation to Gardner, she was on the road, before all reinforcements could be organised.

A recent high-speed pursuit course, combined with fresh bulbs in the flashing two-tone on her grille, ensured she led the race and made it to Thirkleby Hall first.

At such speeds, she struggled with the dirt road after the caravan park on the approach, but she only compromised slightly, despite knowing that a blow out or wrecked suspension were likely.

Eventually, she turned off onto the road which led to the isolated cottage and felt the bubbling anxiety in the pit of her stomach boil over when she saw a Land Rover ahead.

Marsh had already alerted her to the fact that this was Anders' vehicle, and he was currently cuffed to a wheel. She wasn't 100 per cent sure as to the nature of the ex-DCIs crimes yet, but he'd already admitted to Marsh that Riddick had him bang to rights and so an inappropriate arrest was the least of her concerns.

What she was worried about was Riddick, possibly drunk, and completely unhinged, chasing down a dangerous man in the cottage ahead.

She pulled up behind the Land Rover, and despite the darkened glass on the vehicle, she could see Anders' head.

While driving, she'd written off the tremble in her body to the uneven surface and potholes. After killing the engine, she realised that the shaking was a consequence of adrenaline.

She opened the door, stepped out and looked.

She felt the burning twist of dread in her stomach.

Ahead, someone was lying face down on the path. She steadied herself against her vehicle roof as she looked up at the open front door, and then up at the open window above that.

Riddick!

'God, *no!*' She sprinted down the path towards the prone figure. 'Paul!'

For a moment, she was back in that high-rise, approaching the billowing curtain that shrouded the balcony, from which Collette Willows had fallen to her death...

'Paul!'

The figure stirred. *Yes! Please, yes!* 'Paul!'

She froze. It wasn't Riddick.

The figure was wearing shorts and a T-shirt and had a shaved head. He looked up at her with a bloody face and smiled.

Neil Taylor.

Confused, she approached until she was standing over him, looking down. His hands were tied behind his back with rope. She looked up at the open window. If he'd come out of there, he'd be unlikely to be alive. And, if he was, he'd be in a worse state than this. 'Neil Taylor, you are under—'

'The psycho has already done it!' Neil hissed. 'Save it until I get a solicitor and then you can read them to him!'

She looked up at Riddick standing in the open doorway.

Gardner went to help him. The DI's left ear was bleeding, and he looked pale.

'I was going to push him out the window, but I couldn't do it,' he hissed into Gardner's ear.

She looked at him. 'That's enough, Paul—'

'No,' he hissed again. 'I owed it to them. I owed it to Kelsey, to Bradley, to Cherish – all of them, and I couldn't do it.'

'Look at me,' Gardner said, clutching him by the shoulders. '*That's enough.* You're not the same as these people. You're not the same as Neil, and you're not the same as Anders.'

Riddick looked at Gardner. She thought he looked tearful, but it was hard to tell, due to his recent injuries that had left him worse for wear.

'I wish that were true, boss,' Riddick said. 'I really wish that were true.'

EPILOGUE

Gardner put her bag down and sat beside Riddick on the bench at the chapel.

She offered him a tic tac. He showed her a raised eyebrow.

She laughed, reached into her suit pocket and handed him some extra-strong mints. He laughed too.

Then, they sat in silence for a moment, gazing out over the young trees.

'I brought some flowers,' Gardner said, nodding at the bag. 'To say happy birthday.'

'Thanks. They would have been seven today,' Riddick said.

Gardner squeezed his shoulder.

'You know, I haven't seen them in over a month. I mean, I've been here, just... well... you know what I mean.'

'I know what you mean.'

'It stopped... after everything with Anders, it just stopped.'

Gardner nodded.

'Do you know he wants to see me?' Riddick eyed her.

'Yes, I know.'

'What do you think of that?'

'I don't think anything,' Gardner said.

'Truthfully?'

'Yes.'

And it was the truth. It wasn't her place to judge. Riddick had been close to the man for his entire career.

'Well, I won't be going. I just feel that now I've put the ghosts to rest, and Anders is gone, I must try and move on. How does that sound?'

'It sounds sensible.'

'Oh, I have something to show you.' He hoisted his phone from his pocket and showed her a picture.

Cherish was sitting on a bench, cradling Ariah. It was the happiest Gardner had seen the young woman.

'Mother and daughter doing fine,' Riddick said.

'That's wonderful news,' Gardner said.

'I just check in on them every now and again. You know how it is.'

'I do,' Gardner said and smiled. 'You're a good man, Paul.'

'Let's not get carried away. Anyway, I've decided I want to come back to work.'

'I see.'

'I'm ready.' He looked at Gardner. 'I haven't had a drink in six weeks.'

'I know.' Gardner had never told anyone about the drinking and had been there to support Riddick whenever he needed her.

'So, can I come back?'

She looked away. *It's too soon, Paul, far too soon.* 'Let me think about it.'

'That doesn't sound promising...'

You're still recovering. Six weeks is not a long time. And I'm still worried about you. 'Another fortnight, and then I'll speak to Marsh, okay?' Gardner said.

He rolled his eyes. 'Great!'

'How many times? She bloody loves you.'

'Funny way of showing it.'

'Marsh doesn't show emotion.'

'That's for sure. So, what's happening with you?'

Gardner turned away. Operation Eden and her brother's release had taken their toll on her emotionally. She'd struggled these past months, but she'd been successful in keeping it locked away. Burdening Riddick with her demons had not been an option, and she didn't have anyone else to talk to. 'Getting by,' she said. 'Still on a break from Barry. I'm sure it will work out.' *I hope*, she thought. Barry had stabbed her in the back by pulling out of the move up north due to work commitments. It'd sent their already struggling marriage into disarray.

'And you saw Anabelle this weekend?'

'Yes, it was lovely.'

'It's a shame,' Riddick said. 'Because I want you to stay, but I understand you'll have to go back to her soon. Maybe you could bring her up here?'

Not without a custody battle, Gardner thought. *And I'm not putting her through that just yet. Not until I know that my marriage is definitely over.*

'Well, I have another ten months on this secondment first, so you haven't lost me yet.'

Riddick smiled. 'Thank you.'

'For what?' Gardner said.

'For bringing me back.'

Gardner looked away with tears in her eyes, honoured by the gratitude, but at the same time wondering, *who is going to save me?*

* * *

Gardner finished her phone call to Barry, and then finished the second glass of wine that evening.

Promising, she thought to herself. That'd been their longest conversation in over a month. *Signs of life?*

'I'm going to go with *yes*,' Gardner said out loud, pouring herself another celebratory glass of wine. 'Signs of life.'

The doorbell went.

She looked at her watch. Nine o'clock?

The only visitor she ever received at this time was Riddick when he felt alcohol beckoning him, and he needed reassurance and distraction. She went into the kitchen, hid the bottle of wine and the glass, chomped on a few tic tacs to take the smell of alcohol off her breath and opened the front door—

She staggered backwards.

Her brother stood on her doorstep.

Jack looked different to how she remembered him. He'd grown his hair long, and it hung limply down both sides of his face. He also had a moustache and a small goatee. He looked older too. More like a man than the boy who'd been sent down for manslaughter.

He was wearing a pair of cargo pants, and a T-shirt with the band Slipknot on it.

His head was lowered slightly, and he looked at her sheepishly. 'Emma?'

'No,' Gardner said, her heart thrashing in her chest. She reached for the door to close it. 'You don't get to do this. You don't get to come here.'

'Please, Emma, just listen to what I have to say—'

'No. *Absolutely not.*'

'You don't understand—'

'I understand *everything*. I have a life, Jack. A daughter. A good job. You've never brought anything but pain and suffering!'

He continued to look down. His expression was sad. It was an act. He was trying to look submissive, beaten down by life – it was how he'd won his way back into their parents' lives again and again.

'I *need* you, Emma. You're all I have.'

'You're a killer, Jack. There's no place—'

'I've *changed*.'

'You can't change. You know that.'

'According to who?'

'According to anyone who's ever met you! You're not like everyone else.' She started to close the door.

'I have a daughter. Just like you. A little girl. She's seven.'

Gardner stopped closing the door. *No. He didn't. He couldn't...* 'What? How?'

'Before I went to prison. Someone I was in love with.'

Love? No. Not possible. 'I don't believe you—'

'Look,' Jack said, fumbling in his pocket. He handed over a dog-eared photograph of a little girl wearing a flowery dress with her hair in pigtails. 'This kept me alive while I was inside.'

Gardner felt her heart drop. *Poor girl...* 'The best thing you can do is leave this little girl alone.'

'I would... except... I can't do that.'

'You're not able to put someone else's needs before yours. You never have done.'

'It's not that... I would've left her alone... except...'

'Except what?'

He turned around and walked over to a battered old Ford. He opened the back door, reached in and then stood away. The seven-year-old girl from the photograph emerged from the vehicle.

'Dear lord,' Gardner said, and her breath caught in her throat. This couldn't be happening. This couldn't be *bloody* happening.

Jack walked up the path, holding the girl's hand. He kept looking down at the girl, admiringly.

An act. A bloody act.

He stopped at the doorstep. 'This is Rose, Emma.'

Gardner smiled at the little girl. 'Hello Rose.'

'Are you my Auntie Emma?'

Gardner felt her heart racing. She looked at Jack, who had tears in his eyes. She looked back down at Rose.

'We need your help, Emma,' Jack said.

She stared hard at his face. His eyes looked different, somehow. Not cold and hard like they'd done all those years ago in Malcolm's Maze of Mirrors, and in all those horrible times subsequently. There was something in them.

An act. It had to be. He had merely perfected it.

She looked down at the beautiful, smiling girl, and back up at her tearful brother. 'Please, I'm begging you.'

Gardner knew this was wrong. Every part of her being was crying out at her to close the door, walk back to the kitchen, grab the wine and drink herself unconscious. Forget this ever happened.

Every. Part. Of. Her. Being.

'We have nowhere else to go,' Jack said, wiping tears away.

Gardner stepped back to allow them into her home, wondering, before the door had even closed, what this decision was going to cost her.

ACKNOWLEDGMENTS

Relocating DCI Emma Gardner to North Yorkshire has been challenging and exciting, and certainly something I couldn't have done without my extensive support network.

Thank you, Emily Ruston for seeing the potential in The Yorkshire Murders, and offering your valuable advice on delivering Gardner and Riddick's emotional journey. Also, Boldwood Books, who have been outstanding in their support from the first second.

Massive gratitude to my family, who support all of my ambitions, and keep me laughing throughout the most intensive moments of putting together these narratives.

I am grateful to every reader who has taken the time to read my work and listen to my stories, and to the amazing bloggers who have done so much to help me along this journey.

I'd also like to extend my appreciation to my esteemed colleagues at Delta Academies Trust, who work tirelessly to improve the education for the young people in the north of England, and remain forever supportive of me in both of my professions; Paul, Andy, Jane, Ray, Sarah, Becky, Fiona, Sarah, Claire, Paul, Catherine, Helen and Becky.

Lastly, thank you Knaresborough, for being a mysterious, captivating little town that offers me both a wonderful home, and a setting for these intriguing little tales.

ABOUT THE AUTHOR

Wes Markin is the bestselling author of the DCI Yorke crime novels, set in Salisbury. The Yorkshire Murders series stars the pragmatic detective DCI Emma Gardner who tackles the criminals of North Yorkshire. Wes lives in Harrogate.

Sign up to Wes Markin's mailing list here for news, competitions and updates on future books.

Visit Wes Markin's website: wesmarkinauthor.com

Follow Wes on social media:

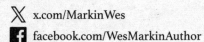

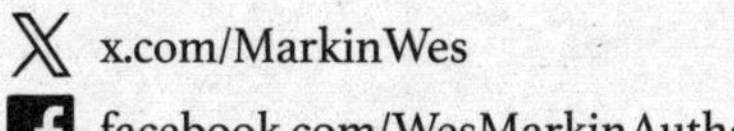

ALSO BY WES MARKIN

The Yorkshire Murders

The Viaduct Killings

The Lonely Lake Killings

The Crying Cave Killings

The Graveyard Killings